THE WRONG END

of the TELESCOPE

Also by Rabih Alameddine

The Angel of History
An Unnecessary Woman
The Hakawati
I, the Divine
The Perv
Koolaids

THE WRONG END
of the TELESCOPE

RABIH ALAMEDDINE

Grove Press
New York

Sections of "How to Greet Your Brother" appeared in slightly altered
form in the *New Yorker* online; "Over the Rainbow" and "How to Make
Liberace Jealous" first appeared in an essay, "Hope and Home," in
Freeman's; "All Hail the Mighty Harold" first appeared, in slightly altered
form, in the book *Bound to Last: 30 Writers on Their Most Cherished Book*.

FIRST EDITION

Published simultaneously in Canada
Printed in the United States of America

First Grove Atlantic hardcover edition: September 2021

The book is set in 12-pt. Cochin LT by Alpha Design & Composition
of Pittsfield, NH.

Library of Congress Cataloging-in-Publication data is available for this title.

ISBN 978-0-8021-5780-5
eISBN 978-0-8021-5782-9

Grove Press
an imprint of Grove Atlantic
154 West 14th Street
New York, NY 10011

Distributed by Publishers Group West

groveatlantic.com

21 22 23 24   10 9 8 7 6 5 4 3 2 1

For Makram and Carine,
Jalal and Yasma

                              Where
And in what unknown depths his bones wander
Seabirds alone can tell.

                    —Glaukos of Nikopolis,
                        "Epitaph for Erasippus"

THE WRONG END
of the TELESCOPE

Round and Round
We Go

He was my people—he and I kneaded by the same hands. He was on the shorter side, my height, not in the greatest of shape. His hair had less gray than mine but was the same shade of dark. We had similar facial features. I would have recognized that he was from the Levant even without the Palestine Red Crescent Society vest he sported. The rest of us, the recently disembarked, were about twenty or so, a motley crew, various nationalities. You would probably say we looked like a painting from a time long past, the late cold light illuminating and shadowing our backs as we stood around the circular belt, a single here, a couple there, waiting for our bags, waiting and waiting. The Palestinian stood by himself to my left. He had a happy face, satiated, like what I would expect Bernini's Saint Teresa to look like postcoitus, postecstasy.

Farther east than Athens, the island of Lesbos was as close as I'd been to Lebanon in decades, yet I stood facing not the glorious Mediterranean but the *chug, chug, chug* of dirty black rubber, a wheel of time if ever there was one—a wheel of time with a few gashes patched with duct tape. The ceiling felt dark and oppressive. I looked for a seat, but there was none. All twenty passengers, with few places to sit, kept shifting their weight from one foot to the other, hips swaying like sluggish, arrhythmic pendulums. The air was nippy and smooth, like velvet.

I texted Francine: Landed. Love you.

I texted Mazen: Landed. Love you. Can't wait to see you.

A book, facedown, was the only object making the round along the carousel. It exited the stage on the far end and moments later entered by slipping under the rubber curtain to my right, the eternal return, each time a little wetter because of the drizzle. A bored-looking young man, Germanic in appearance and attitude, probably still on winter break from college, freshman or at most sophomore, picked up the book and glanced at it briefly before flipping it back onto the circulating belt. The discolored cover was faceup now, a Scandinavian novel of some sort, a murder mystery—a brooding, handsome man, a woman's bare thigh, a pistol. A South Asian woman in a head scarf chatted with a Han Chinese in Malay, her eyes fixed on where her bags might one day appear. An African woman and a European, possibly Greek, both in Red Cross windbreakers and matching smartphones, looked the most at ease. The entire airport seemed to be on a coffee break. Time felt lethargic.

The book reappeared once more, and it had been flipped. I thought it strange. On my left, the Palestinian looked around the room, caught my eye, raised a questioning eyebrow. I scrunched my face and shrugged. He grinned, turned the book faceup when it reached him. He and I watched it disappear again. He was biting at a hangnail. The book returned facedown once more. He gasped in glee and covered his mouth with a fleshy palm, including me in his delight. We had yet to exchange a word and we didn't have to—Levantine nonverbal communication would appear psychic to the uninitiated eye, a brow furrowing or a slide of a lip was worth a thousand pictures, and that was before one included the hands.

The Palestinian waited until the book reached him and turned it over again. All of us were now watching the book's cycle, even the two American men who had conversed endlessly and loudly during the entire flight from Athens but hadn't spoken a word since. The room felt energized. The book came back facedown again. Someone was bored, I thought. We waited for the Palestinian to do the honors. Like an actor performing onstage, hungry for attention, he gauged his audience, acknowledging us with his eyes, and flipped the paperback with a mild flourish. But this time, as soon as it disappeared, we heard the muffled ruckus of the luggage arriving behind the wall, the book returning as it left. Few passengers, yet the resulting commotion was boisterous, buzzing movements like aroused hornets around their hive.

The airport claimed the mighty name of Mytilene International but had only five usable carts that we could see. I would have to lug my luggage. I'd checked a bag for the first time in over ten years, usually traveled with only a carry-on, but I thought it would be a good idea to come with extra winter clothes to donate to refugees: socks, sweaters, long johns, fleece jackets, and woolen skirts that would not fit anyone with my waist size because the discount store had colorful summer ones in abundance but cold-weather skirts only in petite.

My bag was the last to come out, of course. I had bowed the handle with a thin red ribbon to distinguish it, but it turned out I didn't need to since it's an old Samsonite, a model not seen since the 1980s, not produced since the 1970s. I had no intention of returning with it. I began to wonder, not for the first time, what I was doing there. The Americans grabbed their bags and rushed to stand first in line at the Hertz counter, tapping the service call bell a couple of times. I arrived behind them. The stall was hardly the size of a closet, yet its two yellow signs splashed us with jaundice.

The clerk, under the outside awning, heard us, saw us through the glass doors, dropped his cigarette, and pulled his pants up by the belt. He took a long, exaggerated breath and sighed. Behind him was a small open-air parking lot, a rain-slick coastal road, and the aforementioned Mediterranean, yes, glorious. Or was this the Aegean, which Aegeus threw himself into when he thought his son Theseus had failed against the Minotaur? The clouds were such that both the asphalt and the water had the same color, a bluish slate, the color of oxidization on copper with a tinge of periwinkle violet. Off-season on the island, no cars on the road, no boats in the water, purple hills in the distance, east, Turkey in all likelihood, close and not, an hour by ferry if you had the right passport. In the parking lot, a gray van screeched to a stop in front of the Palestinian, and out rushed two women wearing the same white-and-orange vest he was.

They hugged him with such fierceness I thought he was going to tumble over, and without releasing him, they began to jump up and down like pudgy kids on one pogo stick, evidently not minding getting a little wet. I looked around to see if anyone else was watching, but the Americans were in some kind of philosophical discussion with the Hertz clerk, making sure to insist that they were not the kind of men who would be cheated.

If those purple hills were Turkey, then the itsy-bitsy, teeny-weeny bikini of a country, Lebanon, was a few degrees south. I had not been back there in almost forty years, and it was highly unlikely that I ever would. My brother Mazen constantly invited me to visit—come back, come back, he'd say—and I resisted. The dream of my return had died decades ago. He was the only family member I cared about. When I informed him that I was coming to Lesbos, his first response was that I should come to Beirut, which was next door. How could I be in his part of the world and not see him? I explained that I wasn't going to take more time off and he should be the one to come to Lesbos. He argued for a bit, telling me that he would love to see me in my home-town, that I needed to be in Beirut, but we both knew that I had him, that I would win, that I'd always win with him.

The automatic doors yawned open; cold air and the Palestinian came in.

"Would you like a ride?" he asked in Arabic. Blotchy, circular cheeks were most of his face, along with lips—the delicate full lips of a gourmet. Everything about him was round. I pointed to the yellow sign, smiled. "Well, if you wanted to save some money, and you know," he said before briefly pursing those lips, "there's no threat to your honor

with me, absolutely safe." He looked about to burst from
anticipation, waiting for what kind of reply, a boy hoping
I would join his game.

"I'd be more worried about your honor, my dear."

He laughed loudly enough that both Americans glared
as they scurried out the door with their bags.

"I misplaced mine back in Jerusalem," he said, now
in full camp, arms akimbo, both hands clamped around his
waist.

The clerk fake coughed, which led to a fit of real ones
lasting a full ten seconds. I should have taken out my stethoscope, but I only handed him my license and passport, told
him I had a reservation, a small car for the week I was to
spend on Lesbos.

The Palestinian introduced himself as Rasheed. He was
with a group of Jerusalemite nurses and first aid workers,
asked me who I was with and where I was going.

I told him my name and that I was meeting a friend with
a Swedish NGO. "I simply want to see what's happening
here," I said. "My brother is joining me in two days. We'll
help wherever we're needed."

"Come help us," he said, writing his local cell number
on a card. "We can use you. Anyone who speaks Arabic is
good. Well, there are a number of Arabic speakers but few
who understand the culture. There's nothing happening in
Skala Sikamineas. No boats are landing there anymore. All
the refugees used to in the beginning of the crisis, but now
they're landing down here, on these beaches and a little
farther south."

The van honked twice; the clerk shook the car keys.

"Call me, please. I'll explain what we do." He walked off toward the parking lot. The door slid closed behind him, but he turned around and came back in. "I know all the secrets of this island," he said. "If you call me, I'll tell you more." His eyebrows rose teasingly. "You must call to find out." He exited, then turned around once more. "What do you do for work, Madam Mina?"

"It's Dr. Mina," I said in a false huff.

"Oh, come on," he said. "You're not serious. You can really help us. Please, I'm willing to go down on my knees and beg."

You Made Me Do It

You suggested I write this. You, the writer, couldn't. You tried writing the refugee story. Many times, many different ways. You failed. And failed again. Maybe failed better. Still you couldn't. More than two years after you and I met in Lesbos, you were still trying. You tackled it from one direction, then another, to no avail. You were too involved, unable to disentangle yourself from the tale. You said that you couldn't calibrate the correct distance. You weren't able to find the right words even after numerous sessions on your psychiatrist's couch.

I should write this thing, you told me. You called it a thing, flicking your hand with a dismissive Levantine gesture. Every idiot thinks they're a writer; they're not. Every dullard thinks they have a tale to tell; they don't. But I should. I have a good one. You insisted I write the refugee story, as well as your story and mine. This thing.

I told you I wasn't a writer. I could form sentences, present ideas and so forth, but not write a memoir or a book that anyone would necessarily want to read. Who said anything about publishing, you said. I should write my story; no one has to read it. There are enough books out there, you said. Why add more? I should write to make sense of my world, to grasp my story. Writing simplifies life, you said, forces coherence on discordant narratives, unless it doesn't, and most of the time it doesn't, because really, how can one make sense of the senseless? One puts a story in a linear order, posits cause and effect, and then thinks one has arrived. Writing one's story narcotizes it. Literature today is an opiate.

You contradict yourself all the time. You know that, right?

I know, I know. You are large, like Whitman. You contain multitudes.

If writing my story will not simplify my life, will not make more sense of my narrative, if I can't publish and become a gazillionaire, why should I do it?

Memory is a wound, you said. And some things are released only by the act of writing. Unless I go in with my scalpel and suction to excavate, to clean, to bring into light, that wound festers, and the gangrene of decay will eat me alive.

And whatever you do, you said, don't fucking call it *A Lebanese Lesbian in Lesbos*, just don't.

I'm writing now. I'll tell your tale and mine.

I'll write your story for you.

I plunge.

Driving a Stick,
Flying a Broom

It was a small Opel, dark blue, with six figures on its odometer and, remarkably, a stick shift. I hadn't driven a nonautomatic in about forty years, since Lebanon. Hertz had only a manual transmission, which proved not to be a problem. When I started the car, instinct took over. The clutch turned into an extension of my left foot.

Night descended, and I was enveloped in darkness as soon as I passed the little town of Mytilene. The Opel's high beams tilted at a slight angle. I cocked my head to adjust, couldn't help myself. Slow showers had accompanied me since the airport. I hadn't taken off my coat or my overworn Shetland pullover. Everything before me, everything around me, was blued and grayed, pale shapes shifting effortlessly, all ethereal and illusory, as if I were about to plummet into an old memory. The easterly wind was viciously active. I could see tiny specks of luminescence from the whitecaps out on the sea to my right. For the first time in about twenty

minutes, another vehicle shared my road, a light truck driving in the opposite direction with sheep in its cargo bed. In
the rearview mirror, once it passed, I saw orange sparks,
hundreds, splashing from its tailgate before disappearing in
the rain. My twisted brain made me think of roast lamb, and
my stomach growled in protest. The car's tires turned and
turned. Only my breath and the erratic squeak of rubber
on windshield scratched the silence of the drive.

The last time I was on as skinny a road was four years
ago in Tuscany while Francine and I were vacationing. Her
mother had had a stroke back in Chicago; her sister asked us
to return quickly. We were needed. I drove in darkness, in
silence, until we reached the airport in Florence. She always
seemed about to say something during the drive, would
open her mouth, take a breath to speak but then exhale,
nothing. I knew she didn't want me to talk, to say anything.
She needed her space, needed to marshal her resources for
what was to come. When she was melancholic or suffering,
I was to be there for support only. I should be seen and not
heard, speak only when spoken to. She had to train me to
be quiet. A long time ago, before we moved in together, she
insisted we attend couples therapy because I didn't listen
to her, didn't know how, always wanted to fix everything.
That was me, the surgeon. Our friends mocked us for going
to therapy before we were a couple, early even by lesbian
standards. She would be at work now, already eleven in the
morning in Chicago, already with clients.

About a year ago, Francine's twelve-year-old niece
changed the direction-giving voice on my phone to Bugs
Bunny. I thought it amusing at the time, and I didn't correct
it, not that I could have without her help. On this unfamiliar

rainy road, however, I found Bugs butchering Greek names and saying things like "Turn left on Mitilinis–Thermis, Doc" incredibly annoying.

An hour later, no light, no moon, no lampposts, Skala Sikamineas hunkered at the bottom of a hill, down a steep, relentlessly snakelike road without guardrails or tiger-eye road studs. I had a surge of fear as I contemplated the deep decline, but when I made my first turn and my tire sank into a wet pothole, uneasiness turned into elation. Sure, it had been thirty-six years since I set foot in Lebanon, a lot longer since I drove down dark mountain roads, let alone in a stick, but this—this felt ever familiar. I had no problems using the high beams to cut up winding, aphotic asphalt. By the time I encountered another car coming up the hill and we communicated by blinking high and low beams—you go ahead, no please, you first—I was shivering with glee. I was sixteen again, sure of my world.

Except I wasn't sure of my world when I was sixteen. I was not sure of anything. I presented myself as a boy then, a muddled boy, full of false bravado and little hope. I would spend years in high pretense perfecting my confusion.

How I Learned
to Drive

Mazen taught me to drive long ago. I wasn't exactly sure how we thought that was a good idea. He was barely eleven months older, just turned seventeen, no license yet, but our father had taught him, as he had our sister and older brother. Mazen was ready; he was a man. He thought I was. We borrowed our brother Firas's car, a beat-up Peugeot that he'd inherited from our mother, primarily because it was so old that it had the habit of dying capriciously while idling. The Peugeot would then refuse to be resuscitated until a suitable time had passed, say, two minutes, at which point you had to hit a particular spot on the engine with a wrench or hammer for the car to come back to life. My mother worried about being stranded. Her eldest didn't, rarely worried about much. The Peugeot ended up his while my mother had to wait for more than a year to get another car. I remember this because Firas, not my mother, was forced to drive Mazen and me to school whenever we were running late. During those early years of the civil war in Lebanon, driving to school, driving anywhere, was an adventure.

Mazen decided that the best place for me to learn was in the mountains, away from traffic, away from police or the gendarmerie and, most important, away from my parents or, worse, Firas, who would have been none too happy with my learning on his car. It must have been a Saturday or Sunday because I remember we ended up spending the whole day until I got the hang of depressing the clutch and shifting gears. I wasn't necessarily a slow learner, but every now and then I would lift my left foot off the clutch too soon, and the car would lurch as if convulsing with its last breath and die. We'd have to wait for the whupping and resurrection.

In the evening, we had to abort the lesson because the weather was changing. The air turned soft and dense, which in the mountains announced the arrival of a storm. Along our descent, we saw an accident; a black Mercedes Ponton taxi blocked much of the road, its four wheels raised toward the sky like a cat exposing its belly. There were at least four cars parked on the side of the hill, a dozen men milling around. No injuries, no ambulance, no police, just bystanders and a couple of militiamen exaggerating their importance, desperately trying to pretend that they had recently shot someone.

A Little Village
Called Skala Sikamineas

The small hotel stood toward the bottom of the road, not too far from the shore. Between the two was a large plane tree in the middle of what could be described as the tiny main square, which was anything but, more like a heptagon with unequal sides. Everything was charming, if quaint. Even in the mild light I could discern the typical blue-trimmed white walls of Greek villages. The roof's red tiles seemed more Lebanese to me, more Ottoman than Greek.

It took me a few tries to ask the old woman who owned the inn whether Emma was in her room. Since I was unable to fathom her amalgam of Greek and English, the woman — so white haired, so fragile — enunciated her words methodically and loudly, opened her wide mouth to articulate each syllable, as if she were patiently instructing a slow-witted child. I nodded along enthusiastically, too embarrassed to let her know I was only catching every fourth or fifth word. Apparently, Emma was not in her room but was waiting for me at one of the cafés. The owner wasn't sure which one.

The old woman helped me carry my luggage up the stairs to my room on the second floor. She performed a long-winded soliloquy as she ascended, holding on to one side of my heavy bag. A hijab-wearing woman with weary features was mopping the floor, her left foot pushing along a gray bucket. Noticing the owner, she rushed over to relieve her of her burden, but the owner shooed her away with a flick of her head. When she laid the bag at my door, I noticed that she looked livelier, less ashen; color had returned to her cheeks, and her front-buttoned, matronly dress seemed less wrinkled than when we started. She left me at the door with the key.

The light switch was exactly where I assumed it would be, my left hand landing on it on the first try. The room shook off its darkness. It smelled of sleep, of light dust and disinfectant.

I was a tad nonplussed. Emma texted me the day before telling me that she would wait for me at the hotel, and then we would grab dinner. I tried calling, but her phone was off. It felt late, but it was only seven. I wondered whether I should unpack first or go look for her.

The cleaning woman must have been good at her job. The room was spotless—its whites seemed hand bleached, every corner seemed to sparkle—and modest. No amenities here: a twin bed with a single pillow, bare walls, stone tiles on the floor, old French doors that opened to a balcony, and louvered wooden shutters the likes of which I hadn't seen since I left Lebanon. The wood in the room smelled resinous, of fake lemon. A small lace doily on the credenza was the only decoration.

I worried about Emma, fearing she was overstressed. A few weeks earlier, while reading the coverage of the continuing crisis on Lesbos in the *New York Times*, I was struck by a photograph of two dozen Syrian refugees in orange life vests alighting from a small, black dinghy. Men, women, and children, all wet and looking miserable, water reaching up to their knees, marching chaotically toward the shore. In the middle of the photo stood a resolute figure carrying a boy of around seven in one arm, while the other tried to lift another woman, likely the boy's mother, who had apparently slipped and was on all fours in the water. I did not recognize Emma at first. How could I? Soaked, unkempt, her usually perfect hair was a mess, as was she. The saint in the picture was nothing like the woman I knew. I phoned, confirmed it was her. She'd been on the island for a while. She suggested that her NGO could use someone with my skills. Everyone was overwhelmed. The photographs published in newspapers did not come close to showing the magnitude of the disaster. The numbers of refugees arriving seemed infinite, thousands each day, and no one could see the flow decreasing anytime soon. European doors were beginning to close once again, especially after the Paris attacks, and yet more people clamored for entry. Come, she said.

The Trouble
with Emma

I'm not sure you would like Emma. Francine certainly
doesn't, and you two tend to like and hate the same things.
I met Emma in 2005 at a conference on transgender health
in Malmö when she came up to talk to me after my pre-
sentation. Her hair was short and black then, sixties-style.
She wore thick makeup, dark lipstick that would make a
cherry envious, a tight dress that highlighted her slim figure,
and a long cardigan that highlighted the dress. Francine
thought Emma was too hetero, but that may have been
because Emma ignored her, a faux pas that she didn't care
to correct even after I introduced them. Emma and I were
able to be friends because the two of them were good at
ignoring each other.

   Even though I was tired after the long drive from
the airport, hunger forced me to leave the hotel room and
forage for food and Emma a few steps down the hill to
the main square. The only sounds were the soft lapping of

waves from the sea and the squeaking of my waterproof
hiking shoes on the wet tar. It had stopped raining. What I
thought was a jetty turned out to be the harbor, a crooked
black finger that calmed the sea. Three cats roamed the
square ever so silently, as if examining their property for
any damage caused by interlopers while they were away.
The air stood still in front of all three cafés. Two of the cats
continued to reconnoiter, but one stopped and sat on her
haunches, gauging, waiting for me to decide what to do.
A colony of bats appeared out of nowhere, silent in their
flight. Five of them raced ahead of me and began to circle
the roof of a building, probably feeding. Usually, I would
consider that a good omen since I loved bats, grateful for
their insect-free presence, but I figured if the building below
them was a restaurant, I would avoid it even if Emma was
there. I doubted they were feeding on mosquitoes in this
cold.

The first café I came across looked glassed in at first,
plasticked in at closer inspection. It would be open-air in
summer, but this evening, through the not fully transparent
plastic, with the fluorescent light and the cigarette smoke,
the patrons looked embalmed, as if submerged in amber.
And among the preserved sat Emma.

I was trying to catch her attention by waving maniacally when I noticed the boy sitting next to her. The group
of youngsters she was with surrounded her at the table, but
she was seeing only him; she was the collector admiring her
prize possession. There was no one in the square to notice
my clownish gesturing, but a couple of café dwellers playing
backgammon behind the large sheet looked my way with no
little rebuke. I was making a fool of myself as usual, must

have looked like an inflatable air man. I searched for the door in the sea of plastic, went in, and was slapped with the intense white blue of cigarette smoke. For whatever reason, I associated Emma with smoking, always envisioned her holding a thin cigarette in her right hand, taking long drags and exhaling small smoke rings that floated up toward the ceiling, yet I knew she didn't smoke. It was an image seared in my mind that had no bearing in fact.

Other than Emma and the boy she had her eyes on, there were five twenty-somethings sharing the table, three boys, two girls, evidently his friends, not hers. She held court, every bit the star and exotic outsider, and was the last to notice me standing next to her. She jumped out of the chair to hug: how was my flight, did I have any trouble finding the hotel, finding the café, no matter, how was I doing, introductions, Spanish and Italian names, the boy Rodrigo. The tornado that was Emma simply kept rolling, words and gestures swirling in her path. She didn't expect replies to her questions. I had yet to say a word. If I needed to, she'd expect me to interrupt. She asked Rodrigo to get me a chair, but he hesitated; his brown eyes flickered for a moment, and I thought I saw fear, nay, terror. A friend of his borrowed one from another table. I ended up on Emma's left, her boy on her right. After insisting that we two should love each other because of how important we were to her, she made us shake hands once again. He then slipped his hands under his thighs, which highlighted what he was terrified of exposing had he stood up to retrieve a chair, a rather impressive erection. Only Emma and I, sitting on the same side of the table, could see it, and to make sure Rodrigo understood whom his pride belonged to, her hand barnacled it for emphasis, blush red nails encircling a tube worm of brown corduroy.

I had expected the makeup, the earrings, even the garish bouclé blouse. Loud, outrageous attire was her every day and every minute and perhaps would be until her last breath. Her scrubs were so well fitted they'd work as a naughty nurse costume for Halloween. What I didn't expect were the perfectly manicured nails. I couldn't understand how she was supposed to help refugees on boats with them. It took me a minute to figure out that they were press-on acrylics. She was fifteen years younger than me, and Rodrigo and his friends at least fifteen more, yet I looked less of a contrast to the kids. I had my frumpy eternal college student look down pat. My corduroys happened to be brown as well.

The youngsters were all lifeguards. I'd heard of their organization, of course. A number of Spanish lifeguards had been horrified watching the news of refugees drowning when the distance between Lesbos and the Turkish coast was an hour by boat, two at most. They became one of the most effective NGOs working the island. I asked, in my broken Spanish before switching to English, how many of them could swim to Turkey from here. All four boys said they could. The girls hesitated. One of them said she might be able to. The other said she couldn't without serious training for a while, maybe a year, at which point the first agreed that she couldn't either without training, and then she suggested that neither could the boys, especially since they all smoked. A loud, chest-thumping argument ensued, which allowed my mind and eyes to wander.

There were a couple of non-youngsters in the café, two women on the other side, older than I, eating sandwiches.

Both had harmoniously white, hastily bunned hair, pale dresses and cardigans; I wondered if they were sisters. A young man at the table next to ours spoke classical Arabic a bit too loudly, a bit too earnestly, showing off an excellent command of the language for a nonnative speaker. He droned on and on about his studies; I gathered he was a doctoral student in Arabic at a Polish university of some repute. A couple of Arabs at the table next to his, North Africans, I presumed, played backgammon, trying hard to stifle their mirth. For many of us, little is as amusing as listening to classical Arabic being spoken aloud.

A waitress behind the counter, her head shaved almost bald, raised the volume of the speakers. I must have registered bewilderment or surprise, because the lifeguard sitting on my left explained that the singer belting out that ballad was the high priestess of soul, Nina Simone, a true artist, he insisted. Slowly the voices of the customers seemed to gain urgency. The older women asked for the check. They appeared to be in a rush suddenly. It seemed they knew that the mood had shifted, that a match had been struck, and they did not wish to be stung by the fire.

A gravid atmosphere fell upon the enclosed café as if from the ceiling. The boys in the room seemed to sit with more swagger, wanting and failing to look at ease, all of them tense and self-conscious. Laughter would burst out in various corners and die down again. The smell of stale smoke, beer, and pheromones. Kinderstuds preening, kinderlasses coy, hair flips at three different tables. Emma and I looked at each other, laughed, and flipped our hair in solidarity.

"They're young," Emma said, "and high on endorphins from being here and doing good work. Most of them go back to school in a few days, desperate hormones."

"A few thousand years earlier," I said, "and we'd be having a bacchanalia."

"That would have been simpler," she said. "Having all the cute lifeguards at the same time, instead of one at a time."

She explained that Rodrigo, her newest, was returning to graduate school in a few days. She would miss him. Luckily, she said, with the weather being bad, they'd had more time to fuck. Many of these men had never been with a trans woman, she told me, and she intended to correct that imbalance, a public service. My sandwich was tasteless, the cold beer went down with no resistance, and that was all that could be said for it. And then I had the lightbulb moment; interrupting Emma's monologue, I asked what she meant by having more time. She explained that rain and stormy seas meant no boat crossings, no new refugees, and for the next week or so, since this was the holidays, there was an abundance of volunteers, students, Arabic speakers. There were enough nurses on the island that she could take time off until all the disaster tourists left and the refugees returned.

"But Emma," I said, "what am I doing here then?"

Her eyes, which were slightly asymmetrical, widened; her face registered surprise or a small smile, as if she were not fully in control of her facial muscles. Too much time must have passed since her last Botox injection.

"Well, you know," she said, fidgeting in her chair, "I thought Syrian refugees, I thought Lesbos, I thought of you. You're meant to be here. It's destiny. If there's a break in the rain tomorrow, we'll get some boats. I'm sorry, darling. When you called we were overwhelmed, and we will be again soon, as soon as the weather improves and the holiday volunteers leave."

"Emma," I said, shaking my head. "I'm booked for only a week."

"Can you extend?"

"Emma," I said. "You begged me to come. You said you were desperate. The situation was dire, you said. You could really use another doctor. Emma, I put everything on hold to come here. I even asked my brother to come."

"Tomorrow could be worse," she said, trying on a sheepish smile, "or better for us. We might get boats."

"Emma," I snapped.

She began to promise me the world. We would drive to a beach south of Mytilene. A boat had landed there today in spite of the bad weather. She'd heard that there were more volunteers waiting than there were refugees, but I'd still be welcome what with all my skills. It wasn't her fault. She had no way of knowing that many volunteers would show up for Christmas and New Year, but they would all go back too soon. I should stay a bit longer. She spoke without looking at me but at an area on the ceiling, so possessed was she by the intensity of her excuses and the capriciousness of the gods who screwed up the weather for me, as if winter rainstorms would have been unheard of had there not been some Olympian meddling going on.

The truth was that I had not had to cancel many professional obligations. I, too, had time off during the holidays. What I was missing by being here was our thirtieth wedding anniversary. Francine had encouraged me to come.

It was just a date. We could celebrate after my return; my being on Lesbos would be good for me. She felt I'd been bored recently, antsy, spent too much time in my head. I seemed stuck in idle, she said, not shifting gears, and worse, I wasn't communicating, whatever that meant. I needed to be reminded that what I did mattered, that I still lived in this world. She couldn't join me, unfortunately, but I should go, go, go.

The Dance
with Marley

You know, our anniversary is not the date of our wedding. We've had three of those, two ceremonial and one recognized by the state. It's not when we first met, and it's not our first date or our first assignation, which was the day after. Our anniversary, January 6, 1986, is the date of the dance.

Francine was two years ahead of me in medical school, and I'd seen her around. She'd be hard to miss. You told her once that she was the most beautiful woman you'd ever seen, so you can imagine the effect she had on me when we were both still young. That face, those shrewd eyes, full lips I wanted to love bite, the sensuousness, skin the color of dark umber. I remember seeing her once in sea-green linen, in the library trying to read papers while prone on a scabrous sofa, drained, pages falling to the floor as she dozed. She'd pick them back up one by one, arrange them in order, and they would slip once again when her eyes closed. I fell hard before we exchanged one word.

Even then, she had those eyes that could see both angels and demons. I thought, here was a woman who found everything surprising and nothing shocking. Of course I fell. She was what I wanted to be and what I wanted. I was at the height of my awkwardness at the time. Jennifer, the woman I'd mistakenly thought I was going to spend the rest of my life with, had left me nine months earlier. I was going through a phase of thinking no woman would ever want me again. I was beginning to wear a new body, trying it out, shedding what I had been, leaving it behind like old snakeskin along a riverbank while I tried not to drown, tried to come out of the water as who I was and what I truly cared about, allowing myself to be seen for the first time. And there was Francine, seeming to know who she was, what she wanted, ever natural and assured. How could I not be enthralled?

One of the school's administrators held a party of some sort, probably some occasion, but it felt as if the event's primary purpose was to show off her Cambridge Craftsman house to new students. Around a table laden with a cheap, barely edible buffet, soft drinks in liter bottles, inexpensive wine in even bigger ones, fanned paper napkins in various colors, we milled about, doctors, professors, students, pretending to be interested in whatever someone was saying, feeling sorry for ourselves, or at least I was. I couldn't muster enough pleasantness for the inane chatter. I reminded myself that this was the kind of awkward evening that turned into a night of insomnia if I was not careful. I was about to leave when I noticed Francine in the middle of the living room, by herself, a paper plate in one hand. She held up a piece of cheese in the other, floppy and yellow, examined it with amazement, as if bewitched by its incongruous structure and consistency. What substance is this? What unnatural color, what creepy flavor? First contact with sliced, individually wrapped Muenster.

I walked toward her, uncertain and clumsy, unsure of the rules, as if I were moving around within the holy sanctuary of a religion not my own, but I had to halt before reaching the altar. The elevator music in the background had morphed into a Bob Marley song, and Francine pirouetted. Alone in the middle of the room, she and her dreadlocks swayed to the rhythm. Her yellow dress was loose enough that it seemed to move a moment after she did except at the hips, where the belt kept a perfect beat. The skin of her delicious arms soaked up the bad lighting and reflected a divine glow, a corporeal luster. She didn't give up her plate, twirled with it as if with an intimate, a dervish waitress. The hostess followed her example. She too began to dance. She dragged a man out to be her partner. A few others joined. Bless your soul, Bob Marley, savior of bad parties everywhere. We had ourselves a dance floor. Next to Francine, everyone was a pale corpse, the dancing dead. At least three men tried to dance with her, one tried to mimic her movements, looking foolish, another tried to bump hips, the third danced with both thumbs hooked in his back pockets, and she gracefully slid away, spun into her own world. She danced as if she was exploring her body in space.

You can see that this is her people's music, one of the doctors said to another. She was born to reggae. She's Haitian, I said, laughing nervously. Not the same thing, not the same thing at all. I could not remain next to these doctors; I left my spot, their conversation fading like the sound of the freeway at a distance. I found myself circling the makeshift dance floor, hypnotized almost, unthinking, sleepwalking in a way, my eyes not leaving her. A small citrine stone bounced on its chain between her breasts, calling to me. Come, it said. Lick me. A bead of sweat formed on her forehead like a pearl. And I found myself dancing. Not with her, not at first. I too began to explore my body in space, my new body, its shape and how it moved, the curves of my lines. These are what we call breasts; these are my arms. I introduced myself to its new odors. No woman, no cry, but this woman was dancing.

Francine decided to join me. We moved together, two solitudes in sync, following a beat.

I knew that I would belong to her, that I would do anything for her, when she began to look at her plate in the middle of the dance floor. She picked an apple slice, a red one, brought it close to my face. I opened my mouth, her pinky and ring finger caressed my cheek, her thumb and forefinger placed the fruit on my tongue, and it exploded in my mouth, not with taste, mind you, but with possibility.

The Sea, the Sea

I woke up disoriented, my neck awkwardly propped on the unfluffed pillow. I was like a drunkard coming to, unable to put together what I'd done the night before or where I was. The hotel room felt unfamiliar, dark and in shadows. The air flowed around me like cold ink, seemed to settle on my body. Nothing felt intimate. Jet lag felt horrible. My eyes adjusted to the darkness, amorphous shapes coalescing into sense. I leaned toward the nightstand on my left and clicked on the lamp. I stood up, motor functions operating properly. A quick shower might cleanse my mind and wash away the muddle. When I passed my reflection in the mirror a soulful groan rippled through my body. I both was and was not that woman measuring me. The gray hairs befuddled me. I still couldn't get used to their increasing numbers. I thought I'd gained at least ten pounds since Christmas nine days ago. My hips were moons whose gravitational pull forced my breasts to droop. Shower, shower, please. I felt slightly better as soon as I heard the sound of waves hitting the shore not too far from my hotel room.

I can't tell you how much I miss the smell of the sea. You're from the mountains; it can't be the same for you. My father's family lived in Ain el-Mraisseh for generations. I was raised by the sea. Call me Aphrodite, why don't you. I used to love walking the corniche—in daytime, when the boys would dive from high rocks while the bourgeoisie suntanned on lounge chairs, and at nightfall, when the fishermen rowed out into the darkened sea with their awkward boats. I even loved the Mediterranean in stormy weather, the euphonic sound of waves battering those rocks felt invigorating. Salt air quickened my soul.

The first time Mazen and I met after my cataclysmic family expulsion was in Vence, a little town on the Riviera. One of the myriad of remarkable things he brought with him—a jar of fig jam, Fairuz's latest compact disc, the first shirt we shared when we settled on the same size as teenagers and I would no longer receive his hand-me-downs—was a gray photograph of us on a beach south of Beirut. It seemed my mother had thrown out all my belongings and everything else that would remind her of me, but she didn't know that Mazen had a few photos in his possession. We were young, maybe five and six—a serrated photo, glued inside a cardboard folder that had four silver triangle pockets for the corners to fit into, protected by a sheet of embossed, semitransparent paper. Mazen covers me in sand, with only my head showing, whereas he is covered in a dusting of grains, having emerged from his own burial not too long before. My eyes are shut. I look in ecstasy, my gender indeterminate. We were born of the sea, he and I.

When Mazen married his wife, they moved into an apartment not far from our parents' home. He could not live far from the sea or from our awful mother. When his wife divorced him, he allowed her to keep custody of their children, but he kept their small apartment. She left him for a rich man who promised to take care of her. She moved into a glorious penthouse apartment where she could actually see the sea, not just smell it.

Except she ended up not exactly wanting custody of her children. She wasn't a cruel mother, not in the traditional sense. My niece and nephew lived with her — well, ostensibly they did. She put them in the best schools, bought them the best clothes, and hired the best nannies from the Philippines to take care of them. She didn't ask Mazen for a single lira in alimony. The children preferred to stay in Mazen's small apartment, which was what they knew. She rarely noticed that they were not at home, and the nannies loved the time off. The driver she'd hired to deliver them to school began to pick them up at the two-bedroom where they slept atop each other. But they, too, loved the sea's recurring slurring sound. They gave up rarefied air for the salty kind.

You said California suited you better than the East Coast because you couldn't bear the idea of the sun being reborn out of the sea every morning. Apollo's chariot needed to plummet at the end of the day. The sun must drop into the water, drowning and dying for our eyes.

The Art of
the Walk

It was still an ungodly hour. I stood at the edge of the harbor, taking deep breaths, the water giving off a saline, fishy smell, as well as that of motorboat fuel mingled with the acrid tannin aroma of surrounding trees. The sun had not yet appeared and neither had the horizon. In preparation for the rose bloom of dawn, early shadows began to form around the moored fishing boats. The slow lapping of water matched my breath.

I was supposed to have breakfast with Emma, but it was too early. I would walk. East or west, a mental coin flip, and I trudged west along a road not well asphalted, the beach to my right. A cold, intense blue drifted in the air.

I scuffed through mud, among the sodden seethe of leaves, following a bend that looped me around the northern part of the island. The landscape was not as pristine as I'd hoped. Various dwellings interrupted the unpeopled scenery, all occupied by NGOs, it seemed: a house and

garden for Doctors Without Borders, a building blazing
with mildew and a tent campsite for the Spanish lifeguards,
a motor home that distributed food. A confusing cardboard
sign nailed to a pine tree said DOCTOR 16:00–11:00 P.M.,
with an arrow pointing in the same direction I was walking. A sign pointing in the other direction was for a medical bus called Adventist Help, but the cardboard had aged
so much the writing was barely legible, which made me
wonder whether the Seventh-day Adventists had packed
their bus and driven off. Another sign farther along offered
free clothing; underneath it lay a dozen large garbage bags.
Were refugees supposed to take morning walks and then
rifle through the black garbage bags for outfits that fit?
Strange was this world of volunteering. Along a fence full
of constellations of woodworm holes, an aspiring artist had
hung a series of the orange life vests abandoned by refugees
after the crossing, three above each other, then two, then
three, then two, like the workout graphs on treadmills. A
little farther, red life vests were hung in the shape of a heart.

I should take morning walks when I get home, though
that might upset Francine. She takes a power walk every
day along the lake, winter, spring, summer, except if we're
having one of those berserk snowstorms. This is her solitary
time away from me, no distractions. She leaves her phone
behind. It would be selfish of me to take that away from her.
Even if I walked in a different direction, it would still be
an imposition. I mentioned walking to her once years ago.
Fine, she said, but why didn't I walk on an elliptical at the
gym, better for my creaky knees and all that. I did so for a
while, but I didn't like the fact that I'd exert so much effort
and remain in place.

Mazen is a walker as well. When he last visited me two years ago, he dragged me all over the city, from Hyde Park to Rogers Park, from the Loop to Oak Park, for hours and hours. I ended up with blisters. He loved the flatness of the city compared to Beirut, loved the unbroken sidewalks, the lack of car horns. I must have lost five pounds during his time with me, but not Mazen. He was always a mite rotund, even as a child, no weight loss no matter how much he ate or dieted.

I noticed footprints in the mud, different from those I was making. Someone had walked this road barefoot. I could see the heel impressions and the oval depressions of the toes. Was it a volunteer or a refugee? Since no boats had landed on this side of the island for a few days, the prints probably belonged to a drunk volunteer returning late. I turned around and began my walk back to the square.

The village was waking up, the square's pulse weak but getting stronger. The night raised its dark backside gingerly. A young woman inside the aquarium café from the night before took chairs off tables. A fisherman cleaned the outboard motor of his boat. Mourning doves cooed passionately under the eaves of a restaurant. And an unexpected sight in this rustic vista, a cross-dressing villager sitting leg over leg on a wooden chair underneath the plane tree, with a cigarette that glowed into sudden life. An antique bronze kettle of coffee, its top covered with a saucer, waited on the stone wall next to the chair. A calico lay across the cross-dresser's lap, purring loudly, offering her elongated neck for petting. We are everywhere, I thought. I wondered briefly how long I would have to withhold gendering, what clue would be offered. The red dress was much too short for cold weather, particularly without nylons or socks, hairy legs bared; a worn charcoal duffel coat was shorter than the dress. No wig, short, misbehaving white hair, no makeup. He likely identified as a man, a middle-aged guy in a red dress and sensible black pumps. He would later confirm my assumption. He had a smile on his face as he bent forward and whispered to the cat, definitely a morning person. An old Greek widow — stereotypical mourning black including head scarf, cane, and wicker basket — approached him, chatted for a minute. She petted the cat and continued toward the harbor.

When he noticed me, he said something that sounded like kaliméra, hesitated, and followed with a good morning. I raised an eyebrow and pointed to the chair next to him, asking if I could sit. I then had to decline his offer of a cigarette. His English was nonexistent. Did I speak German? No, I didn't. Did he speak French, mais bien sûr, Madame. His name was Nikolaos, of course. I'd known three Greeks in my life and all were named Nick or Nikolaos and so was every other Greek Orthodox boy in Lebanon. He'd spent a couple of years in Paris in his youth, such a lovely city, but not livable. A local man with a large duffel bag and a riotous beard came over, nodded toward me in acknowledgment, then launched into some funny Greek story. Nikolaos, now vibrant and animated, responded with something funnier, because riotous beard guy literally doubled over. He hauled his bag toward the harbor, still chuckling, his oversize stomach rising and falling like a busy pump. I asked Nikolaos what that was about and he unsuccessfully tried to explain. He asked where I was from, what I was doing in Skala Sikamineas. I told him I was a naturalized American, originally Lebanese, my mother was Syrian, and I was here because I wanted to help. He suggested I wasn't like the others. There must have been other trans volunteers, I told him. I knew of at least one.

"You're trans?" he said. "I thought you were, you know, just a dyke."

"I'm that as well," I said.

He said I was different because I talked to him—well, more than talked since a number of the European volunteers did so, but I was willing to have a conversation, not talk at him or tell him what to do. I told him to give me a little time; my wife complained all the time that I told everyone what to do. He found that mildly amusing. He explained that these volunteers, be they European or American, behaved exactly like the German tourists who arrived every summer full of imperious airs and left with shellacked skin and complaints about the chaos that was the island.

"Can you imagine?" he said. "Some Germans would give us advice on cooking. Think about that for a moment."

His eyes slanted toward the temples and bulged as if he had Graves' disease, in the early stages of exophthalmos, which gave him a strange look, almost like he had compound eyes with an abnormally wide angle of vision. What struck me more were his black pumps. How he could walk in them on these half-ass streets was beyond me. I tried wearing pumps a couple of times some thirty years ago, and it was a no-go, no way, not on your or anyone else's life.

Lesbos was a sleepy island. Nikolaos joked that their supply of things to happen had run out when Sappho was laid to rest. Things that happened happened elsewhere. But when the Syrian refugees first arrived, the entire village, the whole island, mobilized to help. No islander would ever leave another human being at the mercy of capricious waves, no matter who they were. That was the law of the sea. Why, that same man with the riotous beard once saved twenty-three refugees whose boat had capsized. He happened to be fishing in the area when he heard screams — men, women, children, and babies. Twenty-three people on that boat of his was neither safe nor smart but necessary. None of the refugees knew how to swim; none of them had even seen the sea before they made their crossing. As soon as a villager saw a boat, there would be a call and all would come out to help, even Nikolaos, though not in his black pumps. The country was in the worst recession in recent memory, no thanks to the Germans, yet villagers opened their homes, shared their meals, donated their clothes. Sometimes there were thirty or forty people sleeping in one house. The NGOs and the volunteers came. They thought they were doing God's work and they expected the villagers to serve them.

"They came because the situation was overwhelming," I said. "The numbers multiplied exponentially. You know that. It's a human disaster."

"Of course," he said. "But all these Northern Europeans think they fart higher than their ass."

I hadn't heard the idiom before, and when sylphlike Emma, also in pumps, made her grand appearance, Nikolaos and I were in the midst of giggling like preteen schoolgirls. I had to introduce them to each other; they hadn't met, which was not a revelation since I knew Emma was not fond of drag queens, let alone cross-dressers. She felt their existence belittled who she was. She turned down our invitation to sit. She wanted breakfast and, more important, a cup of coffee. I startled her by asking Nikolaos if he wished to join us, but he declined, pointing to his coffee cup and the calico sleeping on his lap.

You, the Writer

The weather report for the day was stretches of clear sky alternating with sudden showers. A few boats would make the crossing farther south, Emma said. Once Rodrigo woke up, he would drive us to one of the beaches, and I could begin to feel useful. Even this early in the morning, she smelled delicious, a subtle mélange of jasmine and cinnamon. She had great taste in perfumes and used them liberally, as though she would never wish to give off an odor that was her own. Eat, she said, nodding toward my bacon and eggs. I was going to need the energy. She chugged down half a mug of American coffee. The food was mediocre. I could imagine quite a few Germans who could give this cook a few pointers.

Emma then told me that she'd forgotten to mention it the night before — she was, you know, busy with Rodrigo — but she had seen you. I didn't know what she was talking about at first.

"You know, your writer," she said. "The Lebanese one. You sent me one of his books for Christmas, unreadable, worst gift ever. Why would I care about an old woman who doesn't leave her apartment? Didn't make any sense to me. That's not a story, that's just stupid. Anyway, he was here. Yes, in Skala Sikamineas. The day before yesterday. He looked familiar, but it took me a while to figure out who he was. I couldn't remember where I'd seen him. Who remembers author photos? With normal people I'd have gone up and asked whether we knew each other, but he's not normal. It was as if he had a sign around his neck that said CLOSED FOR BUSINESS. He didn't talk to anybody. He took walks from one end of the beach to the other, back and forth, always silent, constantly observing and judging. Yes, always judging. He'd move from one café to the next. He took walks when it was raining, for crying out loud. How strange is that? His eyeglasses were fabulous, though. Then all of a sudden he disappeared. He was here for a little more than twenty-four hours. I saw him eating dinner all by himself, the nervously smiling man whom no one seemed to know or want to, and then he was gone. Wait, I'm wrong. He did speak to someone, to that homely guy in the dress. I saw both of them sitting under the same tree, just like you."

I Missed You
by This Much

Why did you come to Lesbos? That's the wrong question. Why didn't you contact some organization before you arrived? You showed up and hoped for the best? I asked Nikolaos, who said you told him you wanted to help and you stopped on your way back to San Francisco from Beirut. He said you wondered why there were no boats arriving on the beach, which was why you were here in the village, and you were confused when he explained that boats were landing on different beaches now, on the beach near the airport and those farther south. Pressured by the European Union, the Turks cracked down on the smugglers on the Turkish beach closest to Skala Sikamineas, so the boats migrated south with the birds.

Did you not think of making a plan? Did you approach this like you do your novels, just start and figure things out along the way?

By the way, Nikolaos said my French was much better than yours. Be jealous!

Apparently you spoke to him at the exact time of morning I did, one day earlier. You were jet lagged as well. We missed each other by twenty-four hours.

He said that you were interested in discussing the history of the people of the village, how they were the sons and daughters of refugees themselves, arriving on the island after the Greco-Turkish War in 1922, all of them kicked out of Anatolia by the no-longer-so-young Turks.

You both shared an obsession with the massacres and fires of Smyrna that year. He said you used him as a narrator, an interpreter of stories.

I liked that term. I wondered if that was how you interacted with those around you. You wanted people's stories, not them. You cared for the tale, not the teller.

Here Comes
the Boat

Grayness, soft as amnesia, blanketed the sea. A grayer Turkey interrupted the line where sea met sky. I shivered in spite of multiple layers, including fleece and a rain jacket. I felt the cold of the new year. My teeth clattered sporadically. The morning had matured into a reasonable hour, but it hadn't warmed up. I wasn't just cold. I was uneasy, as if I were back in school waiting for the teacher to hand out an exam.

Emma and Rodrigo had met people they knew on the beach, and they introduced me, but I stood to the side as they talked. Emma furrowed her brow as she looked my way. She smiled when I realized that I was frowning. I tended to squint when I was thinking. My mother used to hate that when I was a child. She once placed clear tape on my forehead so I'd notice when I frowned. Why was I remembering my mother while waiting for a boat on such a cold morning? Maybe it was because this beach was as physically close as I had been to her in decades.

Rodrigo spoke into a Motorola two-way radio, a palm-size black and chartreuse that he had cradled like a newborn for the entire hour drive from Skala Sikamineas. The air crackled, as did the device. A voice spoke. Rodrigo informed Emma that a boat was coming. She flashed me a smirk that said something in between "See all I do for you" and "Isn't Rodrigo hot?" Half an hour out at most, we should be able to delineate the boat on the horizon soon, thirty-two people on a dinghy that wasn't supposed to carry more than a dozen.

"Royalty maybe," said Emma, because many boats of the same size had arrived with fifty refugees or more.

"The runners might be having cash flow problems because of the rains," Rodrigo said.

I felt the first drop of rain on my hair and pulled my hoodie up. I hoped this wasn't a prelude to a bigger storm, that Zeus wasn't patiently waiting to hurl a few of his thunderbolts. Half of the two dozen people on the beach opened umbrellas. Emma decided her multipocketed parka was good enough for the time being. She was dressed down today: jeans, muddy hiking shoes. The head-scarfed South Asian and Chinese women who had been on my plane ran toward a van in the parking lot to wait out the storm.

When the darker speck of gray appeared on the water, everything seemed to change. I shifted my weight from heels to metatarsals. I felt as if we all began coiling our springs. For a moment, I relished the feel of wind on my face. The air turned blue and razor sharp. Two men ran toward a gray truck as old as Sappho, returning with duffel bags — space blankets, Emma called them. So many volunteers, she said, for just one boat. Only two months earlier fifty-seven boats landed in one day and there were only eight volunteers to deal with the arrivals. Unfettered pandemonium it was, she said. More than a hundred infants arrived that day, all of them wailing because of the wet cold.

I had to adjust my hoodie, pull it forward, because rain had direct access to my eyes. Another van arrived in the parking lot, from which nine college-age kids jumped out, five boys, unshaven and in dude drab, each carrying a clear plastic storage box filled with sandwiches, and four girls, two of whom wore long dresses and head coverings, probably Mennonite or Amish, definitely American. One of the boys rushed past me, his tennis shoes flicking sand all about. He had such a deep tan he looked like he'd jumped out of a rotisserie. Emma and Rodrigo did not turn to look at the newcomers, but they sensed their presence, as if the youngsters were unwelcome animals, interlopers in pride territory. Emma bristled, took a long breath, held it for a time.

I was soaking wet before the rain let up. Even those under cover looked shriveled, except for Emma, who seemed unmoved by the weather as she kept staring at the boat. Give her a sword, I thought, and she would look like a painting of Joan of Arc.

Like an epiphany, the embryonic stain on the water transitioned into an actual boat. I could see the orange of the refugees' life vests, the gray green of the dinghy, the black of the wetsuits worn by the three people on Jet Skis—Spanish lifeguards I presumed—herding the boat to shore.

The sun, tired of being ignored, broke through. The sea now looked recognizable, the same translucent blue I

used to step into as a child. Rodrigo unfurled his Oakley
sunglasses, Emma her Prada. She pointed to two Italian
physicians in the group. They'd been on the island for two
weeks, she said. One of them was Giacometti-thin even with
his sweaters and peacoat. He wore spectacles as thick as
a glass paperweight. Looking at Emma's pointing finger, I
noticed that her nails were short and uncolored. The fabulous red press-ons of the evening before were gone.

Before she arrived, Emma said, smugglers bought
dozens of old wooden boats from Turkish fishermen, then
offered them to desperate refugees at exorbitant prices. The
beach at Skala Sikamineas once had over fifty boats piled
on top of each other. Many boats were landing each day
and at night too. One could clean the beaches, pick up all
the refugee detritus — there was a whole network of Greek
salvage guys who would take apart the motors and refurbish
them — but what did one do with the boats? Finally, some
Norwegian divers arrived and began to dismantle them plank
by plank until the area was clear. Rubber dinghies were
more common than wooden boats, which was worse because
they were easier targets for the commandos, dreadful men
in black uniforms and masks who attacked the refugees in
the waters. The commandos drove their boats toward the
refugees, used long knives attached to poles to rip open the
dinghies, and roared away. Sometimes they shot at the refugees. Greeks believed they were from the Turkish government, Turks thought they were Germans, but Emma said
they were rogues among the Hellenic Coast Guard, members
of Golden Dawn, the neo-Nazi party.

The cacophony arrived on shore before the boat:
the motors, the lifeguards on Jet Skis shouting in broken

English, the refugees replying louder in Arabenglish, which brought a smile to my lips as soon as I heard it. Like a giant single-cell organism, the crowd began to inch closer to the shore. I found myself being swept along, still remaining on the periphery. The noise on our side of the divide grew louder as well.

"If a single one of these youngsters takes a selfie with the boat," Emma said, "I'm going to gouge their eyes out."

"What?" I said. "You're not serious?"

"I most certainly am," she said. "I promise I'll do it. I've been saying it for a while now, and this time I will."

"No, I meant you're not serious that anyone takes selfies."

"Oh, darling," she said. "You're so wonderfully naïve. A little girl in the forest is what you are." She pulled me close, hip to hip. "That's really all they want. The perfect photo for Facebook or Instagram or whatever's the latest stupid thing. Look at me, I'm not useless. I'm a humanitarian. Aren't I wonderful?"

For a few seconds, we all stood motionless, anticipating. The peeking sun lent us shadows. The first to land was one of the Jet Skis. The other two hovered for a few moments until the boat beached. My first thought before the rush was that no one should get in a boat like this, ever, let alone get in with thirty people sitting on top of each other. My second thought wouldn't materialize because bedlam erupted.

Women and children were not first. Two young men jumped off at first stop, their shoes landing in beach foam. The shivering children, nine including two crying babies, were handed quickly to volunteers. Emma and I helped an old woman with pink watery eyes disembark, if you could call it that from such a slippery boat. We had to carry her; we gave her a throne by connecting our arms. She was a little wet and by no means a burden, so small and light as to be almost weightless, the bones in her face showing through pellucid skin almost blue from cold. She kept reaching back for her belongings, a tired plastic trash bag the size of a wheelbarrow. She relaxed when she saw Rodrigo carrying it. As soon as we placed her on a blanket, she began trying to unhook the life vest, the only nonblack thing she was wearing, but her fingers were stiff and cold, and she couldn't figure out the latch. Emma knelt in front of her, unclasped the life vest. A man gave her a shiny silver square. He was going from one refugee to another handing out blankets, and she gave his retreating back a look that said nothing if not "What the hell am I supposed to do with this?"

"It's to keep you warm," Emma said, rubbing her own arms to make herself understood. She retrieved the space blanket and unfolded it, gold lamé on one side and silver on the other. She tried to explain by gestures that the woman should change out of her wet clothes, crossing her arms at the waist and lifting them high, but the old woman paid her no mind. She wrapped herself in the blanket, covering everything including her head. She looked like sheet-shrouded cutting-edge furniture. I wanted to speak to her but wasn't sure what to say. I felt nervous, out of my depth. Emma said someone had bags of clothes, but I couldn't remember what part of the beach that was.

The old woman must have not sealed her plastic bag like the other refugees because some white cloth peeked out of it; upon closer inspection it turned out to be old wedding lace. That was possibly her own dress from long ago. I couldn't imagine anyone doing that sort of divine work in this day and age.

A space-caped man in his forties, light greenish in hue, stumbled over, puzzled by the silver mound. He, too, was still in his wet clothes. "Are you all right, mother?"

I shuddered in surprise, a frisson of excitement? Of fear? Of nerves? His simple question rustled the leaves of my memory. I'd recognized the accent, Syrian, from around Deir ez-Zor, the same area my mother was from, although she'd gotten rid of hers long before I was born. But that was not what looped me. It was the way the son called her mother, the Arab way, our way: O my mother. Those words rattled my spine.

The old woman pulled the silver blanket off her head, and her black head scarf slipped down to her shoulders, but she didn't seem to care. Sparse, messy, wet hair was all we saw for an instant before she raised her head and said, "Now you ask me? I died on that boat. The sea swallowed me. I screamed. 'Help me, my son,' I yelled and yelled, but you didn't come over. And when it rained, you stayed with your wife, not with your mother. I lost ten years with every scream, but you didn't care. When the man threatened to throw me overboard, you didn't stop him. But now you ask if I'm okay. I want to die right here, right here in front of all these ugly people and everyone will know that I have an uncaring son. May the earth open up and swallow me right here so I can die this minute."

I wondered if we were related, because that was my mother speaking.

Emma nudged me. "She was terrified on the boat," I told her softly, "and is taking it out on her son."

He had his head down, whether in shame, contrition, or frustration, I could not tell. "I couldn't move," he said. "No one was supposed to. For the balance of the boat. We were as uncomfortable as you were."

A boy of about ten with wide-open eyes approached the old woman. He held out his left wrist, and in his right hand he held an empty plastic bag. "Look, Grandmother," he said. "Uncle's watch is still working. Look, the hand of seconds still turns."

I don't think I had seen a watch that old-fashioned in over fifty years.

The old woman's face broke into what resembled a smile. Visible knots of dilated blood vessels appeared on her cheeks like warrior markings. She sat her grandson on her lap. "I told you it would work," she said. "Your mother knows nothing. You didn't have to take it off. I told you, cover it with plastic. You could cross an ocean and not a drop of water would touch it if you're careful. You're a good boy, not like your father who doesn't care about his mother."

The little boy beamed. His father seemed to be working on his breathing, inhaling and exhaling in a measured way.

The space blankets bent light in the uncanniest way. The silver and gold shimmered, and the volunteers looked as if they were hunting for treasure. One of the Mennonite girls was handing out sandwiches wrapped in tinfoil, more silver. I noticed a kneeling volunteer and thought he looked familiar. When he lit two cigarettes at the same time and handed one to an older Syrian man who had jute hair and looked traumatized, I recognized the Hertz clerk from the airport. Both men took a long drag of their cigarettes and began coughing at the same time. The refugee laughed.

Emma and I turned our heads toward a moan emanating from a woman on our left. She was being cared for by Dr. Giacometti. Her husband and three daughters hovered about. Emma grabbed my hand and walked me over to them.

The beach was a scene from a disaster movie, post-event, when the survivors get together and try to make sense of what happened: was that Godzilla or Mothra that laid waste to our city?

"It seems like there are as many volunteers as refugees," I said to Emma. "Maybe more."

"I told you, only for a few more days," she said. "And then most of the volunteers return home, their holiday over, and everyone forgets that we're here."

Dr. Giacometti was asking for the translator, but she was busy with someone else. The Syrian woman seemed uncomfortable. He kept trying to touch her and she'd flinch. I approached, but Emma was quicker. She suggested to Dr. Giacometti that the woman might let her examine her. They must have worked together before, because Dr. Giacometti hardly blinked. He began standing as soon as Emma began kneeling, mouthing what seemed like "thank you."

"I'm a nurse," she said. "Tell her, please."

Before I could say anything, the woman turned toward her husband. "Don't you say anything," she said in Arabic. "Not one word."

Her husband opened his mouth as if to speak but decided against it. He pursed his thin lips. Warm eyes refused to see anything but his wife. His birdlike face was etched with concern.

"Not one word about what?" I said in her language and watched the woman hesitate. Her husband gasped audibly. The three girls seemed confused. I'm told my bedside manner might be acceptable, if barely, but it seemed my beachside manner needed work. "I'm sorry," I said. "I couldn't help overhearing."

"There's nothing wrong with me," the woman said, but there was. Her eyes were bloodshot with a yellowish tint. She looked much too thin, as well as pale and exhausted, which could have been the result of a boat ride during a storm, of sleepless nights while traveling, of diesel fumes, of many possibilities, but I wouldn't be able to tell without examining her.

"She's a doctor," Emma said in English, whether to the woman or the husband I wasn't sure, but it was the eldest daughter who jabbed Emma with her finger a few times. "She, doctor?"

She couldn't have been more than ten, and she already had a head scarf, which I found strange. During my teenage years, when my father used to take us on trips to Deir ez-Zor, there were few women covered, let alone girls. Emma playfully jabbed the girl back, then jabbed me: "She, doctor." Then she pointed to herself: "Me, nurse." And then to the girl: "You, Tarzan?"

"No," the girl said, in an ardent tone. "Me, doctor." She paused, then extended her hand toward Emma. "Me, Asma," she said. "Me, doctor."

Emma didn't hesitate. Instead of accepting the proffered handshake, she pulled the girl into an intimate hug, wet mingling with wet. "Asma, my Asma," she said. "Best doctor in the world." She stood up, took the girl's hand. "Let's get you all into dry clothes so you don't come down with some nasty cold. Come on, all of you. Let's go change and find something nice for your mother to wear while she stays here and talks to this good doctor."

I had no idea whether the husband and three girls understood a word she said, but they followed her toward a van. As I watched them walk away, the three young girls holding hands, Emma turned around, gave me a smug look. "If you need me, wave your arms in the air like you usually do. I'm watching."

Four refugees stood a few feet away, all young men. One with high-rise hair, his coat soiled with every imaginable sort of stain, genuflected as if praying but made a joke of kissing the beach. When he rose, his face was decorated with patterns of sand, which all four found excruciatingly amusing.

Alone with me on the crowded beach, the woman clutched her swollen 1940s handbag with a terrified and resolute suspicion. I berated myself for my lack of manners.

"My name is Mina Simpson," I said. "Forgive my impertinence. This is my first time here. I was nervous and didn't think of introducing myself properly with all that's going on."

She forced a smile. I did not need a diagnosis to see that she was feeling pain. She consoled me by explaining that social niceties were the first things to disappear in a crisis, although they shouldn't, and she was happy that we were able to correct this minor misstep. Her name was Sumaiya, from a village outside of Hussainiyah, north of

Deir ez-Zor. Her husband's name was Sammy. Easy to remember, Sammy and Sumaiya. They were meant to be together, she said. Her family escaped from Daesh rule and regime bombing, mangy dogs all of them, she was never going back, and still, as much as she regretted it, she was not going to allow me to examine her. Her right hand lay on the upper right quadrant of her abdomen.

"I won't tell anyone without your permission," I said. "This is between the two of us. I'd rather examine you here with just us, instead of waiting until you get to camp, because I don't know what it will be like there. Will you let me?"

"No," she said. "Not here and not in camp. Maybe when we get to the end of the line, where we're supposed to live, maybe then."

And Pallas Athena's wise owl flapped her wings in my brain. I finally understood, stupid me. She was gaunt. Icteric sclerae, abdominal pain, right upper quadrant where she held her imitation crocodile-skin handbag, for crying out loud, Mina. Even her skin looked jaundiced now. Had her loose clothing been wetter, clung more to her form, I would have noticed the distended belly.

"How long have you known?" I asked.

I watched her face register shock once more, except this time she recoiled. Her eyes turned beady with anxiety. I should backtrack. I didn't want her to be frightened. I paused, then held her left hand. She would not look at me.

"I won't say anything without your permission," I said softly. "I promise you." And then, to make it more official: "I swear on my mother and father."

"What do you know?" she asked me, still facing ahead, toward the sea, toward where her past, her home, once was.

"I don't know," I said. "I'm only trying to figure things out. I'm guessing you don't need me to examine you. You know what's wrong, and whatever it is, it's serious, serious enough that no other ailment caused by travel or sea voyage is going to make much of a difference. You're afraid that if we find out, you will be sent back. Am I wrong so far?"

I could no longer read the expression on her face. Was she still afraid? Relieved? Curious? She remained silent, her eyes fixed east. I was right for the most part. I knew that. I might not be an oncologist, but I was not blind. I didn't want to force things. Francine jokingly calls me her bull dyke for many reasons. Don't leave me alone in a china shop. Sumaiya knew it was fatal, not just serious. How to be delicate?

"You're not afraid of being sent back, are you?" I asked. "No, you're not. You don't want your family to be."

She offered a weak smile.

"What kind of cancer?"

"You're doing a good job," she said. "Why don't you guess?"

"I can't," I said. "Not without examining you, but if I'm forced, I'd say liver, or that seems to be what's most apparent."

"See," she said. "You don't need to examine me."

I didn't need to ask if she was on any treatment. Figuring out her medical history would have been next to impossible. I knew that every hospital in her area had been blown to smithereens by the Syrians, by Daesh, by Russia, by the United States. Everybody had had a go at doctors and their hospitals. I wondered who had diagnosed her and how long ago.

"Do you know if the disease started in your liver or elsewhere?" I asked.

"Liver," she said softly, wistfully, without looking at me.

I squeezed her hand, told her that I would do everything I knew how to make sure she wasn't returned, which was highly unlikely in any case. I had only arrived the day before, I said, and knew little about what could be done on the island and who could help, and then I pointed toward Emma in the parking lot surrounded by Sumaiya's family and staring at me from way over yonder. She could help, I told Sumaiya. She worked for a Swedish NGO that had all kinds of doctors, and she would know how to make sure that they were not returned. Not only that, but she was trustworthy. If we told her not to tell anyone, she wouldn't. I extolled Emma's competence and discretion until Sumaiya relented.

I waved my arms in the air.

My Family

My father often drove to Deir ez-Zor to hunt fowl along the Euphrates, all kinds of birds, ducks and geese and quail and grouse and pheasant. Once or twice a year, he would drive for nine hours from Beirut, spend a few days, and return with a bounty that would be distributed to his friends, since his wife cared not one whit for cleaning or cooking the damn things. He went mostly by himself, and I wondered whether his passion was the hunt or the solitude. Since he was married to my mother, I thought it was the latter. But then, Deir ez-Zor was where he had met his beautiful and energetically ambitious wife, and he had already been going there since he turned eighteen, so it might have been the hunt. He was twenty and she seventeen when he brought her to Beirut, much to his family's chagrin since hers was of much lower class. His family shouldn't have worried too much, because she was much more class-conscious than all of them put together. After her marriage, she set foot in her

hometown once and only once, for her father's funeral. My
father kept to his hunting schedule; once or twice a year,
he would drive to Deir ez-Zor, stay with his in-laws, sleep
in their house, and eat with them. She wanted nothing to
do with the town or her family. She could not convince
him not to go, and he couldn't convince her to accompany
him. They compromised when it came to the children. The
three boys could accompany him every few years but my
sister never. Luckily for my mother, no one but my father
cared much for the city or her family: the drive was too
long, nothing to do over there, too hot in summer, too cold
in winter, lumpy beds.

I visited Deir ez-Zor twice only, including for the
funeral of my grandfather, whom I barely remembered.
What I did remember was that my mother made sure we
all dressed in our best and that she'd bought a black dress
we could barely afford.

I would not want you to think that my father and
mother did not get along, not at all. She worshipped him
until the day he died. He was above all for her — and not
simply because of tradition. Whatever his faults, and they
were plentiful, she loved him in both a godly and an ungodly
manner, for he used to look at her as if she'd arrived on a
scallop shell, the smell of sea on her hair. She was his holy
spirit. Their neuroses were perfectly complementary; their
insanities fit together like a jigsaw. The odd piece was mine,
not theirs.

I used to love him as well. When I was young, Mazen
and I would wait for him to get home from work. The first
thing he did upon entering the apartment was unlace and
take off his shoes and hand them over to us. My nose would

detect an ammoniacal odor. One black shoe on each of our laps, Mazen and I would sit on the old storage bench in the entryway, he to my left because he was left-handed. We would hand polish them to the perfect shine, rub them with a clean rag, delicately shove a cedar shoe tree into each, and then store the shoes in separate cotton bags. Before leaving for work the following day, he would unwrap each shoe as meticulously as we had wrapped them. When he returned from his hunting trips, we would have to take his boots out to the balcony for a vigorous scrubbing. He certainly loved his footwear.

When my father died, Mazen, the only family member who crossed my picket line after years of silence, sent me another photograph that my mother did not eradicate, a picture of my father, Firas, Mazen, and me on the one hunting trip to Deir ez-Zor. My father was the center in the photo, of course, holding a shotgun, a round mound raising a Beretta double-barreled over-and-under. Mostly whites and light grays, faded pewter and oyster, the photograph was of long ago, the sixties. His oiled hair was much darker than anything else in the picture, darker than the gun, the metal temples of his aviator glasses whiter than white. I remembered him that way, in that pose, the shooter of birds. When I imagined him, I even saw the vest he was wearing in the picture, its color in real life a diluted beige, wide enough to hold his sizable waist, with four deep, low pockets for carrying shot shells. Firas and Mazen, hyper and overtestosteroned, shot out in different directions, he the sizable sun, they his rays of sunshine. I stood next to him, the top of my head barely reaching his belt. I, his youngest offspring, his little black cloud, drip-drip-dripping tears—*the brute brute heart of a brute like you* — unwilling or unable to step away, my mass too tiny to resist his gravitational pull. That was what I remembered from my childhood. That dear child a false translation of who I was.

I was not surprised that Mazen would send a memorial photograph that included me crying. I was helpless with guns. I remember the exact make and model of my father's two shotguns, one for skeet and one for bird, but nothing about the one he handed me. Was it a fourteen gauge? He gave it to me in the morning and took it away moments later because I almost shot him as soon as I loaded it. He told me in his comforting voice not to fret because I couldn't have hurt him much given the size of the shell, but we both knew otherwise. I couldn't tell you which felt worse to him, the fact that I was hapless with guns or that I broke up in tears when the contraption went off, the pellets exploding right next to his foot, the circle on the dirt barely larger than the diameter of the shell, but I could tell you in minute detail how his devastated face looked that day, the shock, the horror, the sorrow, the open mouth, the white wide eyes with black dilated pupils, as if he'd returned from the ophthalmologist, the globular nose and its oddly circular nostrils, one smaller than the other.

Your Family

I would trade my family for yours any day of the week including Sundays and major holidays. Except for Mazen, he's my bud. And his children, my niece and nephew, I like them. The rest you can have. I can't believe you write about such horrid families even though yours has supported you throughout. When I first read you, I thought you must have been ostracized, disowned, disinherited, blackballed, all that kind of shit. The vast, abrupt chasm between your narrators and their families is clearly delineated, keenly felt. I was sure it was autobiographical. Then I met your family. They adored you, always had. I kept wondering how someone so loved could feel that alone, how you could remain unsated — a congenital condition, I assume. Even Francine wasn't able to figure that one out, and believe me, she's worked with all kinds of desperate people.

Maybe your family can adopt me.

The only person I talked to about my family was Francine, of course. I didn't mention them to friends or to my first partner, Jennifer. I buried them in a chest. I explained who they were to nosy Francine because, you know her, she could finagle any secret from anyone, which she could do effortlessly long before she passed her psychiatry boards.

Take My Kist

Had I not wanted anyone to see the content of my chest of secrets, Francine made sure to tell me long ago, I should have locked it. Not necessarily an elaborate lock, just a sign that the content was private would have been enough of a hint not to look within. Francine called the chest a kist and kissed me every time she used the term. Buy a small lock, she suggested. Wrap twine around your kist; tie a ribbon in its eyelets. She'd know not to snoop. Lock my privates, I joked. Both of us jittery, neither wishing to prod too much, not willing to commit either a silly blunder or an egregious error, to risk the first slight swerving of the heart. Francine had just moved in. During the weekend we brought all her stuff, all her baggage, her kit and caboodle joining my kist. We sat on one side of our bed, mine alone not a few days earlier, now impeccably made with her favorite dusky-brown duvet, the smallish chest between us, facing the closet where she found it, where she'd excavated it from under a myriad of cardboard boxes of books and papers and trinkets. I wished to point out but chose not to that a chest whose top had my original name, Ayman, amateurishly carved into the softened wood with a Bic pen should have given her pause. I saw traces of blue ink in the grooves of the script. It was possible that someone else might not be able to; it was possible that I was seeing the ink I supposed was there that had faded long ago, that I used to see. I knew I was making too much of this situation. The chest was a depository of my past, my book of reminiscences, just the thing I should be sharing with my lover. I should relax, unfurl those tense muscles in my shoulders. But who was I kidding, the strain in my body was palpable. My stomach called out for antacids. It was silly, I could easily talk myself out of this nervousness, could soothe this budding anxiety. I could make a joke. I always made jokes. I was good at that. I could repeat an aren't-we-all-afraid-of-intimacy cliché, any relief. Had I been the seer Tiresias, I'd have come up with a funny line to soften the pronouncement's blow: Listen, Oedipus, remember how your dad said you were getting too old for your mom's goodnight kiss, well, let me tell you . . . Was this a Tiresian moment? My life before and after the opening? I feel ridiculous, I explained. I don't think there's anything more than papers and pictures in here. I want you to see them, and I don't know why I'm terrified of that. Francine kissed me without having to mention kist. I'll show you mine, she said, if you show me yours. That was how it began.

With its old hinges yielding with a woeful moan, I opened the box, pandoraed it, and unleashed my demons unto Francine's world. Don't blame me, I warned her.

The Family

We had to register the family with the police, find them shelter for the night, make sure they left for Athens soon, get Sumaiya diagnosed, on a treatment schedule if possible. She needed stronger pain medication than paracetamol. She'd had nothing else. She must have dealt with such pain. I brought stronger stuff with me, but I'd left it all in my hotel room. Stupid me. Oxycodone? Yes, I bought one bottle. Morphine as well. Half my suitcase was filled with pills of all sorts. I hadn't even unpacked them yet.

I wanted Emma to fix the problems. She knew what to do, where everything was. She chose to commiserate with Sumaiya, holding hands and speaking in soft tones and broken languages. Sumaiya's husband, Sammy, sat on the sand cuddling with the middle daughter. I asked Rodrigo if we should take the family to be processed. No, we were to wait for a bus that would transport all the refugees to a camp called Moria; we couldn't fit all five in our car.

THE WRONG END OF THE TELESCOPE 67

I felt helpless. What could I do?

I was a connoisseuse of helplessness, impotence my intimate. At times, like Orpheus, I felt I could sing to life itself, to defeat the reaper if only for a little while, but I also had to watch in despair as Eurydice was dragged back into the underworld. I'd heard complaints about doctors and their god complex, particularly surgeons. I'd been around physicians most of my life — some were arrogant, some were plain assholes — but I had yet to meet one who thought she was omnipotent. But then neither was god, if she or he existed. We were able to do incredible things every now and then, but often we were helpless. We were godlike in the sense that we were both omnipotent and impotent, and like god, often all we could do was watch and witness.

I took out my phone, went online to figure out as much as I could about hepatoma. I wondered if I should get a local phone number to save on roaming charges.

Asma, the future doctor, unwrapped the top of her sandwich, leaving the rest of the tinfoil to keep it from falling apart. She examined the content between the bread, then took an exploratory first bite. The tinfoil made her look like a bird with a silver beak. She found the taste strange but tried another bite. I explained that it was peanut butter and jelly, a strange American invention. She thought it was much too sweet for a sandwich but kept on eating.

That was not the case with the old woman back where we left her. She was sitting upright now, with the allegedly uncaring son and his family around her. The consummate curmudgeon took one bite of the sandwich and spat it out. A young blond volunteer tried to berate her for spitting out the food, but the Syrian woman simply turned her back to her. Even from a slight distance, the old woman appeared livelier, pinkishly robust in spite of her long trip and longer age. Time, that capricious banker, hadn't yet seen fit to collect all interest due. The college girl tried a different tack, asking the old woman why she didn't like the sandwich, the translation done by one of the old woman's granddaughters. There was some sort of one-sided conversation during which the old woman remained strategically hostile. The college girl showed her an iPhone — the latest, no doubt taken out of its box on Christmas — asking in a theatrically interrogative tone, the kind used to stimulate viewer curiosity at the end of an episode, "Is it okay if I take a photograph with you, and then I can show you what it looks like right here on the screen?"

I wasn't sure if the old woman understood any of the prattle, but she uttered the one English word that made the young girl blanch. "No," she yelled. Where did passions find room in so diminutive a body?

"Eye gouging avoided," I said.

"Don't bet on it," Emma said. "The girl will hit on someone else. Look for the babies, you'll find idiots taking selfies."

I ended up talking shop with Dr. Giacometti from Bari while we waited. He'd been on the island for two weeks, his second stint since October. Sumaiya kept throwing questioning glances my way. I told her in Arabic not to worry, that we were not talking about her. Her youngest daughter, around four or so, napped on her lap while Emma stroked the girl's hair. Giacometti had decided he wouldn't come to meet another boat, preferring to work in the camp, but he was bored on break this morning and thought he'd check the beach. He sang Emma's praises, she who reigned over the island, the best nurse on Lesbos, who could fix every problem. He told me a funny story about meeting his first boat back in October, when he was trying to help a terrified woman disembark and in her flailing she struck his face and his glasses flew off into the water. He wasn't sure what to do. He couldn't see without them. Should he keep helping the refugees off the boat or look for his glasses? He joked that the question became existential: he could help the refugees as a man, but if he were to help as a physician, he needed better eyesight. He hunted for his spectacles like a purblind pelican, to no avail of course, even though the water was calm that day. Then the most amazing thing happened. He noticed an amorphous dark shape plunge into the water ahead of him. Then a shivering ten-year-old Syrian boy emerged, his hand rising out of the sea first, holding Giacometti's glasses.

"I was stunned," he said. "I broke into tears. I was the lady who dropped her handkerchief, and he was my knight in shining armor, a child who should have been sitting in a classroom somewhere on such a morning. Look, I'm about to start crying now talking about it."

I considered giving him a hug but settled on a pat on the shoulder, which was when his colleague approached. "Let me guess," the other doctor said in almost accentless English. "He has told you the story of the boy-knight refugee who risked his life by diving off a high tower into shark-infested waters to retrieve Paolo's eyeglasses." Giacometti pretended to strangle his colleague. We chatted for a minute or so; they cracked a couple of unfunny jokes that made them laugh. I glanced down. Emma hugged Sumaiya, who wept surreptitiously, noiselessly, hoping her daughters wouldn't notice. Her husband held his breath, apparently trying not to cry.

We were duly interrupted by panicked selfie-girl, who asked if anyone had seen her cell phone. She had it a minute ago but couldn't seem to find it. I knew Emma was going to start laughing. Selfie-girl ran from one contingent to the next investigating; each group of refugees and volunteers occupied a precise location, like elements in the periodic table. One of the Mennonite girls offered to use her own mobile to call the missing phone.

A converted school bus appeared, a yellow rectangle in the distance. Everyone gathered their belongings, meager as they were, before heading toward the parking lot. Most of the refugees carried their belongings in large black trash bags. As I passed the old woman, I heard hers ringing.

My Mother and
the Can Opener

My mother arrived in Beirut a young country girl, barely able to read and write, having never strayed more than a donkey ride from her village. She would remake herself within a short period of time and kept doing so for as long as I could remember. She emerged from one cocoon after another, and each butterfly wanted nothing to do with the caterpillar she'd once been. My father was not well-off, particularly when they were first married, but she spent whatever extra money she had on clothes and, more important, accessories. She could wear the same dress for an entire week and make it look different each day. I inherited none of that talent.

A number of her dresses were markers of my childhood. Instructing my sister on boiling rice while wearing a red dress with small blue lilacs spattered across it as if she had tumbled into a bushel of flowers, yelling at me for trying on her precious pillbox hat in a white high-neck number, a sophisticated cut that highlighted her slim figure. For the slap, she had on her popover purple dress. A few days after my ninth birthday, I stood before the full mirror after a bath, drying my hair, noticing that the towel around my head made me look less boy. I wrapped it like a turban, held it high atop my head. I was an African village woman going to market, a desert maiden visiting the well. Naked before that mirror, I moved one thigh in front of the other and disappeared my penis in flesh not yet fully plump. Mazen accidentally opened the door. Stunned, he didn't shut it quickly enough. My mother in purple passed by. She rushed in, smote my African-cum-desert-maiden hairdo without a single word, and slapped me hard. In my late fifties, I could still feel my cheek burning.

I idolized her as a child—well, early on I did. She exemplified the word "fabulous." She used to gesture dramatically with her hands while talking. I used to think that I didn't need to hear her words because her hands explained everything, that those hands of hers were the last practitioners of a lost Babylonian language. Then her gestures matured, became grander, with more flourish, more panache. They no longer illustrated her narrative, were more about style than a need to be understood. I would get lost trying to reinterpret them.

Francine insisted that women like her should not have children, that we only served as garnish. In her own way, my mother loved her children—loved us with a lofty, magnanimous detachment. She air-kissed us goodnight. If any of us achieved anything of consequence, she'd pat us on the head. My brother Firas at seventeen ran the fastest 400 meter in the school district. He received a pat on the head. I had such high scores on the baccalaureate that a Lebanese organization offered to pay my way through Harvard, a pat on the head.

Most of the clothes she bought for us were neutral, blacks and whites and grays and browns, whereas she preferred bright colors. Wherever we showed up as a family, our subdued hues made her shine. It wasn't just us. The walls of our home were a dead white, the furniture beige. Even the carpets were muted. Everything in the apartment had a function: to make her appear striking.

I have one remaining photograph of her in my chest of secrets, from the late sixties, the colors tinted an aging orange. Draped around her shoulders is a white cardigan with red piping. She is going for *Vogue* kitchen elegance on a restricted budget. Her hair is high in the style of the era, an elaborate chignon that required gallons of hairspray; my eyes stung looking at the picture. In front of her, on the Formica kitchen table, mustard yellow, lie a number of kitchen utensils, three bowls, and her newest acquisition at the time, the reason the camera was brought out of its case: an electric can opener. Her hands magically appear from beneath the floating cardigan to direct the viewer's eyes toward her prize. My mother's smile is that of a winner.

Her joy wasn't everlasting, of course. It was a year at most before the electric can opener earned its place at the back of the pantry next to the sealed jars of pickled turnips.

When cans infested Beiruti consciousness, it was about moving up in the world, giving up pesky traditions. My mother desperately wanted to be lifted by the calloused hands of modernity. Nothing spoke to her better then. Look, every single asparagus the same size, not like the idiosyncratic stalks of nature. We were all duly, if briefly, impressed. Canned mushrooms were a particular favorite. The end arrived when in high summer my mother made a compote of canned fruits. I remember looking at the dish before me while smelling the freshly picked peaches atop the sideboard. I wasn't the only one. My father stared wistfully at the overflowing bowl. Mazen held up pieces of the slimy, syrupy fruit one by one. He curled his upper lip and put a slice of mandarin there as a mustache.

Like her pillbox hat and my brothers' psychedelic prints, the novelty ran its course, and we returned to picking fruits off trees. Some years later a forgotten can spontaneously exploded, detritus of botulism and string beans covering everything in the pantry.

The Little Rascals
Go to Camp

Sumaiya and her family rode the bus while Emma, Rodrigo, and I followed in the car. Luckily, we'd decided not to take my Opel that morning. Emma's rental Honda was much more comfortable. In the back seat, I suddenly felt exhausted and sluggish. Drowsiness overwhelmed me. Talking to me through the rearview mirror, Emma suggested that I close my eyes for a bit. It would be at least half an hour before we reached Moria. I fell asleep before she finished her sentence.

I dreamt of my mother, of my father, of sitting before them as an adult, all of us underwater in the Mediterranean, something like that, everything fleeting and hollow. I heard strange knocking noises, as if I were in an aquarium with some child knocking on the glass, my head echoing back. And indeed it was a child who woke me — or rather five of them — four boys and a little girl, all in clothes that had seen better days if they'd ever had a good one. The kids stepped back from the car as soon as I turned, all of them giggling. I'd slept for hours, my head leaning against the rear window.

I had a text from Emma explaining that she thought it would be best to let me sleep, that I should come to the camp when I woke up and call her. I stretched my arms, used the car's roof as support, which made the children laugh louder. I got out of the car, asking them in Arabic if there was something wrong or if they found me generally amusing. The eldest boy, no more than eleven, clad in a multidarned sweater, explained that I was snoring loudly. He could hear my snoring through the car window, he said, but not his friend and lieutenant, pointing to a younger boy, because his ears were filthy. His ears had so much dirt, the eldest boy said, that you could grow wheat in them and make bread. The other boy, whose ears did not seem any dirtier than the rest, was not amused.

It had rained sloppily while I slept, and all the cars parked along the road were still dripping. Shreds of frayed clouds congealed into a dark, menacing mass, covering the light with thickets of moisture. The shadows around me grew fainter.

The children asked me where I was from, then introduced themselves. The leader, his lieutenant, and another boy were from the Aleppo area. The fourth boy was all the way from Pakistan and didn't speak Arabic, but he was fun nonetheless, and the blond girl clad in strident colors was from Iraq and didn't say much because she was shy, but she had to be in the club because the leader's mother would beat him up if he didn't allow girls. And what did their club do? Well, it was formed only that morning, so their objectives were not entirely clear yet, but the main reason for the club's existence was mischief making, as in his mother told him to take his friends and make trouble for other people not her, if he knew what was best for him, and of course he knew. Could they take me into the camp to meet my friend? Of course they could, and not only that, they would explain things to me since I was obviously new, but it was going to cost me. No, not money but a whole chocolate bar, or two since there were five of them, and of course they knew I didn't have chocolate on me. I didn't even have a purse, but I could buy candy at one of the cantinas over there, the boys said. The big one facing the gate had the best chocolate; the owners had given them two bars that morning for picking up all the paper cups and putting them in a garbage bag. Had I ever had coffee out of a paper cup? And it was hours ago since they had chocolate and they were five and it was only two bars, and they could tell me all kinds of things about Moria, the camp to my right, not the city in *The Lord of the Rings*, but they could even explain the movie to me if I wanted, so I should buy them chocolate bars, of course I should.

Cars and vans were parked bumper-to-bumper on both sides of the narrow road. The Iraqi girl took my hand in hers. I thought she was following the universal edict of hand-holding when crossing the street, but then one of the boys grabbed my other hand. They were escorting me across, guides safariing me through this frightening savannah, making sure I wouldn't be attacked by a feral car. We passed a couple of wobbly snack trucks parked along the road; the boys called them cantinas. Apparently there were gypsies the day before, selling new and used clothing out of the back of a truck but nothing nice. We had to maneuver around the numerous cantina patrons, primarily Syrians as far as I could tell but at least two African men and one South Asian, almost all smoking and drinking coffee. Quite a number of them were charging their cell phones. The cantina sold everything anyone in the world could ever want, the boys explained. Did I need a phone, a sim card, coffee, sugar, a sandwich, a foul-tasting banana ice cream, a much-too-expensive soccer ball, a Messi T-shirt, anything my heart desired. And chocolate bars, I said.

I bought them five. I had to. The Greek owner, a woman in her forties, suggested that I shouldn't have because they'd had too much sugar. She'd given them each a bar that morning, free of charge, after which they began to persuade her customers to buy them more. She'd lost count of how many bars they'd devoured. The little tricksters preened. I expected to find canary feathers stuck to the chocolate smears around their lips. When I asked the Iraqi girl how many chocolate bars she'd had, she put up four fingers.

Immediately within the gate to the refugee camp across the road was a large police van, its motor idling, its color a blue so gloomy as to be almost black. I couldn't look at anything else for a minute. It was a beacon of dark in the light, a big blob of bad color. The kids, still savoring the chocolate, stood on either side of me looking at the same van. They were so big, one of the boys said, pointing at three policemen in full riot gear smoking beside the van, helmets off to make it easier for cigarettes to couple with lips. They had not laid their polycarbonate riot shields down. Big boys with machine guns, batons, vests, neck protectors, knee pads—yes, body armor made your ass

look fat. They didn't speak English, another boy said, or
Arabic. They didn't talk except to each other. The cinder
block wall next to the gate shouted defiantly: NO BORDERS
NO NATIONS in red graffiti.

I told the children that I could go in by myself; they
did not have to be my guides. But they insisted. I needed
them, they said. And we had made a deal. Once more they
held my hands and led me across the road. The camp was
contained by high concrete walls and chain-link fencing,
all capped with concertina razor wire, giving it the air of
a high-security prison gone awry because there were hundreds of pup tents in the olive grove outside. There wasn't
enough space inside, the boy leader said. There were more
refugees outside the camp than inside. The Pakistani boy
slept with his family in a tent in another olive grove on
the far side of the camp. The boy leader told the Pakistani
boy that we were talking about him, before turning back
to me and complaining that they couldn't understand each
other and that created a strain in their relationship. One
of the Syrian boys told me that his family had to sleep in
the open air the first night because they couldn't afford
to buy a tent, which was bad because of the cold and lots
of ants, but they were moved into the camp barracks the
second night, and they were going to Athens on a boat
tomorrow, so everything was all right. They explained that
all of them would be leaving within a week or two except
for the Pakistani boy, and they weren't sure how he could
survive without them.

Slight rain welcomed us as soon as we entered the gate,
slight enough that the children hardly seemed to notice it.

The three policemen didn't seem to notice either the rain or us; Cerberus they weren't. These were policemen, the boys said. This was a van, this building was for camp administrators, and they had their own bathrooms. These families were going to the bus that would take them to the ferry that would take them to Athens and then by train to Europe proper. The ship to Athens was huge and was completely safe.

You, the Immigrant

You once wrote that you felt embarrassed when critics and reviewers classified your work as immigrant literature. You joked that the worst immigration trauma you had endured was when your flight from Heathrow was delayed.

Pants on fire! Are all fiction writers liars, or are you just being Lebanese?

Like all of us, you had to adjust.

The Beirut of 1977 could not have prepared you for the Los Angeles you arrived in. You landed in the City of Angels with your father while the civil war raged back in Lebanon. He was there to help you find a place to live and set you up at UCLA. He wanted to ensure that you'd be able to make do on your own for a while. He only had one week before he was supposed to return. No one was sure what would happen to the family as the Lebanese war dragged on.

Your father rented a monster of a car, a Cadillac. That was what one drove on the big roads of America. You stayed in a hotel close to campus. On your second night in LA, you were to visit friends of the family who lived in Pasadena. They had suggested you meet at a landmark, the Hilton Pasadena, and drive to their home from there. On a slip of paper you wrote down the directions given to you by the concierge. Your father suggested you drive. You could use the experience since you would soon be eighteen and would need a car.

He made fun of you even as you settled in the driver's seat. Were you sure you could reach the gas pedal? Ribbing you was his favorite pastime. You thought driving the rental Cadillac was a piece of cake. Your father asked repeatedly if you knew what you were doing. You reached Robertson Boulevard and turned south. You got on the ramp for I-10 and merged into traffic smoothly. You were looking for the Pasadena Freeway, you announced confidently. You turned on the radio, but your dad turned it right off, wanting no distractions.

You reached the second freeway and got on it. Again, you merged into traffic wonderfully. You could see your father smiling. All of a sudden, on your right, among tall buildings, you saw a large sign that said HILTON in red neon. Look, you said gleefully. You were already there. You took the first exit and voilà, you drove right to the Hilton's entrance.

Your father was proud of you. You were his boy for sure.

You used the pay phone to call the family friend and inform him that you'd arrived. He sounded amazed you'd made it that quickly and told you he would be there shortly. You waited in the lobby and waited and waited. No one showed up.

Your father called his friend after half an hour had passed. You began to sweat when you heard him laughing on the phone. You weren't at the Pasadena Hilton but instead at the Los Angeles Hilton. You were downtown, even though the freeway had loudly announced itself as the Pasadena Freeway. You were supposed to take it all the way to Pasadena. How were you to know that? You couldn't conceive of the existence of more than one Hilton in a country, let alone in one city. Why would a country have more than one Hilton?

Your father snickered and said he would be driving.

And like all of us, you did experience trauma.

You wrote about the early troubles you faced as an immigrant, being called all kinds of names during the Iran hostage crisis by classmates at that most liberal of institutions, UCLA. You tried to explain that you were neither an Iranian nor a Muslim, but how could you convince anyone while speaking with a distinct accent?

You were unable to pronounce *Eye-ranian* the way they did.

Someone smashed your car window with a baseball bat in the parking lot of a gay bar on Santa Monica Boulevard, while you were inside the car no less. Would you consider that an immigrant trauma or your run-of-the-mill gay bashing? How unfair. You hadn't even gone into the bar. You'd been sitting in your car for fifteen minutes to make sure that no one was carding at the door and another fifteen trying to build up the courage to walk in.

It was a new car, too, your first in America.

Welcome to Moria,
Ladies and Gentlemen

I saw you standing in the heart of Moria. I looked up the hill, up the cement road, and you were smack in the middle, between the fenced barracks, the prefabricated offices of the NGOs, the tents—so many tents—the garbage dumpsters, the garbage. You were looking downhill, but you didn't see me or the kids I was with. You couldn't take your eyes off the Greek riot police in high butch behind me at the bottom of the hill, with their vans and their batons and their Power Ranger outfits complete with face shields. You stuck out like a mole on clear skin—a beauty mark, darling, a beauty mark. In the midst of misery, you looked more miserable, even from a distance, anxiety discernable in your posture. I walked toward you up the hill, people going up and down, volunteers, refugees, all nationalities. A few sub-Saharan Africans kicked a soccer ball around, a game between pup tents, each with a refugee family guarding its entrance, long lines of people to my left and to my right, and puddles, mud puddles everywhere. Many people, so many. Families, single men, children. The boys pointed out Syrians, Iraqis, Afghans, Iranians, and more, more. North Africans from Algeria, from Morocco, sub-Saharan Africans from Mali, from Congo. Everyone was running away from much, the Syrian regime, Daesh, the Taliban, terrorist groups with even sillier monikers. Lines everywhere, for registration, for food, for clothes, for donations. And white people directing pedestrian traffic.

The kids kept up their job, chattering with each step. That was where they received free tea, here was where they could get extra blankets. The soccer ball belonged to a Greek man, and you had to write your name down and wait to borrow it. Then you had to return it in half an hour. I paid only half attention. As I approached I began to feel concern for you. More than despondent, you looked frightened and disoriented, as if you'd just woken up into a horror of a dream. I wondered whether you were about to have an anxiety attack or were in the midst of one. Something intrigued you, made you turn around. I stopped a couple of feet away. The boys pointed to a prefab structure where volunteers were serving hot drinks and cookies, said they would get in line for their cookies and if I wanted one I would have to stand with them. I told them I wanted to talk to you. They promised to return.

From a few feet away I watched you watch a handsome young Syrian teenager talking on an older-model iPhone, overbundled in sweaters and duffel coat, his eyes shiny and resinous. The small, jutting rock he sat on would keep his pressed pants dry if not clean. He gave the impression of wearing all his belongings. He relayed the details of his journey to his mother back in Syria, the interminable wait on the Turkish shore, the dinghy crossing, the rain, the registration lines. He tried to ask about the rest of his family, but he would be cut short, having to tell her how he was doing, nothing was more important than him. You and I waited for a minute or two. We heard and observed, and then he broke. He wept silently before telling his mother how much he missed her or, more precisely, how much her absence devastated him, and I heard you gasp. Our language is heartrending. You were about to cry, too, but you looked around quickly, noticed me hanging around, and controlled yourself, pulled your face together. He put his phone away and stood up, such a beautiful boy, a breathing kouros, fully clothed, taller than either of us, but then few weren't. I saw you step forward, then stop, then move again. The veins along your temple throbbed and thrummed and expanded. You introduced yourself to the young man, apologized to him, said you couldn't help overhearing the conversation. Could you ask him a few questions, find out his story? Your voice sounded soft and brittle, as if you were a vinyl record played on an old gramophone. He seemed flustered at first but eased up, possibly when he realized you were more nervous than he. Where was he from? From a village outside Hama. No, there was no war or violence in his part of the province, some skirmishes, many deaths a year and a half ago but not now. There was nothing, literally nothing, no work, no school. He was eighteen and a half—he stressed the half—and he wanted an education, to study something, anything. What could he do? His family gathered all its money, his father, his mother, two of his uncles, even his grandmother; everything went into a pot to get him to Europe. He was hoping for Germany, but he would go anywhere that had a university. He would study, work hard, repay all of his family's investment and faith and then some. He would not shirk, not he. You allowed him to walk off when he was done talking, his head down, leaning forward, almost breaking into a run down the hill, away.

The kids returned, asking what I wished to see next. The Iraqi girl was the only one of them still eating her cookie. I told them that I wanted to talk to you for a minute, pointing to where you were, but you were there no longer. You had vanished, poof. Now it was my turn to stand where you'd stood, flummoxed and disoriented in the midst of the refugee camp, wondering what happened to you, not knowing where to look, where east and west were. The riot police were still at the bottom of the hill. But unlike you a few minutes earlier, I had my children around me, the little Iraqi girl holding my hand, the grainy stickiness of sugar in my palm.

You, the Nervous Wreck

You would later say that that incident was your breaking point. You wanted to go back to San Francisco and get a manicure, paint your nails blue, get a massage, get away. You said you ended up in your hotel room in Mytilene behind a locked door, under the sheets, noise-canceling headphones blasting Christa Ludwig singing Mahler's *Kindertotenlieder* into your soul. What breaks us is rarely what we expect.

I had read the essays you wrote about Syrian refugees in 2012 and 2013. They were one of the reasons I came to this Greek island. You'd been working with refugees in Lebanon since the beginning, years before the crisis in Lesbos. You'd interviewed children whose entire families were killed, talked to survivors of massacres, met victims of torture. You interviewed a seven-year-old girl who showed you a drawing of her lost home hanging from a parachute. She said the parachute was needed to keep the house safe in case it had gone flying off with no one to look after it any longer. You talked to a mother in Oslo whose son was being beaten on a regular basis by the other boys in school. She told you Europe may have once been a sanctuary but no longer. Europe was like the light of a star that kept going long after the star itself had died.

Hell, I remember you wrote about the man who invited you into his tent near Zahlé. He was bedridden with the flu and kept smelling a potted sage plant, thinking it a cure. He wouldn't talk to you about what happened to him even though you could see the bandages around both arms and chest. His son finally whispered that his father was slowly skinned while in the notorious Tadmor Prison in Palmyra, a government torturer had spent an entire day peeling layer after layer of his father. That did not break you, but a boy having to leave home to get an education did.

We Could All Use
a Little Break

Like you, I left home to get an education. Thirty-something years ago, I was accepted by Harvard and a local organization offered to pay for the whole caboodle, a full eating-drinking-sleeping-studying scholarship, the prestige of which earned me my family's blessing. *Leave, leave, young man, God be with you — leave and return to us with untold riches and a smidgen of culture to edify.* I left that country, left my mother; I wanted to, and also like you, I surprised everyone by not returning even though I knew I wouldn't from the start. I transitioned in college; I changed from a depressed person to an angry one. The humiliations of my childhood — the don't-do-this, the boys-don't-do-that, the you-must-try-to-be-normal — all those sticks and twigs, dry kindling, burst into a furious bonfire. Everything was my family's fault, of course it was. My cracked cup ranneth over with molten rage that no saucer could contain. My calls home became more obstreperous and less frequent. My side of the

conversation consisted of various permutations of "I hate
you, I loathe you, you never respected me, you never understood me, I'm unhappy and you made me so, I demand
justice, I despise you." Anger was the shape of my breath,
outrage the sound of my voice. I cultivated indignation like
a hothouse orchid. My mother kept insisting I follow her
rules: I should do this, I couldn't do that, I shouldn't think
I was going to get away with whatever. She made sure to
explain that I was giving the whole family a bad name, that
they would be ridiculed because of me and my actions and
the way I was choosing to live my life.

I had been a teenager during the age of rage and carpet-
bombing and obliteration, the age of Baader-Meinhof, Kiss-
inger, and the rejectionist factions of the PLO. I learned
much. I knew how to encase my rampant heart in iron and
plod ahead, and when I left home I most certainly did. I
wasted much then. Profligate, that was me, shedding many
a weight, many a burden, the heaviest my past. I gave up all
its chains. I wooed amnesia. In the Arabic-speaking world,
dissidents and agitators attempted to discard the colonial
past, and in America, I forswore the family name. I became
the continuous revolution, unshackled from bourgeois con-
straints, living in the present. Lot's wife was a cowardly
weakling. I was no prophet's wife. Don't look back in anger
or in sorrow. I galloped forward, focusing on the lure of the
mechanical rabbit before me.

Mistakes were made. I was rebelling against my mother
and could not voice it eloquently. She used many choice
expletives addressing me, and I finally called her a whore.
The decision to cut me off, though, was not hers alone. Both
Firas and my sister, Aida, led the charge and killed me off.

Firas was the one who delivered the news: "You are dead to us."

In many ways, the betrayal by my siblings hurt more than that by my parents, and no wound was deeper than Mazen's silence. The years when he did not speak to me were the worst. Mazen, my Mazen. I could not believe that he had abandoned me. We were supposed to be inseparable. All my memories included him. The earliest and brightest, indelible, was of my following him. He walked the corridor of our apartment up and down, dragging a red fire truck on a string. He told me to follow him and pretend to cover my ears while he imitated a siren: "Waa-woo, waa-woo, waa-woo." I must have been three, if that. That was the oldest memory I had, and he was with me. If he wanted a rupture, I was willing. I was strong. I immured my heart.

The family wanted a break, so I made it official. I changed my name legally. I would not return. I disappeared in that country of unremitting reinvention. I thought I would never ever forgive charming Mazen, but of course I did. He's a slippery fellow, isn't he, and cunning?

Over the Rainbow

Emma said she would come get me as soon as Sumaiya's family settled in the barracks. It should not be more than fifteen minutes. The family had spent a couple of hours registering and had to wait for bed assignments. When I hung up, the little gang leader wanted to know what I wanted to see in the camp. I explained that I had to wait in the same spot until my friend came for me. Another boy asked if I wanted to go to the bathroom, and when I said no, he said I should be grateful because the public bathroom was anything but clean. He knew of a French woman who was so disturbed by the filth that she ran to her car, drove for fifteen minutes to a gas station, and used their facility. He wanted me to know my options in order for me to plan ahead.

A young couple in neon-red volunteer vests walked up the hill, took out their phones a few feet from us. A third volunteer passing by wondered what they were doing in the camp on their time off. The young man held up his phone as explanation. The Iraqi girl tugged on my hand and pointed to a bloated cardboard sign stuck with black masking tape to the concrete wall behind us, FREE WI-FI stenciled on it. I asked her if she'd understood the volunteers, if she could speak English, and she nodded. Every time she looked at me she would narrow her eyes, and her chin and nose would lift, which made her look like a studious resident. Did she learn the language in school? She shook her head, raised her pale, almost indecipherable eyebrows, then spoke her first words: SpongeBob.

Soft raindrops fell on us but were still too insubstantial to penetrate. Only the fetid pool at the bottom of the hill, next to the public bathroom, seemed affected by the drizzle. The Iraqi girl continued to cling to my hand. I glanced at my phone for the time, four in the afternoon. Must be a shift change. The area around us flooded with volunteers in different color vests coming and going. A few moments of chaos before the sun broke through.

Newly arrived families trudged uphill carrying their belongings, pulling rolling suitcases, their voices submerged in the hullabaloo of conversations among the volunteers, the *tap-tap* of hard soles on harder concrete, the bustle of movement. A Syrian family ascended toward us, mother, father, three kids, the eldest a boy of perhaps twelve, his face a picture of glacial determination. A large group of young volunteers in neon-yellow vests walked next to them, boisterous and unselfconscious. One of them, a blond in her early twenties, screamed. Everyone stopped. She screamed again, pointing at the sky. "Oh my God, oh my God." She screamed once more before she was able to form an actual sentence. "Look, it's a rainbow," she yelled. She tried to engage my Iraqi girl, kept pointing at the far sky, spoke louder in English to make herself understood, but my girl wanted nothing to do with her, wrapping her arms around my waist, clinging roughly. As the Syrian family reached us, I was able to hear what they were talking about.

"She's excited because she saw a rainbow," the father said.

The mother shook her head. The twelve-year-old boy said in a quiet voice, not realizing that I spoke his language: "She should shove that rainbow up her ass."

The father snickered. The mother smacked the back of his head, not violently, for they were both carrying heavy loads.

What to Ask
at a Book Reading

You know, I had met you earlier, not officially, at a reading in a bookstore in Boystown. Later you would say you remembered Francine but not me. You signed our books. We didn't talk much.

It was early fall in Chicago, in the midst of a dense snowstorm, of course. You were ill prepared for the cold, making jokes about freezing sexual organs. You were funny and your reading went well, your dial turned to high charm. There, in front of a crowd of readers, behind a rickety lectern, you seemed engaged and alive, vibrant. Your hair called out for a comb, your chin for a razor, your lovely Missoni shirt for an iron. Fancy, idiosyncratic glasses teetered on the tip of your nose. Disheveled elegance you were, an alluring performance, seemingly effortless. The audience adored you as if you were the cutest puppy, all wishing to pet this most exotic of breeds. You talked and talked, divagations galore, the little prince proud of being able to hold court and attention.

I have to say you masked your rage well. No one could see the suppressed fury you habitually unleashed in your books at unwary readers. You almost slipped once. A pompous audience member, a man trying to impress, asked you a question. Beirut was such a crazy city, he said. He wouldn't know how to describe it. No, of course he hadn't been there, but he needed your help to understand it better. If a Martian came to Earth, he said, would you be able to explain the city to him in one sentence? I was taken aback. I heard Francine groan. But you, I saw you cock your head for a moment, your eyes flared as if you'd been shocked with a defibrillator, then a confused smile, after which the great diva returned to the podium. If a Martian landed here, you said with a chuckle, why would you want to explain anything to her, him, it, let alone Beirut, in one sentence? Any other questions?

A portly gay man your age asked if you were ever going to write about the AIDS years again since it had been so long since your earliest book. You were thinking about it, you said. But he surprised you with a follow-up query. What did you think was your biggest loss from those years? You considered the question for a moment. I think the questioner had expected some wise sound bite, a warm idea that you could both share, but that was not where you went. You began with one name, then another, then another, a slow recitation. By the time you reached the fifth, the questioner began naming his lost friends. I heard Francine next to me begin to whisper the names of our friends long gone. Everyone in the room, gay, straight, whatever, repeated names. You had transformed an event to promote your latest book into an impromptu memorial for our collective losses. And then you were making jokes again as the audience wiped their tears. You begged their forgiveness for having a surprise séance, for opening doors and allowing the return of old ghosts.

You seemed solid and confident, a surfer on the waves of life. Do you understand why seeing you frightened and battered by the maelstrom of people in the middle of Moria felt disorienting?

How to Make
Liberace Jealous

Lebanon became home to the largest number of Syrian refugees and to the largest refugee population per capita in the world. In a country of four million, there were more than a million refugees, though the actual number was closer to a million and a half. So much pain, so much destitution. So many refugees. And sometimes it seemed that you wanted to interview every one of them, to provide an ear for all the tales. I remember listening to you on the radio saying there was nothing you could do to ameliorate the situation, that you felt helpless and pointless, but that you thought doing nothing would have been a crime. You could bear witness, you said; observing was the one thing you knew how to do. If you could listen to their stories, maybe their stories could make sense. Only what was narrated could be understood. You traversed the country—granted, it's a pygmy country—talking to all manner of Syrians. You went to different corners of Beirut, down south to Sidon, up north to Tripoli, to the west, beyond the mountains to the Beka'a Valley.

What surprised me after I read the couple of essays you wrote were the details that stuck in my head, the idiosyncrasies of being human. I recalled some of the people in your writings and not others. I didn't remember much about the people you wrote about who were tortured, not much about the suffering of living as refugees. The woman with the sequin pantry, however, was one of those who remained ineradicable in my memory. Though she lived in a tent that had been erected in the middle of an onion field, she refused squalor. This gorgeous woman in her early twenties had an impeccably clean home that was decorated in an understated style except in one respect, the tent's masterwork. She had studded her entire pantry with sequins, with results Liberace would have envied. You thought she must have spent untold hours gluing sparkles onto sheets of wood that would become a pantry to store nonperishables. Intricate and delicate, no spot left uncovered, so over the top that many a drag queen would kill for it.

You desperately wanted it.

You said she seemed embarrassed when she talked to you, admitting that it took her a long time to finish it, longer than she'd anticipated, what with caring for her four offspring, cooking, cleaning, and tending to her husband and in-laws.

"It's good to have something beautiful to come home to," she said. "The children love it."

"I do too," you said with real appreciation. "It's magnificent."

She blushed, then beamed. A shy grin, and her eyes rose to meet yours. "We had a ton of sequins," she said.

In the essay, you wondered what kind of person would think it was a good idea to donate thousands of sequins to Syrian refugees who had nothing left, whose entire lives had been extirpated.

Bright, shiny, gaudy, useless sequins?

A fabulous one, of course, a lovely, most wonderful human being.

How to Become
a Westerner

Another woman I distinctly remember from your refugee interviews was Rania Kassem, whom you met a few months before you showed up to Lesbos. On a Thursday evening in September 2015, under the Viennese lights of the Café Museum, Rania ensnared you in her tale. You spent hours with her. She looked older than her age: only in her fifties, yet the skin on her hands was thin enough that her veins showed violet. She kept brushing a strand of gray hair back from her face. You described her as a woman who didn't seem to care about her appearance—her shirt peeked from below a dark sweater covered with cat hair, a sprinkling of powdered sugar from the apple strudel studded her lips—yet she carried herself with an innate elegance. Her wrinkles became her, you wrote. Though she painted herself as a stranger in a strange land, her steady voice revealed a confidence not usually present in other Syrian refugees you'd talked to.

She lost her husband piecemeal, she said, the scent of coffee surrounding her. She spoke rapidly, as if her mind were racing to find something. She took momentary breaks to dip a sugar cube in her coffee and put it in her mouth for a second. Her husband was disappeared five years before the interview, but it felt as if it had happened the day before and simultaneously, in a different epoch. She told you his political standing was well known. He was your garden-variety socialist with a bit of communist leanings, never pretended otherwise. Everyone knew it, and everyone who was anyone sat at their dinner table at one point — ministers of all stripes, other journalists, his coworkers, and his competitors. Daughters of the president, brothers, sons-in-law. All of them. Even the ophthalmologist showed up for dinner once long before he was crowned their valiant leader. He ignored seating arrangements, requisitioning Rania's chair. She was an ophthalmologist, a real one, so he probably felt the need to put her in her place, which was not to be her usual seat, it seemed. The guests would join the hosts on the living room sofas after dinner, smoking the night away. She usually had difficulty breathing for a couple of days after each dinner. No, they all knew who Rania and her husband were. He was everything to her. They had no children and were devoted to each other.

Demonstrations erupted in various Middle Eastern countries, and everyone in the government was tense, fearful of a possible revolution in Syria. One day, months before the protests in her country began, she left for work at the hospital and she had a husband. She returned home to a husbandless apartment. She didn't panic, not at first. She called his newspaper, and even though she was told he hadn't come in that day, she still wasn't afraid. She assumed he was working on something somewhere. She assured herself that he would show up a bit later, complain about the horrid day he'd had, likely beg to be fed because he hadn't eaten since breakfast. She had the maid serve dinner. No, she wasn't worried. She was a fool.

She fell asleep not frightened and woke up in their giant bed alone and terrified. She began to make calls, but no one knew anything. She may have been oblivious, but she wasn't stupid. She figured out that he'd been arrested. The mere fact that the next morning none of the people who'd been regular dinner guests returned her calls made her certain that he was suffering in some cell somewhere. No one would corroborate anything, and she couldn't figure out why. She had a long talk with his boss at the paper, and he knew nothing. Her husband hadn't recently written a controversial column. He had continued to swing his critical pen, but there was nothing that he hadn't said before, and more obstreperously at that. She wasn't able to discover what had happened, why they'd disappeared him.

She searched for him everywhere. She tried to see the ministers they'd known but that didn't help. She knocked on every prison door in the country. No one would tell her whether he was there. She went to every Mukhabarat office, talked to intelligence agents who wore cheap black leather jackets that were impermeable to compassion. Her husband disappeared, and she turned invisible. The powers that be refused to return her calls and her friends no longer acknowledged her existence. If they saw her on the street, they would cross to the other side. The hospital where she worked fired her for taking time off to look for her husband.

The antique grandfather clock in the hallway stopped striking the hours. It used to chime from one to twelve and then again every day. Her husband was the one who used to wind it, and she couldn't do it with him gone. It remained stuck at the same time, its friendly *ding-dongs* not to be heard. She couldn't pick up the Scottish plaid blanket he kept in the living room for his nap after lunch. Who knew where their belongings were now? The grief, the guilt, inseparable emotional siblings. She spent months locked in her carapace of an apartment with its unbearable smell of memories, not answering the phone or the door, mostly sitting at the kitchen table weeping bitterly, her nose running. She swallowed enough snot and tears for five lifetimes. She was a walking carcass except she wasn't walking. She was mired in a slough of misery. She once took out all the brass in the apartment, the vases, the trays, spent a week scouring them with lemon and ash, a whole week of mindless rubbing four or five pieces over and over again. Then one day she was no longer able to ignore the ringing phone. Her brother in Aleppo was on the line, insisting that she leave Damascus that instant. She should come to him, be among family. If she stayed in her apartment, her life would be forfeit.

She packed a couple of bags. She was sure you'd experienced similar, trying to figure out what to take with you, what to leave behind, knowing that in all likelihood you would never come back, never see your home again. The arbitrary rules we came up with. She decided she'd pack only two suitcases that she'd be able to carry herself if she had to. She didn't take anything that belonged to her husband. She left all that, but for some reason she ended up packing the espresso machine. She suddenly couldn't live without it. She still had it in her apartment in Vienna. If you came over, she'd fix you the best cup of coffee in town.

She moved into her brother's house in Aleppo, but she didn't live there for long. Her brother immigrated with his family to Dubai. They wanted her to come with them, but she couldn't. She still had hope that her husband was alive in jail somewhere. She couldn't leave, but then she wasn't able to stay in the apartment what with cluster bombs falling all around her. She moved to her home village north of Aleppo, into a ramshackle house whose cement floor was broken by weeds and wildflowers. The bombs followed her, however. Syrians, Russians, Americans, they all bombed her at one point or another. She couldn't keep track.

She ended up in Bab al-Salameh, the refugee camp along the Turkish border, the last place on earth she'd ever have expected to end up. She was given a new identity: an IDP, an internally displaced person. Now that was the lowest of the low and she couldn't fall any further. She had to rely on the kindness of international governments and nongovernmental organizations for her survival. She was helpless. She lived in a small tent with five other women and the ubiquitous smell of weak paint thinner. The women took care of her. She had no idea how to turn the coal heater on. Cooking? Forget about it. She'd had a maid who'd done all her cooking for years, and without one, she'd subsisted on sandwiches and eating out of cans. There was nowhere to plug in the espresso machine. None of these gentle women could believe at first how helpless she was. She slept on a raffia mat, woke up with blue bruises on her shoulder and an unnavigable loneliness.

One day, a thirteen-year-old girl in the tent next door stopped being able to move. Rania heard screams in the early dawn, jumped off her mat, and rushed out, only to find a whole host of women blocking the entrance. She wanted to go in, but no one would move aside for her. Whenever a man arrived, the human sea would part for him to enter the tent, but not for her. That's when it hit her. Hold on a minute, she thought. She was still a fucking doctor. She became herself again. She ordered everybody to move aside. Inside, two men tried unsuccessfully to unfurl the girl, each pulling on a different limb. She ordered them out of the tent, everybody out. It had been a while, she said, but ordering people around was like riding a bicycle.

The girl was in a fetal position, catatonic, breathing, eyes shut. That was beyond her expertise. She lifted her. The girl was not too light, but Rania knew she could carry her to the Doctors Without Borders camp. She didn't have to. As soon as she exited the tent, a man from the Free Syrian Army helped her. There were only two doctors in the camp at the time, and they seemed befuddled about what to do. She asked if they had lorazepam or diazepam, and they didn't. They had only ketamine because that was the only sedative allowed in by the Turks. She hadn't heard of ketamine being used for catatonia, but she thought that it should work. It did. They administered it intravenously, and within two hours they were able to move the girl's limbs, within four she was awake.

She returned to her tent a hero. Her roommates kept asking why she hadn't told anyone she was a doctor. She explained that she'd forgotten, not that she'd forgotten to tell them, but that she'd forgotten she was. She was born again.

For the first couple of days after her rebirth, she had not a moment of rest. She had a huge line of patients waiting to see her. Men, women, children, IDPs, FSA soldiers, locals from villages nearby. It didn't matter that she was only an ophthalmologist. She treated them all. Her roommates had to shoo people away for mealtimes. She didn't have to cook for herself again. Not too long after, she was invited to move to the DWB camp. She was back with her peers.

For the eighteen months she was in the camp, she transformed into a different kind of physician. It was as if she were in an intense residency rotation. She had to treat everything, learning on the spot. One of the doctors, a Viennese in his midsixties by the name of Peter, took her under his wing. She had much more experience than him — he'd entered medical school at fifty-eight, a second or third career — but he was trained as an emergency physician, more useful in the camps than ophthalmology. She became a surgeon (bullet wounds and shrapnel), a burn specialist (she wasn't the only one incompetent around an oil stove), an OB-GYN. She delivered more babies than she cared to count.

The Doctors Without Borders camp was separate, but all the camps were controlled and protected by the Free Syrian Army. The joke was that the FSA ran things during the day and Daesh once the sun went to sleep. In any case, FSA men fought alongside the Islamic extremists since their own funding had been cut off and their supplies had run out, whereas Saudi Arabia, Qatar, and other Gulf states competed on who would give more money to their pet religiously criminal group. Now, whatever objections she might have had to Daesh, she still treated the fighters. She would have done the same had someone from the regime needed help. She was a physician. She was able to put aside the problems she had with those bigots. They weren't able to do the same. They had few issues with Western doctors, but she was a local. To them she was a Muslim, no matter if she believed or not. She kept telling them that she was an atheist, but that was even more troublesome. She was an apostate, an outspoken one at that, and a woman. She elicited immeasurable rage in those boys.

Once a young boy of about seventeen called her a slut. She refused to let it go. They'd spent the last four hours in surgery saving his best friend's life, another fighter. She demanded to know the boy's name. He was taken aback but he told her. She chided him on his lack of manners, told him she was presumably older than his mother, who she was sure did not raise him to insult his elders. He turned various shades of red. By the time she was done with him, he was stuttering all kinds of apologies.

But it didn't end there. Peter kept warning her that she should be wary, but she couldn't keep her mouth shut. She felt she had nothing to lose. The men of Daesh kept telling her that they didn't like her clothes, her hairstyle, or her lack of subservience, and she replied with various forms of "mind your own business." She would not cover her hair. She would not lower her eyes. She certainly wasn't about to submit. But then they had another Syrian join them, a thirty-two-year-old orthopedic surgeon. The poor man didn't last three months. He berated a Daesh fighter. He was kidnapped that night. They found his tortured body three days later. Peter insisted that she leave right away. He took her to Istanbul, sponsored her for an Austrian visa, and look at her, she was in Vienna.

She was fluent in German now, she said. At her age, who could have guessed? This was her fifth language. She was competent enough that she could haggle at the markets, but the Viennese were not as fond of haggling as she. A month earlier, she'd bought an antique grandfather clock at the Naschmarkt for only ten euros, a bargain. It was only a case, no pendulum, no weights, gears, or wheels, but it reminded her of her home in Damascus; she had to have it. Her two cats now used the disemboweled clock for nesting.

Of course she was working. She had a temporary job at a hospital, but not yet as a physician. She had to sit for the exams in anesthesiology and pain management the following year. There were many frustrating things she witnessed during her time in the camps but none more than seeing children in pain and not being able to do much because they didn't have the right sedatives or tranquilizers. She was going to be better prepared when she went back. No, she was not afraid of encountering the same problems. She'd be going back as an Austrian. Couldn't you tell how Germanic she was becoming? Didn't she hold her nose high enough? She would be a different person. No one would recognize her. She would pass.

The Ballad of
GoFundMe Jeff

In the middle of Moria, the long line of people on my left inched forward. The small groups who were chatting while they waited began to funnel into a single file, shuffling forward like docile beasts of a recently domesticated species. An NGO was handing out large gift boxes with dried cereal and Barbie Dolls.

I recognized Rasheed's laugh before I saw him or his Palestine Red Crescent Society vest. His face broke into a child-on-Christmas smile when he noticed the kids and me, greeted me like a long-desired present. I explained about the safari guides accompanying me, about waiting for the boat that morning, about Sumaiya and her family. He suggested I leave Skala Sikamineas and check in where his group was, at the Mytilene Village Hotel, which was closer to the camp. I could still go to the beaches for the boats if I wished—they'd be closer in any case—but I would be of better use at the camp. More effective, he said, less sexy, fewer opportunities for selfies.

As if on cue, panicked selfie-girl from the beach made her grand entrance onto our stage. She explained to a new group of volunteers that someone had stolen her phone, that she had traced it to the camp using the Find My iPhone app before the battery died. It was here somewhere, and she was going to find it even if it meant going through everyone's belongings. No, she had not erased all her personal data yet because she hadn't backed up the photos and didn't want to lose them. She seemed about to have a conniption right there and then.

Rasheed explained to my kids what was going on. The little Pakistani boy approached selfie-girl, tugged on her arm, and in broken English said, "Phone in bathroom," pointing to the public bathroom at the bottom of the hill.

She hesitated, gasped as she grasped what he meant.

"My cell phone is in the bathroom?" she said for emphasis before racing down the hill.

The Pakistani boy looked back at his friends, raised his arms in triumph. His friends laughed. The little leader yelled, "You speak English? Arabic?" The Pakistani boy grinned, shook his head, then fled in the opposite direction from the bathrooms. The kids followed him, scampered up the hill through the chain-link fence into the barracks. They didn't say goodbye, but the Iraqi girl turned around behind the fence and lifted a two-finger victory sign before disappearing.

Rasheed chided me for making fun of selfie-girl. These youngsters were a wonderful lot who were trying to do good in the world. If I needed to belittle someone, I should channel my disdain toward GoFundMe Jeff, someone who deserved everyone's contempt.

GoFundMe Jeff was a student at some university in the American Midwest. Rasheed couldn't remember which. At some point in the beginning of the boat crisis, in September or October of 2015, Jeff put up a GoFundMe page stating that he couldn't keep watching the refugee drownings without responding. He was going to take the semester off, travel to Lesbos, and help in whatever way he could. For a round-trip ticket, food, and lodging, he asked for five thousand dollars, an amount that was reached and exceeded in less than three days. It seemed everybody wanted to help GoFundMe Jeff help refugees.

GoFundMe Jeff never made it to Lesbos. For all anyone knew, he was having a good time on a paid-for European vacation. Rasheed wasn't sure which two sins finally tripped him, greed or vanity, probably both. GoFundMe Jeff thought he had the fundraising talent of a television preacher. He went back to his page to ask for more money. In order to do that, he needed photos of Lesbos and of suffering refugees. Easy peasy. He found what he needed on Facebook, posted the photos on his site, and asked for more money. Cha-ching. One of the photos he posted was a selfie of a lovely young volunteer. She looked charming and delightful with a Syrian baby in her arms, and the boy couldn't help hinting that she was his new girlfriend.

Rasheed didn't know how the girl's parents found the picture. Someone might have alerted them. They were furious, since their daughter was on Lesbos with her fiancé. How could she? She didn't of course. She and her fiancé began looking for GoFundMe Jeff. They asked everyone they knew and those they didn't. No one had heard of or seen any GoFundMe Jeff on the island.

What could they do? Not much. Someone contacted the parent company of GoFundMe. Jeff's site was taken down before he reached his second goal, so he wasn't paid again. At least three different Americans threatened to sue, but nothing came out of that. Jeff's Facebook page disappeared. The story died.

Rasheed said one of the photos Jeff had posted of Lesbos was of a beautiful sunset from behind an olive grove looking toward the sea taken by a well-known Greek photographer. GoFundMe Jeff claimed it as his.

Doctors in Drag

I rushed to the barracks when Emma texted that the family had settled in. The barracks were just that, one large room where everyone slept, a house of cards that would have fallen apart had it not been for the clouds of cobwebs holding it together. Symbolic walls, a sheet here, a hanging coat there, were put up around some sleeping spaces. The actual walls, white with a tinge of sulfurous yellow, made every person inside look as ill as Sumaiya. She and her family had to share two thin cots darkened with stains. We hoped that they would not be sleeping in the camp for more than a week, that they would soon be on their way to Athens and beyond. Where beyond, Emma could not be sure, not yet, but she was working with her NGO to see if she could get them to Sweden.

Sumaiya asked if I had had a good sleep. Her two youngest daughters lay with her on the cot on either side, so close that a thread of silk could not pass between them. I could see that she was feeling better than she had on arrival at the beach, yet she was not doing well. At least she was breathing normally. On the little table next to the bed, a small bottle of oxycodone peeked from behind a larger one of local water. No wonder she felt a little better. I asked her how long she'd been on it, whether she knew the right dosage. She looked perplexed until Sammy explained that Emma had given them the bottle. Emma patted the pockets of her parka. You learn not to meet a boat without a good pharmacy, she said. Antibiotics, antiemetics, antidiarrheals, pain medications, she had them all in those pockets. So much to learn, I felt as if I were back in school.

Unadorned bulbs covered in insect flecks dangled from the ceiling, providing even less light than the high windows. The barracks inhaled air, and with each exhale the room turned darker. A few cots to the left, one of those bulbs dimly haloed the tonsure of a reader. I tried to recognize the book he was reading but was unable to in the bad light. A little girl slept on his lap. The barracks were for families, it seemed.

Emma had done all she could for the time being. Her NGO would send a physician the next morning, as well as people to interview the family and hopefully send them on their way. I shouldn't worry. I should come back the next day; she would too. We had to convince Sumaiya to go to the hospital, but for the time being we should return to Skala Sikamineas and let the family rest.

"You're leaving us?" Asma said, surprised. She was sitting next to Emma on the other cot, but her question was directed at me.

Sumaiya explained to her daughter that we had to go because there was no room for us to stay with them.

Asma said she didn't wish me to leave soon because she had questions about being a doctor that she desperately needed answers for. I assured her that I would return the following day and answer any and all questions, but it seemed that one question could not wait.

"Are you a man?" she said.

Her mother gasped. Her father began a harangue. How many times had he told her that she must think before she spoke? She must consider that her words were important, that they could hurt people.

"I'm not offended," I said.

Emma insisted I translate what Asma asked.

"Well," Emma said, "what are you going to tell her? This should be amusing." I could see her eyes light up, an impish grin on her face. "I keep telling you to use lipstick, but you don't listen to me. No, you never do. And those pants are horrific. The things I could do for you if you let me."

I realized that I did not relish being an interpreter.

"I'm not a man," I told Asma. I was still standing, and I felt that I should talk to her while sitting, be at her level, but there was no space on the cots and I wasn't about to sit on the floor, not with my aging knees. "I was born male, but that wasn't who I was."

Surprisingly, no one in the family seemed either startled or shocked. Only Sumaiya's face showed some emotion, and she looked more concerned than anything.

"Oh no, my sweet dear," she said. "That was not what she was asking. Forgive her, forgive us. Let me explain."

"No, let me do it," said Asma. "I can tell the story."

"Not you," said her father. "Your mother can do it."

"What's going on?" Emma said. "Tell me, tell me."

From their small village in Syria, the closest clinic was a half hour's drive at least. There weren't that many doctors before the skirmishes and wars began, and then most of them left or were killed. By the time the so-called Islamic state took over their area, only one doctor remained, and that was because his mother was dying; he had to take care of her. His name was Dr. Fawaz al-Sultan. Now, the militiamen allowed him to treat his mother because she was his relative, but he was not to go anywhere near any other sick woman. There were no female doctors in the area, no other doctor period. These fanatics did not care if a woman was ill. Well, Dr. Fawaz did. He was a good Muslim and a local. Knowing that the punishment for what he did was certain beheading, he put on a full niqab and had his brother drive him to various surrounding villages to tend to the sick. When Sumaiya felt her earliest symptoms, he was the first to show up. During a four-month period, Sitt Fawzieh paid her eleven house calls. The entire family, the whole community adored that poor doctor, who had to work twice as hard because if a village had sick people of different genders, he would first come to treat the men as Dr. Fawaz, then his brother would have to drive him back home and he would return as Sitt Fawzieh. They had to stop at each checkpoint twice. He was a smallish man and not one of the militiamen ever thought of questioning him as a woman. Apparently, Sitt Fawzieh was not to be messed with. Once inside a home, he would take the niqab off and put it back on as he left. No one in the community betrayed him, of course. He was one of them. And so was she.

You in Drag

You were twenty-one when you tried on a dress for the first time. We're almost the same age, so I assume that must have been around 1981. You were on vacation in Rio de Janeiro, a recently out young gay man having fun. The city had the ability to unleash many a desire, and you partook in quite a few. You enjoyed assignations with men of all colors, all persuasions, gay, straight, bi. The demarcating lines were blurred in Rio. But you did befriend a black femme boy, as one should. Even though you and Celso had little in common, you were surprised by how well you two got along, how easily you were seduced by the exoticism of his world, by its sheer fabulousness. Out of little, Celso created the divine. He called you sister. Somos irmãs, he said. He introduced you to friends, accompanied you to the local bars. You watched the Academy Awards on television together, giggling joyously as Bette Midler sent coded messages to her gay worshipers. He asked if you had ever worn drag.

You hadn't, you told him. You'd never thought about it. You must, you must.

He led you into the women's bathroom in the back of a bar one night. Waiting for you were his friends, all in various stages of transformation. They searched through shopping bags until they found the right dress, a dark green, conservative, front-buttoned number with matching cardigan. They wouldn't have to shave your chest or arms. Dark double nylons and no one could see the hair on your legs. No wig for you since they were expensive and not one of them could afford to lend you his. But look, a pillbox hat with a tacky goldfinch on its side and a veil that covered your eyes. They covered your face with so much makeup that you felt like a cadaver being readied for an open casket. But no, you were no cadaver; with lipstick, eyeliner, and a good foundation, they restructured your face, built another atop the one you wore. The face regarding you in the mirror was both foreign and familiar, new but ancient, a mask that covered and revealed. The girls led you into the bar, sat you on a stool, and handed you a dry martini. You took a sip, cast a glance at all the men in the bar, and you freaked.

Thirty seconds was as long as the transformation lasted. No one noticed as you rushed back to the women's bathroom, took off everything, folded it impeccably, washed your face with an assiduous thoroughness you hadn't thought you possessed. Out, out, damn spot. You dressed yourself in your own clothes, men's clothes, and sneaked out of the bathroom, out of the bar, into your safe hotel room.

A gay bar was not a safe space for you, was it? How could any space be when it was peopled?

But a seed had been dropped in fertile soil. How long did it take for you to dress up again, six months, a year? Halloween in San Francisco, not only did you dress up but you shaved your chest because the cleavage of the gown you found fell almost to your belly button. The wig made you look like Elsa Lanchester. I loved the photograph you showed me. You looked young and innocent, full of hope. You sparkled. You greeted many of the one-night-of-the-year drag queens, nodding or blowing a kiss, ignoring the voyeurs. But then you saw the burly policeman. There were two cops ahead of you, a man and a woman, standing, observing, pretending they were there to keep the peace. You honed in on him, the handsome man sporting a facial contortion between an amused smile and a smirk. You went up to him, so close your fake breasts almost bumped his lower ribs, stared up at him, challenged him, and you said, "I look terrible, a disaster, don't I?" He was stunned, pulled back a bit, confusion sculpted his face. But you—you didn't hesitate. Both hands, ten spread fingers pointing to your face, then your magnificent though cheap evening dress. "Tell me," you said. "It's shit, right? I look like shit." The policewoman laughed. The policeman blushed. "No," he said. "You don't look like shit. You look fabulous." You gave him an appraising eye. "Why, thank you," you said, turning your back and walking away.

And the diva was born. With lipstick and stilettos, you could face this harsh world. When Francine saw an old picture of you in heels high enough to make any mortal dizzy, she asked how you could bear it. You said that for her, heels were oppression, but for you, they were liberation.

How many diva incarnations have you had? Lady Orangina, Mezzanine Fleur, Agnes Day, Mimi Chaim-Furst, Gay Ally, Checka Myrack, Lotta Botox, and more, quite a few more. I almost forgot Jane Joyce, who wrote *You Sissies*.

One day you realized you could transform into the diva without putting on a dress or high heels. You never really needed lipstick. It was merely training wheels.

The Women:
Mrs. Peel and Jennifer

Unlike you, I didn't need lipstick when I was younger, not in the same way. I was a peculiar child. I was clearly not a boy, not in how I saw myself. I'm not sure how I saw myself exactly. I knew what was in the picture, but the picture itself was out of focus. What I was certain of at the time was that how the world saw me was not me. In retrospect, I could now say that I didn't see myself as a boy but instead as more of a tomboy. Like I said, peculiar.

I had few role models, of course, and fewer that were positive. At a young age, I found the Lebanese comedians who dressed as women for a joke offensive and, worse, unfunny. I disliked their American counterparts as well. I never understood what was amusing about Milton Berle in a dress. Bugs Bunny in drag, now that I enjoyed.

Even when I began to wake, when I was able to read and, more, when I was able to research, I came across little that shed light on what I was feeling. Most of the writing was about biological males who felt feminine and were attracted to men. I was romantically and sexually attracted to women. I couldn't read my own map.

I recently came across one of your essays in which you described how literature validated your feelings as a young man, how reading Gide and Genet made you feel less alone. The poetry of Abu Nuwas healed you. You wrote that when you were a teenager in Lebanon, a teacher mentioned in passing that many of Shakespeare's love sonnets were written for another man and in that instant your life, your soul, unfurled like a morning glory at the sight of dawn. Yes, you wanted to be compared to a summer's day, you wrote, wanted to be more lovely. The sonnets quenched a thirst you did not know you had. So long as men could breathe or eyes could see, so long lived this, and yes, this gave life to you. I felt envious when I read that. I had no exemplars, no heroes to guide me.

My feelings were in code, and I was a horrible cryptographer, could not find the right key. When I was eight or nine, I watched the British show *The Avengers* religiously, and I worshiped Mrs. Peel—a strong, beautiful woman with a never-to-be-seen husband was someone I wanted to fall in love with and someone I wanted to be. Who needed a cape when one could have her catsuits—serpentine catsuits that pushed and highlighted her breasts as if they were being served on a tray? Good morning, may I offer you my breasts with a martini?

Mazen and I would lie next to each other on the carpet, chins nestling on hands, entranced by her beauty and her Jaguar. Mazen would insist that he wanted to marry her, and I would think that I wanted to grow up to be Mrs. Peel, but I certainly had no wish to marry Mazen.

My parents didn't know what to make of me, the poor sods. I was unlike anything they'd ever come across. I wasn't exactly femme. I wasn't exactly gay. I wasn't exactly a boy. I didn't want to wear a dress but rather a nice pantsuit, tailored just right — now that was me. When I developed my interest in *The Avengers*, my parents were thrilled, ecstatic that I was infatuated with Mrs. Peel. They believed that the interfering Almighty, through grace and timely intervention, had finally responded to their prayers for my normalcy. I thought of Emma Peel as my crime-fighting doppelgänger with gloved karate hands, terribly witty, of course. God's grace didn't even last as long as the electric can opener.

It was in college, Harvard of all places, early eighties, that I was able to formulate who I was. By being around many accomplished women, mainly my professors, I discovered that even though I might be attracted to a pretty girl every now and then, I wasn't one. I wasn't even a girl. I was a woman. Watching my professors, particularly Jennifer, was the true Tiresian moment, the before and after.

I attended Jennifer's introductory anthropology class as an undergrad, and I was duly impressed. That she had command of the subject should have been expected — it was an elementary class, after all — but I was young, and her ability to pull wondrous anecdotes out of various hats felt magical to my untrained ears. Like a good anthropologist, she could spin a tale out of the skimpiest yarn, and hers was hardly skimpy: she was a primatologist. She would look at her students tiered inside the giant lecture hall, swing an arm in a giant arc, and tell stories of gorillas and chimps and bonobos and, best of all, delightful orangutans. She spoke slowly, with many a pause, during each of which I wanted to lift the desk arm, stand up, and urge her on from across the room to tell us what happened. Oh, the epics she spun. Homer had nothing on her. How a community of chimpanzees saved Jane Goodall's life, the first time Dian Fossey bonded with a mountain gorilla. Jennifer's orangutans would descend from Mount Olympus to educate us mere mortals, to frolic with us.

I wished I could turn into a swan to be with her, but of course nothing happened then. As young as she was way back when, she was still a professor, I a younger sophomore. The Fates had to allow us some extra time. Not that I didn't try. I hounded her at office hours. She enjoyed talking and I loved to listen to her, but once the term ended, I could not keep up the subterfuge. I had an inkling that she was a lesbian. It was probably why I was attracted to her. I would later come to realize that even when I sported a male body, I gravitated toward women whose passions were more Sapphic in nature.

I hardly saw her for a couple of years, until the summer I graduated and was waiting for medical school to start. By that time, the relationship with my family was irrevocably severed. Hello, student loans. I noticed her in a café on Third Street, looking regal and beautiful, her dark eyes glued to the pages of a thick book. She smiled as she read, showing three dimples, two on her cheeks and one on her chin. Though it was early summer, she was covered in cashmere. I stopped by her table to say hello. She greeted me, but there was nothing in her rather hesitant look that indicated she had any idea who I was. I reminded her my name was Ayman, and I told her how much I had enjoyed her class. She bloomed as I poured attention, bade me sit with her. We talked for a couple of hours over lattes and pastries. She asked about my future plans. I asked for her number.

I did not believe we would end up having sex, not at first; I simply wanted to be around her. Yet we did have sex. The first time, in her pastel-hued room, under and over luxurious sheets of cotton, she looked at me after her orgasm, rather surprised, as if asking who I was, what kind of being. I did not claim some masculine prowess, not then, definitely not now. I liked her. I wanted to make her happy. I wished to know where her skin was most sensitive, how responsive were her nipples, were her inner thighs more susceptible to a firm or soft touch, all kinds of questions to which her body delighted in offering answers. My coiled ears tuned in to the slightest turn of breath, my eyes recorded the most minute flutter of muscle. I was discovering that one of the best ingredients for great sex is curiosity. I wanted to discover her. All these years later, I can still feel the imprint of her body upon mine. My Jennifer.

She let slip the first time that no man had ever made her feel that way before. Had she made love to women? She'd dallied, she said. Naked, unembarrassed, her hair on the pillow lank, her flush gone. She told me she found sex with another woman more fulfilling, but she insisted that she did not see herself as bisexual. She was right about that. She wasn't.

We rarely left the bedroom that first week. The sex was glorious, and it kept getting better and better. I felt like Wonder Woman, all-powerful and engaged in and with humanity. On a Friday evening, while we were in bed, I told her I should go home, that I needed my toothbrush, a change of clothing, etc. She said I was using her extra toothbrush already, and as for clothing, who needed it if we never left her bed. I laughed, stood up to go to the bathroom. I was stretching my back languorously when I heard her crawling on the bed. I felt her lean forward and reach for my butt—to be more precise, my lower back, right above the cleft of my butt. I told her I would be right back and playfully slapped what I thought was her hand behind me. The slap was much harder than I intended, and as soon as I hit her, I realized that was not her hand. The sound was unmistakable. She was trying to kiss my lower back and I had smacked her face. I turned around quickly. She was sprawled on the bed, her palm covering a cheek that blushed a scarlet red. Her eyes were wide and bright with unadulterated terror, a tear began to form in her left. I started to apologize. I had not meant to slap her. I'd thought it was her hand. I was being playful. I'd assumed she was trying to touch my back, not kiss it. I was so sorry. Yet my apologies elicited an unexpected response. She bawled, mewling, heaving and heaving, a flood of unstoppable tears. She regarded me with such horror I was unsure what to do. I promised her that I had never hit anyone ever. In my life. She cried harder. I knelt on the bed, approached her, and she did not shrink away. I reached out to her; she shifted closer. I held her and she wailed in my arms. I kept repeating I'm sorry, I'm sorry, I'm sorry, until between sobs she finally said it was not me. Not you, she said, not you. We remained enmeshed for a while, until she was able to calm down, to breathe normally.

I tried to find out whether the slap had triggered memories of some past experience. She regarded me as if I were an alien spouting nonsense. She was returning to her quotidian self.

She hesitated, seemed to be considering her options. I told her she could trust me. I would not betray her. It took her a minute or so. In a childlike voice, she admitted that she might be a masochist. She had not done anything of that sort; she could not conceive of doing anything so perverted. She had had these strange feelings since she could remember. She had thought she had everything under control, had her desires stored in a kist, under lock and key. But when I slapped her, all her hells broke out. She had enjoyed it. She wanted it.

The first thing I thought, and it popped right out of my mouth, was that I could work with that. I ran through all the usual clichés. Sexuality came in all shapes and sizes. Yadda yadda. She was neither the first to have these desires nor the last who would. What the unconscious found erotically charged was impossible to explain. Freud tried, but he was a mess, wasn't he? I went on and on, spouting comforting nonsense. I told her we were consenting adults. We could explore if we wanted to, and no one—no one had to know.

I was able to read different emotions on her face, hope, relief, and even titillation. Was I excited by the prospect? she asked. Had I considered sadomasochistic sex? I said I had not but I was turned on by turning her on. I'd loved pleasing her. And in any case, if it came to a choice of slapping or being slapped, I would choose the former. If that was what she wanted, if it was what would make her happy, then I could certainly try out this new role.

That was not the end of the conversation that evening. She was still in my arms, explaining how relieved she felt, how strangely vulnerable and happy. I made my decision right then and there. She had shared her secret. I could share mine. The bed felt safe, appropriate. I told her I was a woman, that I had been for as long as I was conscious, that something about my body, about my existence, felt off-kilter. Jennifer was the first person I told, and until we broke up three years later, the only one. Telling her was a revelation. Speaking it out loud opened both my eyes and my heart, and yes, my soul as well. I felt energized, as if I'd gone through an Ovidian metamorphosis. I thought I could move a mountain or at least fifty pounds of dirt. Francine, ever the yoga practitioner, compares coming out, even to oneself, to a kundalini awakening. If such a thing exists, telling Jennifer slapped my kundalini, shook it, told it to get to work. That evening, I began to be in alignment with my dharma.

I moved in with Jennifer less than a week later, joked that moving in quickly was further proof that I was a lesbian after all.

She and I were happy that first year, lived in a smooth household. I was in medical school. She published three separate papers and was beginning not only to be invited to major conferences but to give keynotes as well. Our home life was stable, our erotic life adventurous. Had she suggested that we get married in the first year instead of the second, I would have done it, but by the time she did I was beginning to have doubts—not about our relationship but about myself.

During a summer evening in Cambridge that made one forgive all Massachusetts winters, Jennifer and I ate ice cream on the porch, spooning it out of three different card-board containers, my feet on her lap. The screens defended us from insects, but we hoped for a glimpse of a firefly beyond. Humidity was high enough that things seemed to be deliquescing about us, she and I so relaxed that we could have joined them. I was complaining about something, my family or my finances, possibly my immigration status, how much the attorney was going to cost. She said it casually, as if it were the most natural thing in the world. Well, we could get married, she said. I knew I was in trouble as soon as I didn't reply right away. She made some nervous joke about fear of monogamy and orangutans, which made no sense to me. I explained that I wasn't averse to monogamy, that since we had been together, I could not imagine an assignation with anybody but her—the usual "it's me, not you." As happy as I was with her, I said, I was unhappy with myself. I was a woman. I knew she saw me as one, but that was not enough. I wanted the world to see me for who I was. Her response was quick. We had each other, what the world saw or didn't see was irrelevant. Who cared about the world? Well, I did.

I couldn't break through to her. I didn't have the skills or the experience to understand how to present myself in this complicated world. I tried that night and on many nights that followed. Even little things would annoy me. I couldn't stand my name, for example. Ayman was the wrong name. It was a male name. Jennifer considered it silly to change my name since no one in America knew the name's gender. As if America were the only thing that mattered. Everyone mispronounced the name in any case, she said. Many called me *Eye-man*, which was how many Americans pronounced

the female name Iman anyway. I did not want to be called
Iman, which sounded too religious, yet I couldn't settle on
a name that felt right, not until we were in Sumatra, glorious Sumatra, but that would not be till 1986. Until then,
we marched on.

Jennifer began making arrangements for a return to
Indonesia, where most of her work with orangutans was
based. I desperately wanted to go; I'd have to miss two
weeks of school, but I knew I could manage that. I was
inordinately excited about the trip. I wanted orangutans, I
wanted monkeys, I wanted jungles, I wanted bananas and
mangosteens and nasi goreng. Because we had both been
busy with work and school, the overseas trip would be our
first together.

We arrived at the airport in Medan rather late at night.
I'd assumed we'd be taking a taxi to our hotel downtown
to rest for the night, but outside, under canopies and high
humidity, a colleague of Jennifer's, Kemala, waited for us.
Her English was better than that of most native speakers of
the language. She'd studied at Oxford, received her doctor-
ate from Leiden, and, more interesting, her classical Arabic
was better than mine. She was a devout Muslim, had studied
the Koran as a youngster, and kept taking university courses
in Arabic literature throughout her life. Both Jennifer and
I adored her. She would be our companion during the trip.
We stayed in a fancy hotel for one night, but I barely slept.
Early the next morning, we threw our luggage into Kemala's
car and headed to the jungle. We'd be staying in her house in
Bukit Lawang, a village on the banks of the Bohorok River,
bordering the rain forest. It would be a three-hour drive, she
told us, even though it was no more than seventy kilometers

away. There was one stretch of road that the locals called Rock and Roll Street, since giant potholes meant that there would be a whole lot of shaking going on.

Kemala, Jennifer, and I walked into the jungle, and my life would not be the same again. I would soon shed the last vestiges of a past life. We had no guide. I was with two women who were experts in the field, but that meant that most of their conversation excluded me. I did not mind. I was buoyed and enchanted by my prelapsarian surroundings, my boots sinking into layers of crackling leaves, my eyes dazzled by colorful butterflies and incomprehensible flora. My companions ignored me for the most part, except for when I bent down to examine what I thought was a tiny worm standing erect on a fallen leaf, waving itself back and forth as if calling me. Well, it was calling me, and Jennifer had to pull me back with the admonition to stay away from bloodsucking leeches.

We observed the orangutans from afar, males, females, families. We were even able to see a courtship and its consummation, gymnastic sex way up in the trees, which made my companions deliriously happy. Neither had ever witnessed a mating in the wild. Jennifer filmed, Kemala took photographs, and I oohed and aahed.

At some point, Kemala said we had to avoid a certain path because we would walk into the range of a semiwild female who attacked human males. We didn't want to risk meeting her, not with me tagging along. Apparently her captors had abused her horrifically. She had recovered at the sanctuary and was friendly to all the women, but she kept attacking the male staff. Since her release into the wild, she had attacked one tourist, an Australian, biting him on the calf, and had terrorized quite a few more. She was to be avoided. Her name was Mina.

Of course, on our walk back to the sanctuary, we encountered the angry lady. Call a demon by her name and she will show up. Mina had ventured far from her usual haunts. We did not realize she was around until we saw her hurtling toward us at an inhuman speed. I wish I could tell you that I was heroic or that I had a smidgen of courage. I froze. Kemala, bless her, reacted quickly but not quickly enough. She placed her left arm across my chest, trying to shove me behind her. I barely moved; my fear grew roots that spread into the jungle floor. Mina rushed at me, but then she froze. Terrifyingly close. I could stroke her face if I reached out. She looked for a second or two before crouching down from her full height, seeming a bit confused, addled. We stared at each other. I heard Kemala whisper not to move, as if I could have. Mina might have been angry, but her eyes were the softest—into them I fell. I knew I was projecting and romanticizing, but I saw the world in those gold-green eyes. I saw wisdom and pain, much pain. Scratch a cyst of anger and the pus of pain will ooze out. That expression, both human and not, the hair around that face, shaggy strands of different shades all pointing toward her eyes, a modish haircut. She looked mature, though there was no gray in her beard. She reminded me of one of my professors, whose prognathism was not as pronounced, of course, but still. Kemala began to baby talk Mina, but the ape ignored her and saw nothing but me. I understood that I was safe. I knew deep down from the core of my being that Mina saw me as I was. She saw me. I heard Kemala say that what was happening was incredible, magical.

I wanted to sit down. I was no longer frightened and immobilized. Before I could do anything, Mina reached out, her hand touched mine, her fingers tapped the dorsal side of my hand, as if she were riffling piano keys in a slow, sultry melody. And she was off, ambling away from the path we were on. Into the forest she went.

"I have never seen Mina behave this way with a man," Kemala said.

"I am not a man," I said.

Dead leaves came alive underfoot. I felt life flow through my roots. My spine straightened. My soul burst into sylvan bloom, healing old wounds. Jennifer had been silent throughout the encounter. She knew. A fire raged through me while hers dulled into a dying ember. I did not have to utter another word. We both knew we were over. She wouldn't admit she was a lesbian, and I could no longer hide. In that eternity, under a gunmetal sky, as we looked at each other, a reversal, Ayman seeped down to the ground and Mina sprang to life.

On the Road
to Skala Sikamineas

The drive back in the dark to Skala Sikamineas seemed endless, a long first day on Lesbos. I did not have to share my fears with Emma because she had already deduced our patient's condition. She was a good diagnostician. Sumaiya was going to die, and soon. A couple of days, a week or two or six, we couldn't be precise without full imaging and blood panels. Her cancer was likely advanced, there for over a year, and unresectable. Any treatment, if she qualified, would barely extend her time by a month. We should convince her to get hospital tests tomorrow, I said.

Sumaiya and her husband had tried to keep the news from their girls, but Asma had guessed that her mother was not going to last long. We wondered how much pain Sumaiya had endured to get to Europe. I told Emma that I had a bottle of oxycodone and if we needed more, I could get Francine to next-day some. Emma assured me that she had access to pain medication, from pills to fentanyl patches.

We had been driving in silence for a while when I received a video call from Mazen, who had landed in Athens. First thing he said was that I was too dark and he could only see me as an undulating shadow. What had the Greeks done to me, what? I missed him awfully. He was going to spend the night in a hotel near the airport and take the first morning flight to Mytilene. I had better pick him up, he said, because he had no idea where we were staying.

I did not wish to spend time in the café-cum-pickup bar with Emma and her Rodrigo. I wanted to be alone, so I took a sandwich back to my room. In the dark corridor on a cheap aluminum chair, the cleaning woman sat, eyes closed, her scarfed head leaning on the wall right below a wooden crucifix that had misplaced its Christ. She stood up as soon as she heard me coming toward her. In Arabic, I told her she needn't get up on my account; she should rest if she needed to. She sat back down, said she needed to catch her breath before she walked up the hill to her apartment. We exchanged pleasantries, and then she asked how long I was staying at the hotel. I realized I had no answer. I hadn't made up my mind, I told her. I was thinking of going to a hotel nearer the camp. She suggested I leave the town. Going up and down that hill could cause me all kinds of anguish, and if I could avoid that, I should.

She explained that she'd arrived on the island six months earlier from a small village near the Iraqi border. She'd traveled by herself; her husband had died in a government jail. Everyone who was on the boat with her had moved on: to Athens, to Cologne, to Malmö. She'd thought about it but decided she was too old, too set in her ways to keep changing. She was staying here. She had a good enough job, never slept hungry. She didn't think she would get a better job in Germany, and she didn't believe what some Syrians were saying, that you would be given a giant color television as soon as you crossed the border. She bade me goodnight; she needed to get home.

I entered my room. Everything was quiet and ever so spare.

Trans Tiresias and
the Great Goddesses

I woke before the quiet dawn for the second day in a row.
No rain, no storms, Zeus must have decided to retire early.
A strip of weak light leaked in under the door. I lay alone
in bed on my one pillow. I'd had a night full of ephemeral
dreams, of lounging goddesses, of Tiresias and snakes, and
of Jennifer. Why was I having so many dreams? Much had
crawled out from the dark reaches of my memory since I
landed on Lesbos, as if the island air had a high concentration of Aricept. Everyone seemed part of the percolating
lava, my mother, my father, my siblings, everyone.

When I told you a year or so later that I dreamt of
Tiresias while on Lesbos, you weren't surprised. How could
I not dream of a transgender Greek prophet while on a
Greek island? Tiresias, a prophet of Apollo, came across
two copulating snakes while walking and hit them with a
stick, wounding them, and *kapow*, Hera transformed him
into a woman for displeasing her. The great goddess made

him in her image as punishment and ended up with a devout priestess. Seven years later, now a married woman who had borne children, Tiresias returned to the scene of the crime. She encountered the same snakes copulating, appreciated the miracle, and Hera turned her back into a man.

Dreamt of a great goddess at night, so of course the great goddess, my wife, called in the morning. She had an uncanny sense of timing. One of the things I was grateful for in my life was that I woke up to her face every day, and on that morning I was also grateful for the technology that allowed me to see her as we talked.

I told her I was thinking about going to a different hotel, one that was closer to the camp. She insisted I do. I was in Lesbos to help, not to hang out with Emma and her coterie of lifeguards. She said that had she been with me on the beach, it would have depressed her to not to be able to smuggle the Syrian family back to our home in Chicago. Even though she had strict boundaries when it came to work, she allowed herself more leeway in her personal life.

Years ago, in the middle of one of the coldest nights in Chicago, we were walking to meet friends at a restaurant when a shivering woman and her teenage daughter stopped us. The mother asked for loose change, explaining to Francine that her husband had kicked them out of their apartment, and they had to raise enough money for a room somewhere. They didn't look destitute, but they were certainly underdressed for the weather. Francine surprised the woman by giving her all the money in her wallet, some forty dollars. It didn't end there. We joined our friends at the table, she opened the menu, but then she stood up, excused herself, and left the restaurant. She didn't have to say anything. I knew she would go back to the woman. I explained to our friends. What I didn't know was that she wouldn't return, and that at home I would find the woman and her daughter taking hot showers in the guest bathroom and ours. The mother, Martha, stayed in our apartment for four days before she moved back to her family's home in Indiana. Esther, her daughter, ended up staying for six months, until she finished her sophomore year. Francine thought it was a bad idea for her to switch to a high school in Indiana during a school year. Both of them still stay with us whenever they visit the city.

You Almost Ran into Me,
Mr. Crazypants

I bade farewell to Skala Sikamineas and booked two rooms in the Mytilene hotel closer to Moria. I texted Emma to tell her I was leaving. She didn't reply for a couple of hours. She wouldn't be leaving her room anytime soon. Her exact words were: "My morning is looking up, up, up, and I'm not going to waste it." She would meet me at Moria at 11:30 with some members of her team. I drove off, a cup of tepid bad coffee my only companion.

There were few cars on the road in the early morning darkness; every now and then the headlights of one would flare and dim. Goats and herds of sheep grazed on the shadowy-green swards of the hillsides beside the road, shepherdless that early. Much like my early childhood home. Geography said Europe, but topography said Lebanon. I thought about Sumaiya, how I could convince her to allow us to examine her, get blood panels and some images. The hepatocellular carcinoma was quite advanced.

No dipsomania. It was unlikely that the cancer developed from alcoholic cirrhosis since she didn't drink. Probably hepatitis B or C, and if so, we should test all three of her girls.

I worried about possibilities for the entire hour drive. Along the way, an old and beautiful oak momentarily distracted me; it was so remarkable I turned off the engine and took a few minutes to admire the aged tree. It was uncomfortably cold that early in the morning, so I basked in the tree's glory from behind the windshield.

It was not too long before Bugs Bunny announced that my destination was coming up on the left. Hills to my right, the sea to my left below, and the large sign announcing the hotel, Mytilana Village Hotel, changing vowels on me. Before turning into the driveway, I noticed a road shrine. Again, so much like our Lebanon. You wrote about them in one of your novels, the kooky commemoration of saints that popped up in the most obscure places, this one on the highway with only the hotel to keep it company. Someone must have had an accident here, probably turning into the driveway as I was about to do. I didn't know as much as you did about saints, wondered if the shrine would be for Saint George. He was always on a horse, which was close enough to being in a car, right? And as I turned, I saw you in your rental Volkswagen driving out. You didn't notice my car till the last minute; you swerved and barely avoided the saint's shrine. You almost uprooted poor George and knocked him off his horse. Even with both of us in vehicles, I was still able to see your eyes and how distinctly they showed such anxiety. You were running away. I thought for sure you were taking the first available flight off the island. But you didn't, did you?

How Not to Treat
Your Child After an Accident

The island seemed to be casting remembrance spells. I was going in circles with my memories as if I were trying to unspool some curse. I recalled the shrine on the steep curve of Araya along the Beirut-to-Damascus road. My mother was driving. We might have been going to some town in the mountains. We were in the Peugeot, before it belonged to Firas, before its numerous capricious deaths and resurrections. He was sitting in front next to my mother. I, the youngest, sat in the middle of the back seat, Mazen to my left and Aida to my right. I must have been eleven. My mother was upset about something. My father was on one of his hunting trips in Deir ez-Zor, staying with her family. She kept telling me to shut up, but I wasn't saying anything, just laughing. Mazen was whispering, pouring pestilent puerile jokes into my left ear. Shut up, Ayman, my mother would yell. What did Batman ask Robin before they jumped into the Batmobile? A question and answer that only I heard, and I would laugh. I swear, my mother said, if you don't shut your mouth, I'm going to slap you hard. What did the doctor say to the cookie? My mother demanded that my sister hit me. Aida smacked the back of my head. Mazen whispered another bad one. My mother reached back and slapped what she could reach, my knee. But then she had to make a hard turn, couldn't retrieve her hand quickly enough to steer. Right next to the saintly road shrine, the car veered toward descending traffic. Firas was the first to scream. A car ran into us head-on. Luckily, both were moving slowly. No injuries. We were all momentarily stunned but only for a couple of seconds because my mother turned around in her seat, didn't ask if we were okay. She simply began to scream at me. It was my fault, all my fault. I was always trouble, ever since I was born. She never meant to have me. I was an accident and a horrible one at that. Even when the driver of the other car walked over to see if we were okay, she did not relent. I was going to be the death of her. The other driver leaned over to check on us, but my mother ignored him. I thought I was smarter than everyone else she said, her eyes crinkling with malice, but I wasn't. I was a monster. Mazen slid closer to me, away from the window.

If You Can't Find a Broom,
Try a Jaguar

In one of your novels, you wrote about an accident occurring on the same mountain curve. Have you any idea what it's like to come across one's own life while reading? Do you understand how glorious I felt while reading a book set in my city, on roads I drove on, among my people, how visceral my reaction? My world was being shared with the world. Do you understand why I love you so much, you fool? How can you hate yourself when I love you so?

Granted, the narrator's mother in your novel drove a Jaguar, not a Peugeot. Mrs. Peel, anyone? The accident was not the mother's fault. You had her drive off the road to avoid a truck that lost control. You had her fly off into the air while the saints in the shrine watched enraptured. I saw myself as her, flying away in a wonderful Jaguar. That was me.

A few years ago, I decided to make my fantasy a reality, to incarnate my dream. I knew that I was in the throes of a midlife crisis, but still, I wanted to buy a Jaguar. I may no longer have been able to fit comfortably in a slinky catsuit, but I certainly could in my fancy car. Francine said she would support me as long as we took some time to think about it. No need to speed through a decision.

You know how she does things. Ever so gently, she caressed the doubts of my desire and nurtured them into bloom. Did I really want such a car in the city? It could go from zero to sixty in about four seconds, which would be great for getting onto Lake Shore Drive unless it was gridlocked. In other words, the Jag might be fun to drive between two and three in the morning. Was the attention a sports car garnered what I wanted? Was it the right image? Did I really want to be envied by every teenage boy watching my dream car idling in traffic?

I didn't buy a Jaguar. She and I haggled over what kind of car I should get, and I won. She tried to make me get a Volvo V60 station wagon, but I would have none of it. I ended up with a Volvo S60 sedan.

That Boy Icarus

You once wrote that Hagar, concubine of Abraham and mother of Ishmael, was the first emigrant, that the Arabic word for emigration was likely derived from her name. You would later tell me that you wrote this because it was metaphorically true, and her tale slid into its place in the book like the last piece of a jigsaw puzzle. You were writing a novel dealing with Arab storytelling. Had it been about Western issues, you would have chosen Moses, or Jesus even, though they arrived on the mythical scene much later. It had to be Hagar and baby Ishmael, how as a poor, destitute exile in the desert she had to forage desperately for food and water for her teeny-tiny prophet. From hill to hill she ran, the same deserted two hills over and over, in case she missed something, a migrant's desperation.

But no, you would say later while visiting me in Chicago, if you were writing about migrants these days, you would consider Icarus the first, his father's only boy.

Daedalus, the artist, had built the infamous labyrinth for his king, Minos. In this impossible maze, the king imprisoned the Minotaur, a monster that had the body of a man, the head and tail of a bull, and happened to be his stepson in a way, the offspring of a salacious assignation between his wife, Pasiphaë, and a hefty bull. Like all rulers throughout time, Minos cared little for artists, ever persecuted, other than how they could serve him. He placed Daedalus under house arrest in a tall tower because the king did not wish the secret of the labyrinth to be known. But you could not keep an artist down, could you? From feathers and wax, Daedalus built two pairs of great wings, one for himself, and another for his beloved son, Icarus. Do not fly high, the father told his son, or low. If too high the savage sun will melt the pink wax, if too low sea foam will soak the feathers. Fly only in the silence of midair. Off into the lapis-haunted sky they flew, escaping oppression, seeking opportunities. Soon the boy, forgetting his father's admonition, enjoyed flying higher and higher until the uncaring sun melted the wax holding the feathers together. Icarus fell out of the sky into the sea.

The spot where his father's beloved perished is now called the Icarian Sea, and the closest island is Icaria, not too far south of Lesbos.

Many have drowned in that small stretch of the Mediterranean between Greece and Turkey, many lives unlived.

Why Icarus, I asked you, of the many myths dealing with migrants, why him? You gave me a strange look, held my gaze for a while. You proceeded to prove to me that no matter how normal your appearance was, you were anything but. A strange, neurotic bird, that's what you are. You lifted your butt off the seat, removed a folded sheet of white paper out of the right back pocket of your jeans. You unfolded a list you'd copied by hand off Wikipedia, a list of wheel-well stowaway deaths. Your list didn't include deaths of people who tried to escape by hiding themselves in an aircraft's cargo hold or its spare parts compartment, just those who stashed themselves in the landing gear bay. Your forefinger slid down the names and dates. You skipped those who had died by freezing when the temperature dropped at high altitudes. Your finger did not stop at those who died of being crushed by the wheels or by decompression sickness. You read aloud only those who fell from the skies, not in any particular order.

In 1969, a man fell from the sky on a flight from Havana to Madrid.

In 2001, London to New York, an unknown man fell from fifteen hundred feet on the jet's approach to JFK.

In 2004, Su Qing, all of thirteen years old, fell from the sky shortly after takeoff from Kumming.

A year later an unknown boy of ten would fall from the sky in Western China.

A boy of fifteen, Ilgar Ashumov, fell from the sky out of a Baku-to-Moscow flight.

Qassim Siddique, Lahore to Dubai.

In 2003, a man from Mali died on the way to Paris, falling from the sky not too far from his destination when the landing gear came down.

In 2018, Marco Vinicio, seventeen, and Luis Manuel, sixteen, fell from a Boeing 767 after takeoff in Guayaquil. They were hoping to reach New York.

And Carlito Vale, the young man from Mozambique who dropped out of the sky onto a nice suburb of London in 2015.

More and more and more.

"Who would keep a list like this?" I asked you.

"Wikipedia," you said.

"No," I said. "I meant who would keep a list like this on his person?"

"Me?" you said. "I mean, someone has to, don't you think?"

How to Rob an Armenian Jewelry Store

The hotel was in deep hibernation. The pool looked dour without its water. The few chairs left outside looked miserable without their cushions; a few clung to each other, entwined, hugging and cuddling until spring. The umbrella stands without umbrellas, the deep holes in the round stones, felt the loneliest of all. All things gave off a faint smell of cider and firewood. Persephone was still wintering in the underworld.

I waited for Rasheed and his Palestinian contingent in the hotel's frayed dining room. The breakfast buffet was sparse and none too fresh. Only the white cheese called to me, so I had it with a couple of slices of bread. The paint on the walls was yellowed all the way up to the ceiling; a corner at the top showed cleavage. Across from my seat was an indentation, tabletop height, that looked like some powerful god had punched the wall by accident, or Bacchus had kicked it with his hoofed foot. As decaying as the hotel was, it was still an upgrade on the one in Skala Sikamineas: at the off-season rate of forty euros a night, my room with its sea view was costing more than twice what my previous one did.

Two young boys tumbled into the room. They pushed the swinging doors roughly and fell as soon as they entered, as soon as their squeaky sneakers landed on the wall-to-wall carpet. They were back up and running before the rest of the family made their appearance. The dining room felt as if it had awoken from a deep sleep. The boys, drenched from being caught in the morning rainstorm, zipped past my table to check out the buffet. The family sat two tables away. The mother asked the boys to quiet down, to no avail. They were all chatter, me, mine, mine, mine, chatter, chatter. The accent screamed Damascus or not too far from there. The father acknowledged me with a nod. He had the kind of face that suggested he'd been punched in it a few times; everything about it seemed recessed save for the pop-out ears. The teenage daughter would not look up from her cell phone screen, her hand tweaking a gold necklace with a turquoise evil eye pendant that was meant to thwart the venomous intentions of any wicked onlooker.

I never had one of those. My sister, Aida, did. My mother gave her an evil-eye-thwarting pendant when she was a toddler, and she held on to it like it was a dragon's treasure. She even wore it as a necklace at her wedding, where it bounced in the valley between the two hillocks all evening. My mother gave Firas one, too, at the same age, but he lost it. By the time Mazen and I came along, she'd had enough of evil eyes. I didn't think I cared that much, but I surprised myself when I visited a jewelry store in

Chicago as soon as I became financially solvent. I had no intention of buying a turquoise, but I left the store with one, an amulet dangling from a delicate bracelet. Of course, I misplaced it in less than a month, probably when I took it off while scrubbing. I never wore jewelry again, not even a wedding ring.

The two young boys had a gigantic mound of soggy scrambled eggs on their plates, topped with fruit, cheese, and potatoes. The father, a small man with a big stomach, called the waiter over, asked for yogurt in Arabic, and the waiter did not comprehend. He asked his daughter if she knew what the word was in English, and she shook her head, still not looking up from her screen. The manager joined the waiter. Neither could figure out what the family wanted. The father used hand gestures, using an imaginary spoon to scoop out of his cupped hand. The boys giggled. The father asked his daughter what the word for cheese was. That she knew. The best phrase the father could come up with in English was *cheese water*. The boys laughed louder. I told the manager in English what the family wanted.

All five looked toward me; even the girl lifted her eyes briefly. The father said thank you in English, and I replied in Arabic. I ended up having to give the short version of "I'm American of Lebanese and Syrian origin." The girl returned to her cell phone, the boys to their clowning. The father wanted to know which region in Lebanon I was from, a code for what religion I belonged to. He wanted to know, needed to, a Levantine need born long before either of us. Once he heard I was from Beirut, he began to tell me how much he loved my city, that they had lived there for the last four years. The children went to school there. The family had left Syria and settled in Beirut in the beginning of 2012. A garrulous fellow, he spoke at me from across the room. Only his wife paid him much attention. My mind began to drift, though I did want to ask him why he was in Lesbos if they had been living in Beirut, but I figured I would not have to wait long and I was right. He launched into his story.

When the Syrian troubles began in 2011, they had no idea things would escalate into a war. He spoke like an actor reciting lines from a well-practiced monologue. Peaceful demonstrators demanding—no, asking for—their rights, rather nicely, he thought. But then the world was flooded and he fled with his family to Beirut. He was able to find a job, of course. He was a master jeweler, always in demand. He had done well even though his shop outside Damascus was not in the best area, because, as any sophisticated person (as I undoubtedly was) knew, gold was important even to poor people, or more so—to a pauper, gold was as important as the very air he breathed. I still had not said anything since I mentioned Beirut. The girl had the evil-eye necklace, but no one else in the family wore jewelry of any kind, which was to be expected. Had one of the Turkish smugglers seen any, the price of crossing would have quadrupled, and the family would have been robbed. But in Beirut, he said, he couldn't open up his own shop. Who would back him? He had to work for an Armenian jeweler who was not a good man, didn't know much about anything let alone jewelry and had no idea how to make money. Still, the father worked there for three and a half years. It wasn't as if everyone was rushing to hire Syrians, so he worked diligently for an ungrateful man. Of course, he did not wish to imply that all Lebanese were unappreciative and churlish, just the Armenian ones. About a month ago, he began receiving phone calls from a malevolent man with a shifty voice who threatened to kill him if he didn't help rip off the store. He was afraid at first, terrified really, but decided to ignore the calls even as their number increased, at least one every hour, then two, then three. He stopped answering his phone. But then the criminal sent a couple of policemen to the store to threaten the father. The police, would I believe that? They beat him up, shame-slapped him with such disdain, punched him in the stomach three times. He was in excruciating pain but didn't check into a hospital because the policemen had warned him not to tell anybody. He called in sick the next day and the day after that. He thought if he hid in the family's apartment, the criminals would leave him be. But then another policeman approached his wife while she was buying groceries at the market. He told her they knew where the family lived and where the children went to school and they would murder them all if her husband refused to cooperate. The police-man warned that he would do unspeakable things to their daughter before he killed her, the father said, while point-ing toward the girl, who was still engaged with her mobile. What could an honest man do? He couldn't tell the police that the police were threatening his family. They bought airline tickets to Istanbul, bus tickets to the coast, and boat tickets to Lesbos, except they were cheated on every leg of the journey. The boat was the worst because they were told they were getting business-class seats on a ferry and that they would enjoy a full meal aboard. His wife nodded her head in agreement with the last comment.

Rasheed and two other Palestinian nurses, the same women who picked him up at the airport, saved me by coming into the dining room. The two groups exchanged morning pleasantries before the nursing trio joined me. The father made sure to tell me how pleasant talking to me was. I did not wish to bring up the subject of the family with Rasheed while the gossip object was sitting not too far. I didn't have to. As soon as Rasheed sat down with his pitiful blue-banded breakfast plate, his back to the Syrian family, he raised one eyebrow, the left, asking in a soft voice: "Which version of the sad story were you lucky enough to get?"

Every Country Gets
the Refugees It Deserves

Although I'm not as much a gossip lover as you—what was it you wrote, gossip is the fuel that stokes the fire of your soul?—I do love a good story. You had chatted with the same Syrian family the evening before, and as I did, you had to translate their dinner order since they did not want anything on the menu. Across tables, the man regaled you with the family's story, replete with violence and valor, with ardor and adventure, narrated with no little glee. The master jeweler part of the tale was the same as mine, but yours had the Armenian himself threatening the man because the perfidious owner wanted to rob his own store to collect insurance. No policemen in your story, just three Armenian thugs who beat him up, threatening his wife and daughter. You told me you thought at first he might belong to the Syrian regime's secret police, sent to spy on the refugees, but then you realized that couldn't be the case. The Mukhabarat, like all state terror organizations, was evil and stupid but not dumb enough to have one of its agents improving his cover story with each telling. If he and his family were an undercover anything, they would be staying in the camp, mingling with other refugees, not calling attention to themselves by staying in a hotel, as reasonably priced as it was. No, you realized he was lying without having to compare his stories. And you decided that he was running not from stray bullets, not from falling bombs or fighter jets. He was the one who robbed the Armenian jewelry store. Rasheed came to the same conclusion.

I wish we could have asked him. Did he rob the store himself? How much was the haul? Did he hide it in their suitcases? Was he terrified when they went through customs in Istanbul? Did he sleep with one eye open while waiting to board the dinghy to Lesbos? I should have asked. Not having answers at the ready bothered me. In one of your essays, you wrote that a novelist had to be able to "sit with the not-knowing," which was not something I was comfortable with.

You had a conversation with the wife, whom you found more bearable than her husband, though not by much. You were trying to find out whether any of the refugees cared to immigrate to the United States. Not one refugee cared to, not one on the entire island. All of them wanted to go to Germany, to Sweden, to Denmark, and that was before the imbecile president of America was elected. You asked her where she hoped she would settle. She said she didn't much care. It could be Berlin, Paris, Frankfurt, or Copenhagen, but definitely not Athens. She'd already told the United Nations people that she didn't want to go to there. She'd told them that she didn't leave Damascus and Beirut to end up in a place like Athens.

What happened to that family? Where were they? Unlike you, I tried to find out. A couple of months after I returned to Chicago, I asked you if you knew, then I asked my contacts, Emma, the other doctors. Nothing. Of course, I didn't know their names because I hadn't asked. I would describe them as: "you know, the jeweler and his wife, two young boys and a teenage girl, stayed at our hotel." But then Rasheed knew their name. He found out through a friend where they were living a year later. The family had ended up in Florida, Tallahassee of all places, which seemed appropriate for some reason. Of all the refugees you and I talked to, that family was the only one that immigrated to the United States, as if the reputation of Syrian refugees needed more damage in America.

At least the family settled somewhere. They were lucky, as was Sumaiya's family. They arrived in Lesbos while Europe was in a quandary as to what to do with them or, more accurately, while European nations were trying to figure how to stop the refugees from entering without appearing monstrous for doing so. The November 2015 Paris attacks increased the influence of the anti-immigrant factions in Europe, but those forces had yet to mature into their full fascistic power. During a brief window, Syrians, particularly families with children, were allowed to trickle into Western European countries. Processing was difficult when we were on the island but would become next to impossible not too long after. Within a month after we left, the European Union began to smother refugees in more and more bureaucracy, the empire's most effective weapon. We were there a few weeks before Europe all but closed the borders. I understand that these days families wait for months to get a red stamp and then wait for many more months to get a blue stamp, more for yellow or green, if they're lucky and aren't sent back because they turned out to be color-blind. You and I were lucky. We were in Moria before it morphed into a callous prison camp, before the riots and arson, before the refugees had to be forcibly returned to Turkey, returned to whatever home the authorities deemed was theirs. With the dumb tenacity of moths the refugees kept coming, and from behind the cold pane of Moria, they longed for the unattainable warmth.

Lesbos was a somewhat humane mess when we were there. Shortly thereafter it became an inhumane one.

A Terrorist by Any Other Name Is Still a Terrorist

Of the Syrian reputation in the United States, I should tell you about a friend's family. Once known as Lina Abdullah, a nurse at the Chicago hospital where I worked, she took on her husband's name when she married in 2006. She had considered the custom of assuming the man's name to be misogynistic, and she certainly had not expected to be doing it herself. Yet there she was now with a new name. When she made her resolution to keep her last name, she hadn't thought that one day it would elicit such Islamophobic fury from strangers. After the World Trade Center attacks, she had to delist her phone number because she began receiving random hate messages. The things she was called, the virulent attacks on her character by anonymous people, terrified her. It grew worse during the invasion of Iraq. She spent years in therapy, yet the situation improved only after she changed her name. She was finally able to sleep through a night.

The irony is that Lina is Jewish.

Her father was Morty Abdullah, né Mortadda Mohammad Abdullah from Aleppo, arrived in the United States
with his family when he was seven years old. Muslim by
birth, he grew up not terribly religious, though he was
instructed in all the rituals and rites of Islam. He was popular at Schaumburg High School, attended some college, and
ended up supporting his family by owning three gas stations
in the northwest suburbs of Chicago. He hadn't changed
his name legally, but for all intents and purposes, he was
Morty, never Mortadda or Mohammad. That would get
him in some trouble after he died.

Morty married Elena Finkelstein, née Elena Midamasek from Damascus, arrived in the United States with her
family when she was three. Her name was changed at Ellis
Island. When her family landed, an inspector decided that the
name Midamasek — Hebrew, meaning "from Damascus" —
was not pronounceable in English, so he baptized the family
with the name Finkelstein. When I first heard of the name
change, I had some doubts, thinking that a more English-
sounding name would have been chosen, but then you came
along and told me you had a friend with the exact same name
and story. The surname of your friend's father was changed
from Schwarzberg to Finkelstein at Ellis Island. One might
come to the conclusion that there was an inspector there who
really truly loved the Jewish name of Finkelstein. *You're a
Finkelstein, you're a Finkelstein, and yes, you over there, wouldn't
you like to be a Finkelstein too?*

Morty and Elena Abdullah had three children who,
though raised rather irreligiously, identified as Jewish. They
grew up in Skokie, Illinois, after all. They had a typical

suburban upbringing. Lina once claimed that the only difference she saw between her friends' parents and hers was
that Morty and Elena spoke Arabic when they didn't wish
their kids to understand what they were saying and that
her mother's cooking was way better. She did not realize
that her parents had different religious backgrounds until
she turned fourteen or so, since neither Morty nor Elena
believed much.

Somewhere around 1999, Morty realized that Elena
was having problems. It was only little things at first. Elena,
who was an exquisite cook, began to serve meals that were
mediocre at best. He grew terrified when one night she came
out of the kitchen with a cauliflower stew that was missing
cauliflowers. He called on his kids, who lived in the area.
The family would take Elena to the right doctors, and even
though the diagnosis would not be confirmed until later, the
neurologist thought that Elena had early-onset Alzheimer's.

Morty was Elena's caregiver for a year or two, but
her decline was swift. He was unable to keep up. After she
had a frightening fall in the bathtub (no broken bones), her
children convinced their father that she should be moved
to a facility where she could receive twenty-four-hour care.
He hesitated, tried to persuade his children that he could
care for her if one of them would move in with him to help,
but none were willing or able. Unfortunately, the day they
decided to move Elena to the memory care facility was September 17, 2001.

Years later, when a local television station reported on
the events surrounding Morty's death, the correspondent
stated that Mortadda Mohammad Abdullah's wife left him
after the World Trade Center attacks. I don't have to tell

you that the story was picked up by Fox News, albeit briefly before being dropped, and of course there was no apology for the erroneous reporting.

In 2010, Morty had an incapacitating ischemic stroke that sent him to an assisted living facility in Skokie. He lasted until his eighty-second birthday the following year. Toward the end, he was only able to get around on his motorized wheelchair. And that was why his death turned traumatic for many.

Morty's fatal heart attack occurred in the corridor heading toward the dining room, right after the call for dinner. A teenage girl, Melissa or Marissa, visiting her grandmother with her parents, happened to take a video, the one that went viral. When interviewed on television, she said that she was bored, hadn't wanted to visit her grandma, but her parents forced her because it was Tuesday night prime rib at the facility. The residents, with painfully slow gaits and varied syncopation, ambled to dinner.

Morty, too, was on his way, looking forward to his prime rib, but he died quickly, probably painlessly, and his wheelchair took off. Into the corridor it whirred.

The video showed the carnage from behind the wheelchair, which looked like it was being driven by a ghost, since Morty's slumped head could not be seen from the back. The most memorable moment was of a frail, elderly woman in a flowery smock, lifting her walker, the tennis balls on its legs rising like two yellow suns to face the oncoming wheelchair in an attempt to halt the inevitable. In total, dearly departed Morty ploughed through six other residents, all of whom survived. The injuries were severe, many broken bones including hips, but no one died.

Once Morty's name was released as Mortadda Mohammad Abdullah, two wire services reported the incident as a
terror attack — a suicide terror attack. Most were certain of
the dead man's malicious intent. All American lips seemed
to carry a curse for Mortadda Mohammad Abdullah. As
with everything, the brouhaha barely lasted one news cycle
before everyone moved on to more ridiculous commotions.

Lina told me that she received a phone call from an
FBI agent the day after Melissa/Marissa's video surfaced.
The agent apologized, explaining that she was simply doing
what she was told, that they had to investigate because of
all the calls the office was receiving. So the stories about the
FBI investigating the wheelchair terror attack were both
true and not exactly.

And by the way, Lina Abdullah is now Lina Finkelstein. Yes, she married a Finkelstein. Definitely no relation.
Her husband's family was already Finkelstein and remained
so after being processed at Ellis Island.

How to Greet Your Brother

I came to appreciate Mytilene Airport a bit more on my second visit. It was so small that I saw the plane land a few minutes before I reached the airport and knew that it was Mazen's from Athens. I worried I'd be late, but parking my rented Opel was easy and literally a walk of twenty seconds to the terminal.

More rain was coming. The bits of insanely blue sky seemed to be shrinking like an encircled army already defeated, turning paler and more vulnerable, the sun less convincing. On the pavement outside the squat airport building, a man in some kind of uniform sprinkled seeds, pigeons forming a wreath around him. Into a plastic bag his hand would dip, returning with more seeds to be flung. The circle of pigeons expanded and contracted like a pumping heart.

Mazen had his back to me as he contemplated the eternal mystery of the luggage carousel. I did my inflatable air man wave, but he was picking up his bag and didn't notice me. The bored, seated guard wouldn't let me through, asking me to wait behind the yellow line next to him. Mazen, rolling his bag, passed me, looked left and right. I came up from behind and hugged him, my hands snaking under his elbows and around his torso. My ever-trusting brother didn't even flinch. Why would he be surprised? Didn't everybody receive unexpected hugs at airports? When we were kids I liked to jump on him, particularly when he had his back turned to me. I'd end up holding on to his neck, my legs around his waist. We were both too old to repeat that these days. We were the same height, though, the same weight. We spooned perfectly together.

"Good morning, madam," he said in the softest of voices. He held my arms but did not turn around yet. "May I interest you in our newest fund, which I believe has the right risk-to-reward ratio that someone like you would appreciate!"

We both chuckled. The childish joke was in reference to an earlier conversation when he asked me what he would do in Lesbos, how he could help the refugees. He'd said that the only thing he was remotely good at was selling stocks, if that. He was a stockbroker at Merrill Lynch in Beirut. He didn't think he could meet the boats with the latest investment portfolios. *Pardon me, ma'am, would you like me to explain how a family savings plan works?*

A memory came back to me. He was eight, I seven. In our bedroom, on the floor, we sat side by side, touching at the hips, as if we were two trees, bough grazing bough, our roots, our legs, intertwined. This image—this memory had not crossed my mind in decades. Mazen held a housefly in his loosely closed fist. He repeated the gesture that our father performed each time it was his turn at backgammon. Mazen shook his hand roughly as if it contained a pair of dice, made me blow on it for good luck, and with great panache threw the dazed insect onto the floor. We watched the flummoxed fly try to regain its bearings. Below us, the insect dragged itself and its confusion in small circles, unable to lift itself into the air for a while. We did this every time we caught a fly.

Mazen, my Mazen.

He and I had a blood pact, literally. I was eight, he nine. He had heard that if two people shook bleeding hands, they would become blood brothers. We would do it. We didn't consider that we were already siblings. We thought the ritual would make us as close as two people could get. We would stand side by side even if attacked by sword-wielding monsters or fire-breathing dragons. With a pin from a thistle flower, we pricked our forefingers and shook hands, sealing our contract.

When the familial umbilical cord was scorched, I was so furious with my mother and with my father who always took her side that I felt I could live with that break. I may even have convinced myself that having nothing more to do with them would be a welcome relief. But Mazen cutting me off? That—that I could not abide. I directed my dispro-portionate rage at him first. I decided I would not speak to him ever again, even if he came begging forgiveness. If he crossed a desert on his knees to atone for his sin, I would not relent. No, I was certain that I'd never forgive his betrayal. I encased my heart in iron and chugged along, a clean break.

But then breaks are never ever clean, no such thing.

In 1987, a few years after the rupture, I received an envelope from Beirut, from Mazen, containing nothing but a black-and-white photograph. Standing before the cadre of mailboxes in the dark lobby of my building, I tore open the envelope and tried to figure out why Mazen would send me a picture of himself and his bride. No note, not one word, just a cliché of a wedding portrait: the couple coming out of the church, a young Mazen, plump and fleshy, beginning to follow in his father's footsteps, dark suit and tie, a beaming smile on his face, grains of rice stuck to his meticulously gelled hair. Clearly besotted, he was gazing at his bride, while she, coiffed hair streaked with highlights and gardenias, looked seductively at the camera, her leer proclaiming: *I'll give him the wedding night, and then all bets are off.*

Had we been speaking, I would have warned poor Mazen. They were divorced after ten hellish years. She left him for some sleazy millionaire with whom she'd been having an affair.

At the time I didn't understand what he was trying to do. If he wanted to make contact, why send me a picture? Why not a letter, a phone call? Did he think this inanity would make me forgive his duplicity? We had a pact. He was my closest friend, my only friend. Cosigners of a covenant, we shared a bed till I was ten, pressed together against the same sheets of cotton. When I had a nightmare, I would sidle closer and hug him fiercely. He poured comfort into my ears. The nightmare was not real, he would tell me. And then he abandoned me. Did he think my fortified heart would be easily pierced?

I hesitated, not sure what to do. I wished to hurt him. Damn him. I decided I would treat him the same way. I sent my reply, a photograph of Francine and me and my budding breasts. She and I were young and in love then, and the picture reflected it. We were atop each other in Cambridge Common, haloed by glorious sunlight and a furious cloud of gnats.

Mazen sneaked back into my life, slipped into the water with a silent paddle. We sent photographs back and forth for years, but no words were exchanged; our relationship was reduced to a visual correspondence. It was only later, when he came to visit for the first time, that I learned he'd sworn an oath to my mother: he would chop off his tongue if he uttered a word to me; he'd saw off a finger if he wrote a single letter to the family freak. At the time, though, I wanted him to say something, anything. I wanted him to send me more than a photograph, but I refused to ask. Instead, he'd send me a picture of himself on a Beirut beach, and I'd return one of myself walking the Lakefront Trail. I received a snapshot of his son and returned a photograph of my cats. I refused to break. I was the strong one.

When I began my first job, the hospital's newsletter published a grainy photo of the chief of surgery and me in pristine white lab coats, the obligatory stethoscopes around our necks. How Mazen found that newsletter I do not know. I received a picture of him hugging his daughter as she sat on his lap, his left hand holding the newsletter, my new name stationed where his heart was supposed to be.

He broke first. In 1997, I received a four-by-six portrait of his son with a slightly bleeding nose, taken hastily, badly lit, likely by a bathroom bulb. On the ten-year-old face, a thread of blood trickled from nose to upper lip, curved an ogee around the corner of the mouth and down the chin. The boy was in no pain; he looked inquisitively at the camera, probably wondering why his father had had the urge to bring it out.

I held my breath for a beat or two or three when I saw the image. On the back of the photograph Mazen had written, "I keep seeing you."

Iron is iron until it is rust.

When I was ten, a bullyboy at school pushed me into a wall. My nose bled. Mazen, eleven at the time, took me to the lavatory and helped me clean my face. We missed two classes, hiding and holding each other in the bathroom. The boy's face in the photograph was a replica of the one I saw in the mirror that day. Mazen's son looked more like me than like his father.

My response didn't include a picture. Like him, I began with only one sentence, the incipit of all further conversation. In the middle of a white sheet I wrote, "I have never stopped missing you."

Avoid Getting
Liver Cancer if You Can

Sitting cross-legged on the floor between the family's two cots, Sammy was the first to notice me. He graced me with a weak dimpled grin. He began to stand up as manners required, but both Mazen and I gestured simultaneously that there was no need: right hand, palm down, slowly moving downward, then up to the heart. Rasheed, who accompanied us inside, performed a similar gesture. Sumaiya lay on the cot to her husband's left, and three women sat on the one to his right. All three greeted us with soldierly handshakes. A gray shopping bag filled with the family's belongings nestled next to Sammy like a loving pet. Sumaiya looked awful, more jaundiced, more wan, and when she glanced my way, I noted something off-kilter with her eyes. Dust motes wandered aimlessly through the air as if on a mild narcotic. Introductions were made: my brother Mazen; the women, two of whom were journalists and the third their interpreter; and Rasheed, who wanted only to meet the family before he started his shift. Both journalists were strikingly blond with safari outfits and matching ponytails that gave the impression of having been deftly pulled into position years ago and remaining like that ever since. They wanted to write stories—personal and poignant stories, they made sure to explain—detailing the suffering of Syrian refugees before and after the great crossing. I couldn't tell whether they worked for a magazine or were freelancing. One was English, the other Belgian. Their Dutch translator spoke classical Arabic fluently, a PhD student in a green woolen sweater and khaki pants. I complimented her on her language skills, and she told me that her Arabic argot was improving on a daily basis since she'd landed on the island.

"All they do is talk," Sumaiya said a little too loudly.

She said it to me, but it sounded as if she were announcing it to the entire group. Sammy reached out and squeezed her shoulder. He seemed frightened, even horrified. The translator straightened her shoulders. I could see she was about to say something, but she held back. The two blonds were oblivious, perfunctory smiles glued on their faces.

Rasheed chuckled. "They all do, and we have to suffer them," he told Sumaiya in Arabic. He didn't elaborate on who *they* were. "And on this lovely note, I beg you to excuse me, for I have to get to work." He promised to return later to check in on her and asked me to walk him out. I noticed Mazen sit on the edge of Sumaiya's cot, close to Sammy and the three women. The rusty hinges moaned as we opened the barracks door to exit. Rasheed halted right outside. Under a suddenness of sun, his eyes blinked concern, his head moved jerkily, checking that no one could hear.

"She should be in a hospital," he whispered. "If she can't be checked in to the one in Mytilene, there are a couple of medical tents. She shouldn't be in the barracks. I assume I don't have to tell you that. She's not doing well at all."

I told him that we'd get her examined today, once Emma arrived. I explained Sumaiya's concerns, that she did not want any help until she reached her final destination.

"Her final destination is probably this island," he said. "She has late-stage liver cancer, unresectable, not that she could get any surgery anytime soon. You knew that, right?"

I nodded.

"I've seen it a few times before. Tell her husband not to squeeze her shoulder the way he did. She bruises easily. If she doesn't now, she will soon. Her stool might be acholic already. She's going to get weaker and weaker, anemic as well. Watch for that. I doubt she'll be able to travel."

"I know," I said.

On our right, a middle-aged man with an eggplant-shaped physique lectured a lump of young volunteers who regarded him with the silent skepticism of cattle. Berate, berate, chide, chide, in a raspy voice, the man wanted the yellow vests to treat the refugees differently than he was treating them.

"The Swedish NGO has good doctors," Rasheed said, "but I can help if you need me. The hospital in Mytilene is not well equipped. No MRI, not much. I doubt she'll be able to get the medical care she needs on Lesbos, and I'm not sure we can get her transferred to Athens anytime soon."

I found him endearing. He looked like one of those drunk monks in Renaissance paintings or one of Bacchus's companions—cherubic and amused, in spite of the miserable surroundings. Actually, he looked a lot like my brother and reminded me of him, which was probably why I'd liked him at first sight. Mazen would whine about his whole life falling apart with a sneaky grin on his face or would witness the atrocities of the Lebanese civil war with eyes that refused to give up on joy.

"I'm thinking how much I appreciate your being here," I said. "Thank you."

He beamed liked a Boy Scout receiving an extra badge. "I'll be back soon to check in," he said. "WhatsApp me if you need anything. Oh, and get some Benadryl or hydroxyzine. She might develop hyperbilirubinemia and get quite itchy. They won't help much, but they're definitely better than nothing."

Butt Sniffing in the West

Emma and her people would not get to Moria for another half hour or so. The barracks were less crowded than the evening before. All the refugee families were out, working on getting their papers. The tonsured man was still there on his cot a few feet away, still reading, and I still couldn't see what book it was. I would find out later that his daughters had befriended Sumaiya's and were somewhere out in the camp with his wife, leaving him alone with his treasured book.

I settled down on Sumaiya's cot and listened to the journalists' questions.

No, he was not an Islamist, Sammy said. He wasn't sure what the word meant. Yes, of course he was a Muslim. I realized that the translator wasn't nearly as good as I first thought. Her English was impeccable, her classical Arabic proficient but lacking any of the nuance of the spoken language, let alone any understanding of the Syrian dialect.

The creaky conversation confused Sammy. No, he did not practice his religion. He was a Muslim. He did not need to pursue Islam; he was born a Muslim. Of course he prayed the requisite amount. He was apologetic, asking what that had to do with practicing.

I did not butt in. I should have, but I was too intrigued. I watched how the women sat, upright and matronly, how they approved of what was being said with an easy glance between them. I was a primatologist observing a strange species in its natural environment. The various forms of asking "Are you an Islamist" were the human equivalent of dogs sniffing butts.

But then Mazen intervened. He told Sammy not to worry about the questions, that the journalists were trying to get to know him, but they were not extremely bright. It wasn't his fault. The Dutch interpreter did not translate that.

Sammy said the family didn't have much of a problem when Daesh began to control the area, particularly early on. The Daesh men—worshipful, callow boys mostly, all peach fuzz and pistols—allowed him a lot of leeway in the beginning because he was well known in the area for being antiregime. He was able to drive his beat-up truck to work without slowing down for either checkpoints or potholes. He did not understand how horrible Daesh was at the time. His village was too small to matter, so everyone went about their business without much ado. For him, anything was more acceptable than the capriciousness of the regime. Why? He was arrested once, a long time ago, long before he met Sumaiya, when he was a teenager.

"He's my hero," Sumaiya told me, almost yelling. She nudged my thigh with her elbow. "He asks me to tell him he's my hero whenever we get romantic." Sammy turned his head toward us, his eyes as wide as porcelain plates, mortified, but she simply went on, her voice avid and light. "In between kisses, he keeps saying, 'I'm your hero, isn't that right?' He's quite sweet, you know."

Mazen cracked up. "Who doesn't love a romantic hero?" he said to Sumaiya.

I smiled at her, but I was perturbed. Was this hepatic encephalopathy? Her behavior was not normal, yet I could not be sure if that was because she was confused or if it was simply a general change of attitude. I needed help. She needed help.

The journalists wanted to know why Sammy was arrested. They listened to his story without moving, sitting on the cots with their backs firm and erect, like well-mixed concrete; you could pull out all the supporting steel rods and they would still be straight.

He was young, Sammy said. He talked too much, not knowing when to hold his tongue. He had criticized the regime to a friend, saying something innocuous, like you could only get a job in Syria if you knew someone important. Nothing significant or subversive. Then he said that if you knew the ruling family, you could steal money, and no one would say a word. Well, that friend told someone who told someone who informed on him. He ended up being arrested and tortured. He was in jail for six months.

Tortured?

Sammy lifted his shirt, showing pale scars, three long, off-color lines on his back, and one on his chest that began a little below his right nipple and ran all the way across toward his spleen. The security services whipped and cut him without interrogating him. They didn't need information from him, although he would have willingly offered anything they wanted. They hung him by his wrists from a pipe in the ceiling for days for no reason. They sliced into him as he spun like shawarma.

"That's funny," Sumaiya said. "I think I've heard that before. He repeats a limited number of jokes, but they still make me laugh. You know, a prison guard taught him barjees because he needed someone to play with. He didn't do a good job, though, because I beat my husband every time."

The translator seemed unsure whether to translate Sumaiya's running commentary. She looked toward her masters, the journalists, and they ignored Sumaiya. She followed suit.

Daesh did the same things as the regime, Sammy said, as did other Islamic groups like Ahrar al-Sham or Jabhat al-Nusra. Friends informed on friends, family on family. Daesh also set up a system to provide social services, and they cleared out the various criminal gangs in the area. Sammy didn't pay attention to what was going on for the first few months, grateful that he and his family were safe and that the regime's security services were no longer anywhere near their village.

"That's because he's a man," Sumaiya told me. The Dutch woman glanced up at her but still did not translate. "I knew the situation was going to be bad before they arrived, so did every woman in the village. Our lives would become unbearable. No school for my daughter, I would not be allowed to leave my house without being accompanied by my husband. I did not need to wait until the killings started to know they were repulsive human beings."

I whispered in her ear, asking if she was in pain. She said of course but no more than usual, and the pills from Emma were helping. I asked because I wondered if her loquaciousness was drug induced. I brought a few more pills, I told her.

"Why are they talking only to him?" she said. "Why don't they ask me what happened to my family? Is my story not good enough fodder for them?"

Sammy began to guess at the danger they were in when he first heard of the murders. Anyone who disagreed with Daesh was killable. Christians, Muslims, it didn't matter, Sammy said. If they didn't like you, you were either an infidel or an apostate. They executed many and sent severed heads back to the families. Sumaiya and he understood that they should leave the area, go anywhere else — Turkey, Lebanon — but they were worried about their families. His parents had passed away a long time ago, but he had four brothers and two sisters. Sumaiya's mother was still alive. She lived about an hour away, which meant they were seeing her less and less. Still, they couldn't take her grandchildren away from her. They stayed — suffered and stayed until they were left with no choice.

"I was willing to leave," Sumaiya told me, loudly enough to interrupt her husband. "And he was listening to me. We would have left much earlier, but then I became sick. It wasn't awful in the beginning, but I had pains in my stomach and I was nauseated. I felt that I should wait to feel a little better before beginning a trek. I wanted to take my daughters away, but I didn't know I was not going to get better. By the time I knew, it was too painful, too late."

Still the translator said nothing. Sammy began to squirm. He adjusted his seating position and reached out to his wife. She had openly admitted what she made him swear never to reveal. He looked toward me, pleading.

"We're going to the hospital as soon as Emma shows up," I said.

I noticed a swatch of pink sticking out below her left hip. I reached down to find out what it was, and she momentarily flinched. She turned curious as I pulled a child's sock out from under her. She took it from me, squeezed it in her hand. I covered hers with mine. She didn't seem to mind. I tried to smooth out the rucked up sheet next to her shoulder. I was about to say something, but she beat me to it.

"I like your hair," she said, "and I like that you leave it natural, like God intended. All the gray makes you look older, but that's how it's supposed to be. And I like that you don't cover it."

"You don't have to either," I said.

"Oh, no," she said. "Your hair looks good uncovered. Not mine, definitely not mine."

How to Trans in Raqqa

In an early essay, you wrote that one of the more remarkable Syrian refugees you interviewed in Beirut was Hiyam, a trans woman who had arrived from Raqqa with her mother. By the time you met her, she had been in Lebanon for a couple of years. She worked as a receptionist and grant writer for one of the queer rights organizations in the capital. You said that you had not realized how firm some of your preconceptions were, marble hard, and as you talked to her, as each minute passed, fissures and cracks appeared in the stone.

A transgender person from Raqqa?

Well, yes.

How did she get access to hormones?

Pregnancy pills, she said. One makes do.

A trans woman wearing a hijab?

She wore one as soon as she could.

Still wearing one in Beirut?

Well, yes, as you can obviously see.

A million and a half Syrian refugees in the country, and yet she, who barely finished eighth grade, found a stable job writing grants?

Well, she was one of a kind, she sure was.

When she first reached Beirut, she was a sex worker. She had to survive and she had to take care of her mother, who couldn't work. Yes, she wore her hijab in public and took it off when in the bedroom with a client. You asked questions that were much too personal, but she didn't mind, she said. She was a free woman, an open chest of drawers, nothing hidden.

A Lebanese trans woman explained to Hiyam that she could get assistance from gay rights organizations, everything from housing to classes to stipends. If she was a queer refugee, she qualified, and she most certainly was. She received aid, and in gratitude she began to volunteer at the organization. She sat at the reception desk and welcomed the gay refugees. If someone was desperate enough to claim that they were gay, then they needed help. She admitted that she tended to believe any refugee who maintained that they were queer. It wasn't as if Hiyam was going to ask when was the last time a boy gave a blowjob. She wasn't as curious or as inquisitive as you. The Dutch government and various gay organizations in Europe were offering grants. The NGOs were mostly based in Holland, a few in Scandinavia, one or two in Germany, but of course not a single one in the United States. She started helping with grant writing, with research at first, presenting cases, but as her language skills improved, she wrote a bit. She was hired full time.

She prided herself on being able to get many boys and girls off the shady streets.

What was her life like before all this? How did she manage being trans in Raqqa? Very well, thank you. Most people left her alone, her mother was loving, Hiyam had a job, and yes, she had a boyfriend who loved her. They had been together for two years. Her troubles began when the first so-called Islamic militia overran the town. Don't you nod your head as if you know, she chided. You know nothing. The militiamen did not have a problem with her. They did not bother her much. It seemed they did not believe trans women to be apostates. They did have a problem with her boyfriend. Whether it was because they considered him gay or an adulterer, she wasn't sure. All she knew was they beheaded him. She left with her mother as soon as she heard. She could not bear living in that hell.

Yes, she was dating a man in Beirut. It had only been a month or so. But no, he was not her boyfriend. She was still mourning.

Marriage Does Not Become a Ten-Year-Old

The journalists wanted to know what Sammy meant by being left with no choice except leaving. What had happened? What changed?

There was a certain man who wore his religion garishly. He rose up the ranks in the newly assembled army because of his ability to quote wide swaths of text from the holy book and, more important, because he was artful in belittling those unable to recall the Qur'an as well as he. Rumors were that he murdered both his parents and slit his two brothers' throats for not being assiduously devout. Every Daesh fighter called himself Abu this and Abu that, but he called himself Abu el-Nabi.

"Father of the Prophet," the translator explained.

"May God forgive him," Sammy said.

"May God blind him," Sumaiya said, "and burn his religion. May God never forgive him!"

Abu el-Nabi was a graduate of the infamous Tadmor Prison in Palmyra. It was said that before he was arrested, he considered religion an afterthought, that he'd never fully contemplated the role of Islam in his life. But the electrocutions he suffered, the beatings with thick PVC pipes, the torturers whispering into his ears that they were going to turn him into art, bringing forth many different colors on his skin, all that transformed him into a believer. The villagers over whom he and his cohort ruled mocked him behind his back, suggesting that he was once a tall man, but the security apparatus broke enough bones that he graduated from prison a ridiculously short one.

In a Baath Syria he would have been a nobody, a puny homunculus of a man, but in the Islamic state he was a giant. He had two wives and he wanted a third.

And one day, not too long ago, five Daesh men, well scrubbed and in their best clothes, knocked on Sammy and Sumaiya's door. The emaciated dog of the neighborhood understood everything and he barked and barked, trying to warn Sammy not to open the door. Abu el-Nabi looked comical in all-over sea blue, that whitebait of a man drowned in a shalwar kameez. The men were invited in, offered tea and welcoming conversation. It was half an hour into the unscheduled visit when one of the men stated the reason they were there. They had come to ask Sammy for his daughter's hand in marriage. They had heard only great things about ten-year-old Asma, and they were there to vouch for Abu el-Nabi's incredible qualifications as a husband. He was brave and courageous in battle, his men had the utmost respect for him, as did his wives, and most important, he followed the correct path. He was nothing if not devout.

"He was nothing if not a son of a bitch," Sumaiya said, "a most despicable man. May God never grant him health. And short too. Asma was already taller than him. Everybody was."

The men said they would have preferred, for propriety's sake as well as tradition, to have had their women with them at this most glorious occasion, but there was a war going on and the situation was difficult. Sammy announced that he would of course give permission, how could he not? Granted, his daughter Asma was young and had her whole life ahead of her, but she wouldn't be able to find a more worthy husband than Abu el-Nabi. The family would be honored to have such a man as one of their own. What family wouldn't? Truly, a blessing had descended upon the house. Sammy explained that Sumaiya was rather ill and they would need a little time to prepare Asma for her future life. The men should return in a couple of days or one week. Yes, they should have the marriage contract signed the following week with a feast to end all feasts in celebration.

"He thought one week would give us enough time to sort everything and leave," Sumaiya said, "but I had had enough of those sons of whores."

They packed as much as they could as soon as the men left. They woke their children, and everyone squeezed into the family's thirty-year-old pickup truck. They drove to Sumaiya's brother's house, where they stayed for two nights before continuing to the Turkish border.

"We drove as if we were being followed by jinn that first night," Sumaiya said, "so fast that I threw up twice before we reached my brother, had to put my head out the pickup window and regurgitate into the dark night." She paused and took a short, labored breath. Her husband offered her a look full of concern and utter devotion. "There was no light anywhere," she said. "We had to drive the whole way with the headlights off because we were afraid of snipers. We were used to the sound of low-flying planes, of artillery and rocket launchers. Everything appeared gloomy and purple, yet I was able to see olive groves as we drove along, cucumber fields and bushes of sumac. Will I ever see their like again?"

Sammy wrung his right hand with his left as if squeezing water from a cloth.

Who Is Us and
Who Is Them?

"Tell him he's a hero," the Belgian journalist with earnest blue eyes said to the interpreter.

"Me?" Sammy replied. The slow movements of his hands and arms as he spoke seemed jerky because of the immobility of the women interviewing him. My brother watched him intently, and the subtle arcs his hands made seemed to replicate Sammy's.

"Yes, yes," the Englishwoman declared with schoolmarmish intensity. "You're a hero." She nodded as if she needed to emphasize her words to herself.

"He's my hero," Sumaiya said. Only her husband, Mazen, and I paid attention to her. She was no more than elevator music to the three women. "He's my hero, not theirs."

"And you're mine," Sammy told her. "I belong to no one but you."

"See?" Sumaiya said. "I told you he's the sweetest man."

Then to my brother, "You should be sweet to the doctor here. She deserves the best."

"Yes, you should," I said to Mazen. "You definitely should."

I wanted to call Francine and tell her she was my hero, that I belonged to no one but her.

Emma entered our universe. She didn't look our way at first, only at her two companions, neither of whom was Rodrigo. She seemed generous with her accessories this morning, superfluously so. Her jangling bracelets rang a higher note than her laugh. She spoke Swedish, and I couldn't figure out what she was saying to the couple with her. All three wore orange neon vests, but hers clashed with everything else she wore. Unlike the attire of the other man and woman, her pants, sweater, and jacket were not neutral—nothing about her was ever neutral.

The journalists kept repeating that Sammy was a hero. He shook his head. He wasn't one, he insisted. He did what any man would do for his family, what any husband and father would do. There was nothing special about him. The journalists asked the interpreter to explain that he must accept that what he did was exceptional and that he should be lauded for it.

I was glad Emma had arrived. Sumaiya kept asking why the women were hero-worshipping her husband and why they wouldn't leave him alone.

"Well, what you did was remarkable," the Belgian said. "You're an unusual man."

Mazen couldn't sit quiet anymore. "Why do you think he's atypical?" he asked in English, probably more gruffly than he had intended.

"He saved his family," the English journalist said.

"You consider that unusual?" he asked. "Most of the people in this camp are here because they wanted to save their families. They're all heroes."

"No," she said. "Not all. This man wanted to save his daughter. He endured much hardship because he loves his daughter."

"Of course," Mazen said. "What father doesn't?"

"Well, they don't really love their daughters. Not all of them."

"What?" I asked as calmly as I could.

"What?" Mazen screamed. Loudest I'd ever heard him.

Sumaiya was nudging me, asking what they were saying. I was relieved that the translator hadn't translated.

"What do you mean?" Mazen demanded, losing the last shred of civility. Rage added a rosy tint to his cheeks and brow. "Who is this 'they' you speak of? Who are they who don't love their daughters? Why don't you tell us?"

All three women sat unmoving, faces blanched and terror stricken. I was about to stand up and move to them, face-to-face, when out of seemingly nowhere Emma's hand locked on to my left shoulder.

But Mazen — Mazen did not have a hand holding him back. "Fuck you," he yelled. "Fuck you and fuck your stupid ignorance." He sounded American when he swore, though his rage was pure Lebanese. "Why don't you tell me to my face that I don't love my daughter? Just say it. I dare you, you fuckwits, I dare you. Say it, and it had better be loud and clear. Say it!"

"I think it's best you left," Emma said to the women, walking into the middle between the two beds with a gesture that included her companions, my brother, and me. "We have to process this family."

The women rushed out, shuffling as they tried to make sure they hadn't left anything behind. My brother, adrift in his own seas, kept yelling: "Fuck your blasphemous stupidity."

Emma, grinning ear to ear, said, "Hi, Mazen. Welcome to Lesbos!"

How to Process Rage:
An Instruction . . . Maybe an
Example . . . Oh, Never Mind

Mazen apologized to Sumaiya for exhibiting such rage. He assured all of us—Sammy, Emma, the Swedish doctors—that he was quite all right or would be as soon as he went outside for a moment to inhale some fresh air and expunge the negative energy. He gently picked up a confused Sumaiya's hand and kissed it. "I'll be completely sweet from now on," he told her. "I promise you."

"But what is going on?" Sumaiya asked me. "What happened?"

What I wanted to do was walk the barracks from one end to the other, along the corridor between the serried cots, at a fast pace to slow my own anger, but I could not do so without worrying or frightening Sumaiya. I had trained myself to set aside my feelings for a time while I continued doing what had to be done—or at least not to exhibit these feelings around people. I settled on briefly telling Sumaiya about the exchange and apologized for the screaming. She didn't understand my anger or my brother's. How could one not love one's daughter, she said dismissively. The women were stupid.

There was a time when rage was my intimate, in my late teens and twenties. I was shy and confused as a youngster, to the point of being taciturn, afraid of saying the wrong thing, of behaving inappropriately. I spent my youth terrified of being seen and desperately wanting to be. I held secrets within secrets within secrets, wrapped myself tight in dissimulation. By the time I arrived in the United States, I couldn't hold anything in any longer. Like the can my mother stored in her pantry for so long, I exploded, and what spewed out of me was venom. My mother cut me off before I changed my biological sex. She declared me dead because of my wrath. I was unable to speak to her without screaming across international phone lines. Such fury, such indignation.

Luckily, I did not remain wrathful for too long. Time away from my youth and its triggers softened the edges of my anger, ameliorated its harshness. I could get furious every now and then, but my temper was no longer as easily lost, and I grew adept at regaining my composure when that happened.

Mazen, on the other hand, never got angry.

Francine wrote a paper about outsider rage. I don't have to explain it to you, do I?

Choosing the Best Song to Play at a Mass Drowning

When Nikolaos, the cross-dresser of Skala Sikamineas, described your conversation, he said you kept balling your fists and digging your fingernails into the palms of your hands, as if trying to not lose yourself. Tales of the Smyrna fires were what upset you. I was intrigued by the fact that he said you knew the history of the area better than he, that you'd researched the subject extensively, yet you still couldn't control your temper, particularly when he told you what his grandmother, a young girl at the time, witnessed while she was stranded among the terrified crowd at the port of Smyrna.

His grandmother was seven as the Ottoman Empire imploded at the end of the First World War. Her Greek family lived in Smyrna, Izmir now. She was happy in the cosmopolitan city. Christians, Muslims, and Jews lived and worked there, Armenians, Greeks, Turks, Arabs, Kurds. But then the Greek army invaded at the behest of the Western

allies, specifically the British prime minister, David Lloyd
George. Get your land back, the Greeks were told, the land
that the Turks thought of as Turkey, the one the Greeks
thought of as Greater Greece. Oops.

She was ten or eleven when the Greco-Turkish War
ended in 1922. Turkish nationalists drove the Greek forces
all the way back to the city where she lived. And her idyllic
life shattered. Her entire family was killed except for her
and one sister, two years older. You empathized with the
young girl's tragedy, but what captured your imagination
was the Great Smyrna Fire.

Three days after the Turks took back control of Smyrna,
a devastating fire erupted and destroyed at least half the
city—the Christian and Armenian neighborhoods but not
the Muslim or Jewish ones. Depending on who was writing
the history or who was telling the tale, anywhere between
ten thousand and a hundred thousand Greeks perished.

But that was not what upset you, was it?

Most of the Armenians and Greeks who survived
ended up suffering a bit more than death by fire. Many
of the women were raped. Most of the refugees were sent
into the interior of the country, where they died an even
harsher death. Thousands of deaths, some historians claimed
as many as one hundred thousand.

Definitely upsetting, but that was not what made your
blood percolate in its veins.

When the fire started, Nikolaos's grandmother and
her sister ran to the port along with thousands of Greek
refugees. They crammed the waterfront. Many ended up
jumping into the water to escape the flames even though they
could not swim. Allied ships docked at the harbor refused

to pick them up. The allies were supposed to be neutral. They could not get involved.

No, even that was not what made you as angry as Achilles.

To alleviate the discomfort of the sailors who had to listen to the cries for help from drowning refugees, the British ships played loud music on their speakers. Refugees wailed while listening to popular tunes of the time.

Nikolaos told me you kept asking him in your bad French if his grandmother recalled any of the songs that were played. She didn't. He wasn't sure she remembered, but he was sure that she didn't tell him before she died. Nikolaos said you were hoping that it wasn't Al Jolson singing "Swanee." You wanted to know, desperately wanted to, as if knowing what song thousands of refugees were forced to listen to as they drowned could help ease your suffering.

Choosing the Best Way
to Deal with an
Ill-Mannered Boor

Francine wrote the outsider rage article in 2009 after an incident where she behaved unprofessionally — unprofessionally according to her but certainly not in my book. A colleague working at Chicago Lakeshore Hospital called her in to consult on the case of a twenty-two-year-old Guatemalan woman diagnosed with mutism. The patient had not spoken for nine months and exhibited symptoms of depression and anxiety. She had episodes of hiccups that lasted for hours. Francine read the patient file and noted that the young woman had been brought to the hospital by her sister and not by her husband, an older white male. The patient, though remaining mute, was responsive with Francine, going so far as to smile once.

Her colleague asked Francine to join him in explaining the situation to the husband. She did not like the man, was predisposed not to from looking at the file, but then he exacerbated matters by ignoring her and speaking only to her colleague, who also happened to be a white male. She would speak, and the husband wouldn't even look her way. He interrupted her a number of times, until she'd had enough.

She told me she wanted nothing more than to slap him and she almost did. It wasn't just that she'd been wondering whether he was abusive to his wife. It wasn't just that she'd deduced that the marriage was unequal, a colonialist betrothal. He had married his wife while on "vacation" in Guatemala. It was the fact that this man dared to treat Francine as unworthy of his attention, to treat her as a subaltern, an outsider. She seethed, something almost as rare as a unicorn sighting, as you know. If the man only looked at her, she was sure she would knock him over with her venomous eyes. She was about to slap him, truly, wound up her arm to do it, but her hand stopped at his cheek. She held his face between thumb and palm, sternly telling him he was an ill-mannered boor.

Now, that would have been a fireable offense had she been working for Lakeshore. Under normal circumstances she might have lost her medical license. But the man was terrified. He didn't file a complaint. One of the nurses joked that he turned mute — mute with stupefaction. Her colleague was stumped, unable to fathom why she'd lost her temper. He told her that of course the man was offensive, but he'd seen her brave much worse without batting an eyelash. Her impassivity was legendary.

The three nurses who witnessed the exchange, two black women and a Puerto Rican gay man, were not flummoxed by her behavior. They were standing behind the boor, and all three gave Francine the thumbs-up.

She was furious with herself for reacting. She began to write the article as soon as she got home.

I told her one of my favorite bad surgeon jokes: no one would dare insult me because they knew I'd cut them up.

Choosing the Best Lipstick Shade to Wear to the Hospital

Before Sumaiya would get into the ambulance, she had two major concerns. The first was who would watch over her daughters while she was away. Mazen offered to do it, but I wanted to bring him along with me. The tonsured man and his wife ended up the volunteer babysitters. The second concern was how Sumaiya was to go to a hospital when she looked grotesque. How indeed? She explained to Emma and me that she had not packed any makeup while preparing to flee for her life, an oversight. She rarely used much, but she preferred not to be seen by strangers without a good foundation. I felt almost certain then that she had encephalopathy due to high ammonia levels, and she was going to get worse, with progressive delirium. Emma extracted a tube of lipstick from the horn of Amalthea that was her pocket, but Sumaiya thought it too bold. The tonsured man's wife was able to help, since she had remembered to pack some makeup while fleeing for her life. Not well packed, though, she said, it was damaged during the sea voyage. The powder was damp and lumpy, the lipstick verdigrised. Sumaiya was happy, I grateful.

Even though the ambulance did not have its siren turned on, I still had a lot of trouble following it. The pressure of being in the middle of a short caravan with Emma and the Swedish contingent in a car behind and the ambulance ahead strained my nerves. That would not have been as bad had I not made the mistake of turning on the GPS on my phone. The ambulance had different ideas than my mobile on how to get to the Mytilene hospital. Bugs Bunny sounded not too happy.

The ambulance would drop Sumaiya off at the emergency entrance of the hospital. Sammy and one Swedish physician were with her, whereas Emma and I, in different cars, would have to search for the hospital's parking lot. She had mentioned that the one time she'd been to the hospital she had to drive in circles at least three times before she found it.

Without my having to say anything, Mazen turned on his phone and had his GPS direct us. He picked up my mobile from the cup holder and turned off Bugs Bunny.

"Your driving is astounding," he said. "After all these years, you're still able to handle a stick shift like a champion. Whoever taught you must have been a genius. He should be given a Nobel Prize in physics."

At a stoplight, a middle-aged Greek woman crossed the street. She hunched in a gust of wind that tore at her ancient, patched cardigan. She looked Syrian, like a relative of ours. She glanced back at the ambulance, perhaps wondering why it didn't turn on its sirens and run the red light.

"What happened back there?" I asked Mazen.

I wondered whether this was the right time to talk about his apoplectic tantrum since I wasn't sure I'd be a good listener, what with being on edge behind the ambulance. Yet he and I were alone in a car at a stoplight. In a way, the red light made it seem appropriate.

"I got angry," he said.

We looked at each other askance, which was our way of telling each other: *That was the worst joke ever* or *Are you kidding me?*

"I'd say I was surprised *you* weren't angry," he said.

"Oh, I was. Only I didn't end up screaming. I haven't seen you this upset before. I'm not sure I've ever seen you angry, for crying out loud."

"Well, I stopped smoking," he said. "It's nicotine withdrawal."

"You stopped smoking eight years ago," I said.

"I'm still suffering. You don't know what it's like."

I lifted my hand off the steering wheel as if to slap him.

"Okay," he said. "I shouldn't have gotten so angry, but I couldn't help it. I loathe these Westerners who have fucked us over and over for years and then sit back and wonder aloud why we can't be reasonable and behave like they do with their noses up in the air as if they're smelling shit. I hate their adulation of their own imaginary virtues. She actually said they don't love their daughters with an upper-class English accent. May Satan tie her forked tongue for eternity. Maybe I was furious because I miss my daughter immensely. Ever since she moved to Dubai, I hardly ever see her. Maybe it was because I want to kill my daughter since she refuses to give me a bushel of grandchildren, goddammit. I've been good. I deserve grandkids. Maybe I raged and you didn't because I'm not as used to those assholes. Maybe because I wanted a cigarette. Maybe I went ballistic because I should have. What's the word you used to describe your rage all those years ago?"

"Righteous," I said.

A housefly buzzed out of nowhere and landed on the inside of the windshield, bulbous iridescent body, gold-skeined wings; a prisoner in the car, she rubbed her hands in consternation or in glee. The swiftness with which Mazen caught the fly still impressed me after all these years. He shook his fist and held it before me to blow on for good luck. With the usual panache, he threw the dazed insect onto the dashboard.

"Yeah," he said, looking ahead, into the distance. "Maybe it was righteous."

How to Steal a Bath

"You're wrong as usual," Mazen said. "You've seen me angry many times. I'm insulted that you don't remember."

"I don't," I said. "I assume I must have, but nothing comes to mind."

"What about the bath?"

"What bath?"

"When I tried to get you to steal the bath," Mazen said with an exaggerated huff, "and you failed miserably."

My laughter burst out suddenly, accompanied by a fricative snort. My fingers tightened around the steering wheel. I'd almost forgotten.

I was ten, since Mazen and I still shared a bed. As I was walking back to our bedroom, I noticed the door to the bathroom open. The tub was filled with the most enticing water, limpid and blue—a beckoning, hot spring lake in a snowy white room. The late-afternoon light forced

the steam to dance along the water's surface. I must have
sighed when I walked into our room, because Mazen, lying
on the bed, wondered what was going on. I told him I'd
never wanted to soak in a bathtub as much I did now. He
jumped off the bed to see for himself. We heard our sister
talking to our mother in the kitchen. He led me by the hand
toward them, but we stopped right outside the door. In the
most nonchalant tone he could muster, Mazen asked Aida
if she'd set up the bath. When she said yes, he told me to
go jump into the bath while he went into the kitchen and
distracted her. I undressed down to my underpants in my
bedroom, as usual when taking a bath, then went into the
bathroom with my comics because that's what one did, soak
in a tub with a comic book. I peed before stepping into
the tub. I'd taken too much time. Only one foot was in the
water when Aida rushed into the bathroom, grabbed me
under my armpits, and hauled me out of the tub. She was
sixteen then and much larger than I was. She dragged my
limp naked form across the bathroom and pushed me out
the door. Humiliated, my buttocks pressed onto cool stone
tiles, my legs splayed before me, I saw the streak of kanji
my wet foot had traced on the floor. My white briefs landed
on my face. Mazen cracked up. Aida made sure to tell us
that we, her sons-of-bitches brothers, were not as smart as
we thought we were, not smart at all, as she slammed the
bathroom door and locked it.

     "No," I said. "You're the one who's wrong as usual.
You weren't angry. You were laughing and mocking me."

     "I yelled at you," he said. Pink bubbled up to his cheeks,
and his impish eyes reminded me of the boy he was. "I

couldn't believe you didn't lock the door. Who doesn't lock a bathroom door?"

"No yelling," I said. "You were on the floor laughing."

"Yelling, I tell you," he said. "I was angry at you for not locking the door, for screwing up my genius plan."

"Laughing."

"Yelling."

One Hospital
Is Much Like Another,
One Job Same Same

I had been with Sumaiya as she waited to get an X-ray, but I felt like a fifth wheel, so I left the room. Emma stayed with her. The doctors knew where to find me if they needed a translator. In the corridor-cum-waiting room, my brother and Sammy were deep in a whispery conversation that halted as soon as they noticed me. I answered their unasked questions. Nothing yet, no news. I sat on an apple-green plastic chair on the other side of Sammy, asked what the two of them were talking about.

"Your brother was telling me all about his wonderful children," Sammy said.

"A bit of boasting," Mazen said. "My apologies. I shouldn't have done that."

"Not at all," Sammy said. "You should be proud of them. I would be as well. My greatest wish is for my daughters to grow as accomplished as yours."

"From your lips to God's ears," Mazen and I said at the same time, even though we both were blatant nonbelievers.

The hospital might have been more worn, might have looked different, atypical, but it felt quite familiar. White walls, white walls. Crow's feet radiated from the eyes of the windows. A sickle of pale light fell on my boots.

Sammy kept trying to sit up, as if he needed to be at military attention, but within moments he would be bent over again, his head nearing his knees. He was probably exhausted, definitely nervous. Each time someone opened the door on our left, spurts of cold, shallow wind would force him to put his hands in his coat pockets.

"She's not going to make it, is she?" he said, and a look of profound desolation crossed his face.

I hesitated. He seemed to have resisted the false entice-ments of optimism without much help from me. The Syrian phrase he used was a bit odd. Translated literally, it would be: "She's not going to finish," the object not specified. We use the same phrase—also meaning "she's not going to be saved"—more often than "she's going to die."

"No," I said. "She's not going to make it. We're trying to figure out a more accurate diagnosis in order to see how we can lessen the pain, maybe ease her way."

Upon our arrival at the hospital, the admitting nurse, wearing a heavy fleece coat over her scrubs and a suspicious eye, asked us what the problem was. She seemed the type of nurse I got along with best: smart, not young, compassionate, even-keeled, and she'd seen it all. When the Swedish doctor explained Sumaiya's condition, the nurse faltered for only a second. Her face showed a "why are you bringing her here" expression before she told us in a tone that combined sympathy and helpless resignation that there was little she could do. No MRI machine, a blood panel would take some time to return from the lab, and even then would not be complete. Still, she said, we should do what we could. A person untrained in nursespeak would have erroneously thought her uncaring.

I did not blame her for wondering why we brought Sumaiya to her hospital. We all knew of the country's financial crisis. Hospitals were stretched to the limit.

Sammy remained quiet with his thoughts for a while. His bronzed hands poked through tightly fastened cuffs. I wished Francine were with me. She knew how to deal with situations like this much better than I. Her mere presence was comforting. I felt nervous, if not outright afraid, when I had to tell patients and their loved ones that there was no hope. I'd done it numerous times, of course, part of the job, but I had yet to be inured to it and never improved at it, whereas Francine had the ability to be intimate with grief and the grieving, to hold wounded souls in her hands.

"She knows," Sammy said. "She didn't think she would make it this far. She made me promise to keep going if she died along the way. She wanted me to leave her body unburied and keep on going, as if I could have done that."

"She made you promise?" I asked.

"Yes," Sammy said. "She was sure she wasn't going to make it to the Turkish border, let alone all the way to Izmir. She didn't want us to slow down and waste time. She made me promise, so I lied. I told her we would leave her wherever she dropped. For the sake of the girls, I said, I would let her be. But I knew and she knew that I would never leave her. I wouldn't be able to stand as a man if I left her unburied. Just the thought. She wanted to believe that she wouldn't be a burden, so I promised. But she grew stronger along the trip, I swear. By the time we were in the boat and everyone was getting sicker, she was getting stronger."

I didn't have to ask any questions, barely needed to utter a word. I wasn't sure he cared about who his audience was or remembered who was listening to him. He rambled on in a dolorous tone, his head still bent, as if he were addressing his knees. He hadn't been able to talk to his daughters yet. Asma had understood how badly her mother was doing all on her own, but the younger two knew only that their mother was ill. They were waiting for her to get better. Everything got better, everything always turned out all right. Wasn't that what Sumaiya and he told them?

How would he take care of his three girls? No family around him in a foreign place where he knew nothing. Why him, why his family? He had tried to be the best man he could. Sumaiya—Sumaiya was the best woman in the world, the most decent. Everyone loved her. Why was God testing him harshly? Was there some lesson behind all the disasters that had befallen them?

His unhappiness was that of a man who felt he was about to lose more than what he already had. He went on, kept talking, worried and bemoaning his fate, until Mazen changed the subject, asked him what he did for work. He was a farmhand, working a modest field belonging to one of his uncles. No education, he said. Neither he nor his wife had gone past middle school. He had to work at an early age since his own father and brothers couldn't make enough to feed everyone.

"But my life could have been different," he said. "When I was seventeen, I worked for a well-educated man, a professor at the university. He visited our village because he was studying the geography of the area. He needed someone to take him around, so he hired me. I was a gofer at first. Do this, get me this, take care of that. I did everything. I loved it. After a couple of weeks, I noticed that he was trying to draw maps, but his fingers were old and swollen. I had a great facility for drawing, always had, and I suggested I do it. I became a cartographer, and he taught me all the time. I was so good that the professor promised he would enroll me in a school for mapmaking. I would have a great career. But then I was arrested, and everything fell apart. Even though I was released and all, the professor no longer wanted anything to do with me. It wasn't that he liked the regime, he said, but he couldn't take the risk of crossing the powers that be. No one could. I was unable to find any work for a couple of years after that. The only one who would hire me was my uncle because I was family. And now another disaster. I've heard that Syrian doctors can only find work as taxi drivers in Germany. What's a farmhand like me going to do?" And he devolved back into lamenting his horrid luck.

As soon as the door to the X-ray room swung open, Sammy was on his feet, a forced smile on his face. The Swedish physician, his hands swallowed by the sleeves of his ill-fitting lab coat, explained that we couldn't see anything we didn't know before. We couldn't admit her to the hospital, but we should move her and her family to another refugee camp, Kara Tepe, where she would receive better medical care. She could stay in a special tent where refugees who were ill would be away from the hustle of the camp.

He used the word "hospice," but I didn't translate that. Not yet.

When You Don't Know
What to Say, Have a Cookie

We had to split up. Sumaiya was to ride in the ambulance to the Kara Tepe camp while Sammy went to Moria to pick up the kids and their belongings. I wanted to go with Sumaiya since no one else in the group spoke her language, but she maintained that Emma and I should help her husband and kids. She was only going to be moved to a new bed, as she put it. The Swedish doctors would take her. She did not need to understand anything they said. As soon as she arrived at the bed, she was going to sleep. In the wheelchair, she looked exhausted, barely able to speak. Her eyes insisted on drooping.

But then Mazen said he'd go in the ambulance. He could translate if need be. "I'll make sure to be really sweet to you," he said to Sumaiya, which delighted her.

In Moria, while Sammy went to collect his kids, Emma and I waited outside the barracks. Amid the lugubrious decay of the camp, she looked shiny and ultracompetent.

With raking fingers, she pulled in strands of hair that had gone astray. She wanted to know if I had any ideas as to how to tell Sammy that he had to test his daughters. Sumaiya had tested positive for hepatitis B. We would leave it to him to explain to his daughters that their mother was not leaving the island. Emma's organization could speed the Swedish registration process. They would have been able to move the family to Sweden within a day or two had Sumaiya not been sick.

"We are moving camps," Asma said, coming out of the barracks, followed by the dank, stuffy air of the building, the smells of bodies and cold sweat. "We're going to a better one."

"Oh, yes you are," Emma said after I translated. "It's better for families, and we can take better care of your mother over there."

Asma looked up at us. Her gloved fingers plucked at one of the extra-large buttons of her overcoat as if they were playing some ancient instrument whose music only she could hear. Her face, encapsulated by her head scarf, was gorgeous and questioning. She hesitated briefly before bluntly asking: "Is my mother going to die?"

Emma wanted to know what she'd said. I translated, and Emma gave me a look. "Tell her we don't know when something like—"

"Yes, she is," I said. I crouched down so Asma and I would be at eye level. I wasn't that much taller. "Your mother is sick and declining. I don't know how long she will continue to live, but she can't stay much longer."

Asma, aspiring doctor, seemed to shrink. Her lips quivered, her eyes welled, but she didn't cry, not until Emma bent and hugged her fiercely. I watched them weep into each other's shoulders. Asma was the one who pulled back first. Through tears she said she didn't want her sisters to know, didn't want them to see her in this state.

"Cookies," I said.

Hand in hand, Asma and I walked the downward-sloping twenty steps or so to the tea and cookie dispensary. It was afternoon; there was a long line. We were heading toward the end when I noticed Rasheed and his Palestine Red Crescent Society vest at the front of the line, almost at the window. He grinned sheepishly, rubbed his stomach. "I need my afternoon tea and cookie," he said, shouting so we could hear him across the distance. "I shouldn't have sweets, but it's not my fault. I blame British colonialism!"

I pointed to Asma and mouthed "cookie." He nodded. We walked beyond the line a little, stood on a ridge of chilly dirt watching the refugee tents below us. The Greek riot police still loitered at the bottom of the hill. An American in his fifties, big man, rugby-build physique, talked to a group of refugees on the cement walkway quite a ways from Asma and me, but I could hear his slurry, adenoidal accent clearly. He was indicating where the refugees were to sleep that night. Another family waited to talk to him, a thin, lanky mother with worn men's slippers on her bare feet, her four children wrapped around her like cotton candy on a stick.

Francine, Francine, help me talk to this young girl.

I pulled Asma close to me, my hand on her shoulder, and she gently squeezed it. At the end of the middle finger, her glove had a hole with a wreath of jagged stitches around it. The tip of her nail poked through the wreath.

The cold afternoon light had a sheen, like air behind a windowpane. We observed the scene below us, the pup tents, the impromptu soccer game with no goals, the triple-strand concertina razor wire, the police vans, the far horizon where the sea and sky were joined by a thin blue thread that was never straight, as if sewn together by an incompetent seamstress. Quite a bit for the eye to fix on if it wished to avoid the discomfort of intimacy.

Below, to our left, was a static line, much longer than the tea and cookie one, where families, mostly women, waited for another gift box from an NGO. The women had a demeanor of calm anticipation peculiar to people accustomed to waiting. This package would be magically imbued with their dreams of respite, with their hopes of comfort, of a sudden change of fate. This was a box that would return everything to normal, a miracle of light and purity that would heal their family's pain. Even though the package of the day before contained nothing but a box of cereal and a doll, today's was sure to break the cycle. And the line began to inch forward little by little.

"I have dreamed of our house every night since we left," Asma said. "It's a small house with a small sitting room and two small bedrooms, but in my dreams it's huge and warm and pretty and the courtyard is even bigger with a giant oak tree in the middle of it. I know we left our home, but my dreams don't seem to know that."

"Are you okay?" I asked.

"Yes," she said. "I'm fine. She told me this was going to happen. She explained it to me. She said I have to be strong, and I am."

"Yes, yes, you are." I said. "Everyone can see that."

Good, I thought to myself. That's handled.

At one of the tents, next to a small campfire breathing a little smoke, two women sat one in front of the other on a small tarp as if in yoga positions. The younger of them, wearing a green head scarf, knelt with both feet under her behind as she combed the hair of the other, who seemed to be in a half-lotus position, an assiduous combing to rid the wet hair of even the tiniest tangle. On the other side of the women, looking utterly out of place, was a small pot of wilting geraniums wrapped in pink crepe. Francine had a black dress with a pattern of tulips the exact color of that pink.

No, I had not handled that.

"You are strong," I told Asma, "but it's difficult when we lose someone we love." I made sure to look at her, to see her. "My father died a while ago. I hadn't seen him for a long time, but I loved him. I was sad for many months. A piece of my heart was taken away. I had to be strong because I had people who needed me. I had to go to work in the morning. I had to talk to all kinds of people. I would be strong and operate on a patient. But then I had to find time to cry by myself. I couldn't help myself. I would cry and cry until I had to be strong again."

"How long did you cry?"

"Oh, a long time," I said. "Two months, maybe more."

"And then what happened? Did you stop?"

"I don't know what happened," I said. "I think I started crying less and then a little less. I was still sad, but it didn't hurt as much." I crouched before her once again, face-to-face. "I'll tell you a secret. You can't tell anyone. As

I'm talking about my father now, I want to cry. I'm still sad, but the sadness isn't as strong anymore. I still think about him. Just today I was talking to my brother about him."

Rasheed showed up with chocolate chip cookies for each of us, and Asma had hers in her mouth in an instant.

One Should Listen to
a Soprano During
a Refugee Crisis

All that time, while Mazen and I were with Sumaiya at the hospital, while I helped the family move to Kara Tepe, you locked yourself in your room and refused to leave. You checked yourself in to the fanciest hotel in Mytilene, affordable during the off-season, and waited to leave for San Francisco. You were out of it; you didn't have the wherewithal to simply take an earlier flight. Whatever penalties you would have incurred for changing your reservation would have been cheaper than those three nights in Mytilene. You were a zombie.

You didn't leave the room for twenty-four hours. Thankfully, the hotel had room service. You burrowed under almost-lush sheets, listening to one soprano after another sing the great tales of woe.

Kindertotenlieder? Oh, yes.

Der Rosenkavalier? For sure.

Das Lied von der Erde? Hit me.

You'd flown all the way to Lesbos to help refugees, and you ended up hiding in a hotel room. Only you.

The next morning, you were able to sneak out of your room briefly. You had breakfast in the hotel restaurant and rushed back to your room.

Female Trouble

The next morning during a break in the rains, I was back in Moria waiting for Rasheed, standing on the same ridge as the day before, looking at the same scene. That morning's viewing included an unbridled horse promenading in an orchard up the hill behind the camp's wall and razor wires. Luminescent in the distance, the animal didn't seem to be eating or doing anything in particular, just taking in the air on a stroll in its backyard.

I'd promised Rasheed three hours of my time before I checked on Sumaiya and her family in Kara Tepe. I was his to use however he saw fit, which meant that Mazen belonged to him this morning as well. One of his Jerusalem group's primary focuses for the last couple of months in Lesbos had been helping with cases of physical and sexual abuse. Being Palestinian, speaking the same language, Rasheed and his friends were better than Westerners at interviewing refugees. A Farsi-speaking group performed similar interviews with Afghan and Iranian refugees. It seemed that Rasheed spoke some Farsi but nowhere near nuanced enough for native speakers.

"Do you mind?" I asked Mazen. "It might not be much fun for you."

During the rains in Moria, everywhere there was the smell of the sea—of electricity, of ozone. After the rain, the smell of way too many humans returned. Mazen took in some air and stood more erect for a moment.

"And you think it's going to be fun for you?" he said. "You're here to help, and I'm here to help you. I'll do whatever. And make you feel guilty so you'll have to buy me a big present for my birthday."

I heard the thick, wet thud of Rasheed on the muddy dirt behind me, but still he startled me when he appeared next to us, full of morning cheer. Every time I saw him I wanted to pinch his cheeks as if he were a little boy. He was our age, closer to sixty than to fifty.

"Did you remember your stethoscope?" he asked. The white-and-orange Palestinian vest seemed to have shrunk on him since the day before. "I have an extra if you forgot." I took mine out of the side pocket of my cargo pants and showed it to him. "No, no," he said. "What's the point of having it in your pocket? You won't be using it much. It has to drape around your neck in the official stethoscope position, announcing you're a physician. People trust doctors. They can reveal the most intimate of secrets. They won't lie to a doctor."

"Oh, you'd be surprised," I said.

"No, seriously," he said. "I'm a nurse, and when I wear the stethoscope, the women seem to trust me more. It makes you more godlike. You'll be a great help."

For a moment, Rasheed and Mazen seemed to be appraising one another, and then both smiled, in approval, I hoped. I found it intriguing that I considered them similar, not only in personality but also in looks. Both on the plump side, round faces that seemed to have no cheekbones, yet both were nimble and agile in their movements. Their facial features highly Semitic, the brown eyes, the scimitar nose. The hair was different. Rasheed's remained relatively dark, cut short. Mazen's thick, curly hair was unruly, and strands floated above his head in every direction. All his life he looked as if he needed a haircut, no matter when he'd had the last one. His hair was all gray now, much more so than mine.

We spent the morning interviewing, or to be more precise, listening. We talked to women exclusively. At times, their husbands tried to butt in, not wanting their wives or daughters to talk to us without their being present, at which point Rasheed would gesture toward me and say the doctor wanted to talk about private female issues. To make himself less threatening to the men, he would become a touch more feminine. As you did whenever you returned to the United States from abroad, he instinctively knew how much to camp it up for the husband, as if saying, "Look at me, I'm no threat to your wife at all."

It was a gray universe, a gray room, a converted shipping container called an Isobox, which wasn't small but still felt cramped and airless. A tiny window provided scant daylight. I didn't understand how we could discover if a woman had been abused unless the physical evidence was obvious. Rasheed wouldn't ask directly, and I wasn't sure the Syrian women would admit it if they had been. They did talk, though, talked and talked. Some of them regaled us

with tales of bombing campaigns and sniper fire, of maraud-
ing gangs and arbitrary arrests. They talked about how they
left Syria, the routes they took, the journeys lasting days and
weeks. They walked, drove cars, rode buses whose ticket
prices tripled or even quadrupled if the drivers figured out
how desperate they were. There were explosions over here,
bombings over there, yet the buses moved slower than fig
jam. Livestock blocked traffic, oblivious goats strolling this
way and that, drivers cursing and yelling at shepherds, the
smell of dust and milk, the smell of cordite, sheep lying dead
and bloated on wounded fields that had turned into battle-
fields. The women ran on and on, moved from depression
to optimism and back down again.

Mostly, though, they talked about their ailments. The
physician was in the building. Every other woman had cold
and flu-like symptoms, as did the children. Headaches, diar-
rhea, catarrh, trench foot, and many had menstruation issues
caused by stress. Ailments that were minor became gigantic
because of the paucity of services. By the time we'd been
there for half an hour, we had a sizable if haphazard queue
of eager women and their children waiting to talk to us.
Mazen ended up doing what he did best. He handled the
line of people, talked to them, told stories, became their
entertaining and charming host as they waited. I wrote down
diagnoses on pieces of paper so other physicians could read
them. We handed out NSAIDs right and left. One woman
had fungus forming tiny sculptures on her feet. Another had
a rash on her neck that she'd been trying to heal by covering
it with a convoluted homemade poultice containing sage,
marjoram, and three other herbs I'd not heard of. Luckily,
I had a tube of hydrocortisone cream.

A woman in her early thirties sat in front of me with her seven children, all under ten. Birth control, I thought. I should be talking to the women about birth control. The children sported kohl around their eyes. I had heard of the long-ago practice of putting kohl around a newborn's eyes to keep away the evil eye, to keep Satan and his jinn at bay, but when I asked the mother, she said that what kohl kept away was conjunctivitis. I spent ten minutes disabusing her of the silly belief, explaining about viruses and bacteria, rather loudly so everyone in the room could hear. Most of the women we interviewed were not as superstitious, at least not when it came to medical cures.

A farmer told me that she and her husband had the most fertile plot of land in the entire universe. She was able to grow anything on her farm. Citrus? Of course. Olives, peaches, cherries, apples. All kinds of vegetables, cucumbers, tomatoes, and onions so tasty they'd make you weep before and after you cut into them. She missed the smell of flowering apricots. She insisted that even if she were blindfolded, she could tell precisely where she was on the farm by feeling the earth through her soles. She had all kinds of trees on her land, and she could name every single one of them. She knew the names of all the wildflowers she encountered, the names of all the grasses she walked over. But what good was all her knowledge now? She would have to learn names in a language not her own, on land not her own.

It was then that I realized that as poor as these refugees were, they were not the most destitute of Syria's population. The Turkish mafia charged a thousand dollars per passenger, a bit less for children, and you might be able to haggle a discount if you were willing to leave at odd hours or during reckless storms. Those were exorbitant fees. Where was the money coming from? Where was the money going?

When a young widow who had left Syria on her own — her husband's family having abandoned her seeking refuge in Jordan the year before — kept smoothing her skirt while sitting on the cot before us, I wondered, Did she have to barter? I surprised both Rasheed and her by asking a somewhat more direct question: "Did you encounter any problems trying to book a place on the boat from Izmir?"

She shook her head no a couple of times. A bit tentative, awkward, she interlaced her words with serious pauses. She would not look at me. She seemed to examine her hands as they lay on her lap. I wondered if I should push, but again I felt out of my depth, not just as a physician, as a human.

"It must have been challenging," I said. "Hard."

She suddenly stopped fidgeting, looked up; her eyes found mine.

"Thank you for asking," she said. "I did not have a problem getting on the boat. I did have a problem earlier, right after we crossed the border, but I handled it. I've had to deal with the problem before. It wasn't difficult." She grinned and her eyes lit up. "But yesterday is gone. It's a new day. I must forget where I came from."

Either You Are with Us or You Are with the Terrorists

Every nation needed an enemy, you wrote, every group a nemesis. Quite a statement, though you should have left it at that. But you added that the stronger a nation was, the more defined the enemy needed to be. I thought that wasn't right. I know it was one of the characters in your novel who said it, not you; nevertheless, it gives me pleasure to point out that you were wrong and your character too.

Who would have expected that the new enemy would be *terror*? Who would have thought that we'd declare war on an abstract noun?

That speech, that fucking speech.

Either you are with us or you are with the terrorists.

You and I had a similar reaction to the bombing of the World Trade Center, beginning with the shock of it and on through the grief. You were alarmed, but more so when the president gave that speech days later. You knew, just as I did, that our world would soon spiral into horrors hitherto unimagined.

They hate our freedoms.

You knew, I knew, everyone from the Middle East knew. Hell, every immigrant knew. Our country was redefining the enemy and it was us.

But first let's bomb them over there. Shock and awe, baby. Let all of us who *believe in progress and pluralism, tolerance and freedom* blindly destroy their countries, shatter their political systems, economies, infrastructures, and create millions of refugees for generations to come. Bush called that civilization's fight.

Even grief recedes with time and grace.

But not before we damage the world for eternity.

You had to adapt; you were good at that. First you were an enemy because you were queer, but suddenly being a Middle Eastern immigrant was a bigger threat. A shift of wind. A sailboat has to adjust to the whim of the wind, not the other way round. You adjusted. Every time you returned to the United States from Beirut, the new Homeland Security people gave you a funny look, until you figured out how much the sail needed trimming, how to jibe the boat. You learned how to camp it up at passport control, a sashay here, a seductive grin there, a small drop of the shoulder, as if saying, "Look at me, I'm no threat at all." Worked like a miracle.

And the true revelation arrived on a flight from London back to the United States after you'd visited Pakistan. You were worried that you'd be interrogated, that the customs officials and the Homeland Security agents would conspire to delay you at the airport for an hour or more. You would be exhausted after such a long flight. The woman in the seat next to you was polishing her nails a delightful pink. You told her you loved the color; she told you she was willing to share. Of course you partook. Of course you did.

And when you arrived at the desk with hot-pink nails a stark contrast to the dark blue of your American passport, the agent simply opened the little booklet, briefly glanced inside, returned it with a smile, saying: "Welcome home."

Look at you. Building any kind of explosive device would ruin your manicure.

No one at a US port of entry had ever welcomed you home before. Every day now, hell might be shadowing your soul, but stark nail polish is your companion as well and maybe a touch of eye shadow.

And Wellbutrin.

After Lesbos, definitely Wellbutrin for you.

But How Butch Are You?

Rasheed told me this story about two Iraqi gay men who had arrived in Lesbos a few months earlier. Processing for Iraqi men took much longer, and that was if they were lucky. They were gay, they explained to anyone who would listen. They had to leave Iraq because they would have been killed, maybe beheaded, stoned to death, you never knew. They were a couple. They had been together for eight years. They were a family with nowhere to go.

Well, no one seemed to believe them, Rasheed said. At first the couple assumed that it was because their English, though passable, was not up to par. They asked for a translator, but then the translator would cock his eyebrows whenever they said they were a couple. They would point to their rings, yet their application would go back to the bottom of the pile. They could not understand.

They watched as Syrian families were processed and moved to Athens on their way to new homes in Europe.

They saw new couples arriving on the island and being given prime real estate inside the camps, while they had to sleep in a small tent in the olive grove outside Moria. It was cold and wet and muddy and awful. They wondered at the unfairness of it all. They had thought there would be less discrimination in Europe, that they could live more openly in the West.

And then Rasheed came along.

Done with his shift, he walked down the Moria runway.

"All right, I pranced down the hill," he said. "Let's say that the boys saw me, and right away one of them said hello. I turned around, and before me was my ultimate sexual fantasy. Mamma mia! I wanted to be sandwiched by those two gorgeous bears from Iraq. They were almost thirty years younger than me, but in my fantasy, they would find my aging body charming. We got to talking, they told me their story, and I was aghast. They explained that they were not sure what they'd been doing wrong. The boys had another interview the next day and were worried. I told them that I, gay superhero for the ages, would fix it.

"I took them with me to my hotel. No, shut up, it wasn't what you think. I put them up in their own room. They were my people. I had to explain that they were having trouble because they were much too masculine. Of course, I had to listen to the usual but this is who we are, blah, blah, blah. I told them the system was unable to compute two masculine men in a relationship. They would have to femme it a little, just a little, or at least one of them had to. They panicked. Would they be able to do it? Could they pass? I told them not to worry. It wasn't as if they were going out in drag. They didn't really have to become feminine, only a touch less masculine. Gay superhero for the ages could help, no problem. They couldn't decide who would become the less masculine one. I decided for them. Both, I told them. I had them shower, shave their beards, and yes, shave their chests and backs just in case. They spent an hour in the bathroom, and I could imagine what went on in that shower. When they were done, I took them down to the restaurant for dinner and showed them how they should behave, how not to overdo things. It was only little things, slight adjustments, instead of putting ankle over knee, it's the back of one knee over the other. Very simple. Smile more often. You want whoever is talking to you to like you. No, not because you want them to process your application. You want them to like you because you're a gay man. You get used to smiling because they have power over you, not just when it comes to an application. Wherever you go, they will have power over you. Appeasement is your friend. Always smile nervously. And for the coup de grace, I showed them the secret weapon. I told them that when they pointed to the rings, it had better be a certain way. I showed them Beyoncé's video. Luckily, I only needed the first thirty-five seconds, because you know how slow the internet at the hotel is. My hero points to her hand and sings, "Put a ring on it." I had them memorize how she moved her hands. I told them if they could Beyoncé, everyone would know they're gay. Smile nervously and Beyoncé.

"They're now in Berlin."

Heavy Words

A woman, head covered with a simple scarf, asked to speak to me alone, without anyone else listening in. She looked to be around my age, give or take a few years. She apologized profusely to Rasheed and Mazen, saying she needed to discuss a private matter with the doctor, a medical condition. Rasheed, more experienced in dealing with overtly devout women, asked her whether she needed the men out of the room. No, she said. She only needed to talk. She did not say anything until my companions were at the other side of the room.

"I have a problem," she began. She looked both left and right to make sure no one was listening. As she did, she set off waves of spicy fragrance, some combination of basil, ginger, and olive oil. I couldn't be sure where exactly the scent emanated from, but I assumed from under the head scarf, probably some homemade hair-care oil.

I nodded encouragingly, making sure my face remained noncommittal.

"Ever since we left home," she said, "I haven't been able to speak."

I did not say anything, just raised a questioning left eyebrow. She understood. The vertical wrinkle running down her forehead deepened.

"Oh, I'm speaking now," she said, "but not the right way. My words seem heavy and slow, much too slow. And sometimes I can't even form words."

"Forgive me," I said, "but I don't understand what you mean by your words seeming slow. It appears to me that you sound normal."

"No, I don't sound normal," she said. "Not like before. My tongue has expanded. It's quite swollen, much too big for my mouth." Shoving her head forward toward me, she opened her mouth wide, drawing her cracked lips apart with both forefingers. "Look," she said with a distorted lisp. "Look."

She wished me to examine her mouth like you would with a horse. Unlike her teeth and her dry and stretched lips, the tongue looked healthy and pink. Her uvula, hanging like a fleshy polyp at the top of her throat, seemed normal to my naked eyes. I asked her to lift her tongue and she did. Nothing.

"Does it hurt?" I asked.

She shook her head sideways. It didn't. I was now certain that the lovely spice scent originated from her hair.

I told her to keep her mouth open for a minute, but that there was no need to use her fingers. I wondered what

I could use for a tongue depressor without having to abandon her to look for one. I didn't have a spoon on me, a Bic pen would have to do, and I did have alcohol wipes in my pocket. There was no sign of a problem, not on her tongue or in her throat. No discoloration, no movement issues, no swelling, no pain, no polyps, no apparent symptom of any disease I recognized, not diphtheria, no visible tumors. All I could see was a possible abscess in one of her teeth, but I was no dentist. I could not figure out what was going on.

"I don't see anything wrong," I said. "And you have no pain, right?"

She seemed disappointed. I wondered whether it was a neurological problem or a psychosomatic one. Why did she want the men to leave? I asked her if she could be more specific with her descriptions. How did it feel to have a swollen tongue? What did heavy words sound like? She shrugged.

"I think you should see a dentist," I said.

"My teeth don't hurt either," she said.

She thanked me politely, stood up, and walked away. She sat on her cot across the room, took out a large plastic bag brimming with clothes, and began to rummage through it.

I wished I could refer her to someone. I wanted to explain to her how the brain works, what the nervous and endocrine systems were, but nothing came out. I wished to say kind words to her, anything.

My words were too heavy.

Another woman moved up the queue and sat before me.

The Old Woman's Theory of Loss

As Mazen and I descended Moria's little hill to get to the car, I saw the old woman from the beach trudging up in the opposite direction. We were in heavy traffic, feet shuffling up and down the walkway, except no one could figure out the lanes, let alone stick to them. The old woman still carried her black plastic trash bag; it looked a little less full, less heavy than the last time I saw it. She must have felt tired, because she plopped her behind on a protruding stone next to the cement walkway, seemingly oblivious to all the people around her. I pointed her out to Mazen, telling him that the last time I saw the woman, she had stolen a young volunteer's iPhone.

"Good for her," he said as he pulled me by the hand, weaving through the crowd to go introduce himself.

She regarded us suspiciously as we approached and clutched her bag closer to her bosom, almost disappearing behind it. Thin and bony, she looked as if a caricaturist could capture her in no more than a couple of strokes. Her shaky body seemed about to run at any moment.

"What do you want?" she snapped. "I have nothing for people like you." Her tone had the right measure of disagreeable, giving each word a particular weight and value.

"We only want find out if you're doing all right," Mazen said, using his most pleasant salesman tongue. "We were wondering if you needed anything."

"I was there when you landed on the beach," I added, hoping to make her feel less anxious. "I'm the doctor." I wondered if I should take out my stethoscope and drape it around my neck.

"I don't need a doctor," she stated emphatically, looking up at us standing before her, challenging us to disagree. "Didn't need one then, don't need one now."

"I'm glad your health is good," Mazen said, sounding serene. "Do you have everything you need here? Are you missing anything?"

"Here?" she said. "Here where? In this awful camp? How can I have everything I need in this place? How can anyone?"

I took a long breath and shoved the air out with a sigh, whereas Mazen seemed to perk up. The woman reminded me too much of my mother, a small evil sprite, malevolent and ungrateful.

"I understand, believe me," he said. The left collar suddenly peeped from under his sweater as if it wanted to jump out in glee. "After losing so much, being in a foreign country, in a place like this, must feel terrible."

Her eyes turned skeptical again. "What do you mean, losing so much?"

"Having to leave your home," he said, still not breaking stride. "The war, the destruction, things like that."

She rolled her eyes, and her face went slack. "You young people don't know anything," she said, "and you're no longer that young. What hope is there for the world when it's run by young people who know so little?" She was in all black — black dress, black head scarf — except for a pair of sparkly blue Adidas sneakers that someone must have given her recently. "You can never understand."

"Maybe we can," Mazen said, ignoring my tugging at his sleeve — tugging so hard that his other collar popped out. "We're from Deir ez-Zor, or our mother is. I have been there a few times, the last time not too long before the troubles began."

Her hand let go of the bag to flick itself in the air, dismissing everything around it. "That's worse," she said. "You should understand, and you don't."

"Tell me," he said.

"When you're my age, you've lost everything over and over again," she said.

"I understand," he said, "but I was talking about your home, the belongings you left behind."

"You're like my son," she said. "Not bright in the head, are you? My son is up there weeping like a little girl for what he lost, all the dolls that he can't play with anymore. How is he going to be able to get new dolls in a new country? Wah, wah, he blubbers every evening, until it's time to go to bed again. He shuts off the light, settles down, straightens the damp pillow, and tries to sleep. He wakes up and starts crying again. You're all children."

My attention was caught momentarily by a squawking seagull that alighted on the roof of an Isobox. Slowly, the old woman lifted herself off the stone, stretched her back as if she had not a care in the world. She was shorter than us by almost a hand.

"You know, this is my son's second wife. His first died twenty years ago. Oh, he mourned her, keened and cried, said he wasn't going to be happy again, and married a much younger girl within three months. I found her for him, me, just so he would shut up. Did he ever visit his first wife's grave? Of course not. He doesn't remember what her face looked like. She has vanished with the dead. Now he wails because he has lost everything again. Even toddlers are smarter than him."

"Help me understand," Mazen said, still grinning.

"Help you understand that you're stupid?" she asked impassively.

One should not generalize a single person's behavior to the larger population. However, since she behaved so like my mother, I was tempted to conclude that all women from Deir ez-Zor were ornery and downright insufferable. Except Mazen was not only suffering her but enjoying her company. It was then I decided something was amiss in this conversation. The old woman started out feeling imposed upon but no longer. She was enjoying the exchange too. She could have walked away, but she remained standing, waiting for Mazen to get back to her.

"Yes," he said, his face still set to impish. "Please tell me how come I'm stupid."

"Well, at least you're smart enough to ask for help," she said. She actually reached up and pinched his cheek, and he beamed. She was pleased with him and immoderately pleased with herself. "I didn't lose much now. I've been losing everything for as long as I can remember. So have you. My son weeps for his home, but he lost it a long time ago. It's not the same one he was born in. Everything had changed, and he wasn't paying attention."

"The apartment we grew up in is still in Beirut," Mazen said. "My mother still lives there."

"She lives there alone, doesn't she? Her children have left. You think that's still her home, your home? That's even worse. It's a hollow shell. Not living, no soul."

"True, but I would still feel sad if we lost it," he said.

"Fool," she said. "I'm telling you that you've already lost it."

"You know," he said, "my mother left Deir ez-Zor to get married when she was a young girl. She returned only once, for her father's funeral. My father insisted she return for her father's memory. She would have preferred never to set foot once she left. She'd wanted a clean break. She wanted to forget her past, bury who she was."

"A smart woman, your mother."

"This one here," he said, pointing at me, "hasn't been back to Lebanon. Not once has she come back to visit me. Giving up our roots is a family specialty."

"Everything I grew up with is gone," the old woman said, a touch wistfully. "The school I attended as a child is now a Pepsi-Cola factory. The house where I was married is now a supermarket. My home, the one where I had four children, well, my son decided to build two more stories on top of it and rent each to strangers. All the places I truly loved are gone, and countless people. The regime destroying my house can't hurt me. I lost everything a long time ago, and I will outlive them all."

Mazen agreed that she would outlive everyone but disagreed with everything else she said. She told him in no uncertain terms he was an unbridled idiot. Back and forth they went, she insulting him, he laughing it off, until she finally suggested that he help her carry her heavy bag up to the barracks.

I bet you wouldn't have disagreed. In one of your gloomy essays you wrote, "What is life if not a habituation to loss?"

Loss of the Loss That Was

Miriam was one of the first refugees to arrive in Beirut from Homs, one of the first you interviewed. You told her she should have been a philosopher. She had no idea what you meant. She loved being a hairdresser—well, would have if only someone in Beirut would offer her a job. Everything she had ever worked for was erased overnight by the war: the home she had decorated, the plants she had loved and watered, the clients she had nurtured.

There must be a name somewhere for what's not there, Miriam told you on her second interview. A few years had passed since you last spoke to her. She grieved for what she'd lost when she first arrived, her family, her apartment, her job. But one day she woke and the grief was gone. Poof!

She had lost too much, she had a hole in her heart, and grief had rushed in like a high tide to fill it.

In time, her grief withdrew.

She now had nothing except for the hole.

My Theory of Loss

Francine and I met Lubna when she married our friend
Syl and moved to the United States to be with him twelve
years ago. She was Syrian, from Damascus, and being fifty
at the time, she found the transition to Chicago a culture
shock, even though she'd always been cosmopolitan. She'd
met Syl at a conference in Lausanne, and for the first eighteen months they followed each other at conferences in
Europe, in South and North America. Living in America,
however, surprised her. It was the little things, she told me.
She couldn't figure out why everyone went to bed early.
That was her number one grievance. I explained that I did
because I would be exhausted the next day if I didn't have
enough sleep, to which she replied that she would as well
but she napped every afternoon. She couldn't understand
why siesta was not more popular in Chicago. She trained
Syl to nap daily. They were both university professors and
refused to schedule classes in the afternoon.

Yes, she was a woman after your own heart.

The little things she missed. Even though she was Christian, she missed the adhan at dawn, what she considered the most beautiful symphony as one mosque after another called the devotees to prayer. She missed the smell of verbena. Why did few buildings in the United States have balconies? She wanted to drink her morning coffee on a verandah. With neighbors. She'd lived in the same building downtown for years and the neighbors hardly acknowledged each other in the elevator. They were too busy staring at the floor numbers lighting up one by one. She was grateful that she'd been in Chicago for years when her city was bombed mercilessly, but why couldn't she find cotton candy that didn't taste like chemicals?

We were going to cook lunch together one day, and we visited Whole Foods to do our shopping. She told me that the first time she tried to make kibbeh, she bought the wrong kind of mint, since in Syria, there was only one kind.

"Here I was trying to show off to my husband and his friends, and instead of making kibbeh, I ended up with Chiclets."

I remember that Whole Foods excursion because she saw small jasmine plants at the entrance, about twenty in all. She quickly grabbed two and began calling her Syrian friends in Chicago, and her friends called friends. By the time we left the store a little more than half an hour later, there was only a tired one left. A Syrian contingent had descended upon the store. She insisted that I buy the last plant, as droopy as it was. Didn't I miss the scent of jasmine?

Of course I did. Of course I bought it. Of course I killed it within two months. Jasmine in Chicago?

What's That Smell?

What were your father's last words? In the hospital bed, before he passed on, he told you he smelled cardamom. Within that sterile room redolent of disinfectants, his mind conjured memories of the magic pod.

I too dream of cardamom. I don't think of using it while cooking. None of the recipes require it. I no longer drink Turkish coffee. But in bed, after a long night of dreams, I sometimes wake up with nostrils inhaling the spice's soft scent.

It is not just the land that binds us, not just the red earth, the fig tree, the lemon, or the olive. It's more than the city of Beirut, the surrounding mountains, or the Mediterranean. You and I are bound together with the aroma of cardamom.

And cloves.

Saffron.

The Faculty of the Mind

Emma was able to expedite the application of Sumaiya's family. They could take the ferry to Athens as soon as they were able to and then all the way to Malmö, not far from where she lived. The problem was that Sumaiya had been deteriorating rapidly ever since she settled in the medical tent. Her children were visiting her that morning when she had multiple nosebleeds, which terrified them.

The medical tent in Kara Tepe was not one. There was canvas, but it covered the structure, two windowless rooms constructed out of sturdy wood. In the bracing cold of late morning, it looked like an unassuming chapel on some back road. Sumaiya lay on one cot; her husband sat on the one next to her. Between her right arm and her hip, she held her imitation crocodile handbag, mustard colored, now matching her skin tone. She was already using a nasal cannula and an oxygen ventilator. In some ways, her husband looked worse. When I first saw him on the landing beach,

I thought he looked much younger, frail and wispish, as if he carried an eternal boy within him or a serious, studious college student. Before us, on the cot, the boy looked lost. Sammy seemed morose, his heavy head in his hands as he mumbled quietly to himself. He didn't notice that the four of us had entered the tent.

And what a foursome we were, Rasheed, Emma, Mazen, and me. The two nurses quickly walked over to adjust Sumaiya's breathing tube, which was askew. Rasheed was there first. Sammy stood up when he saw us, bowed his head, both as a greeting and a display of respect. Emma, using Rasheed as a translator, began to explain to Sammy about "the next part of their journey," as she called it. They spoke in soft whispers.

And Sumaiya blinked her eyes open. Her first reaction upon seeing me was a wide grin. She never ceased to surprise me. Her eyes sparkled, as if all this were some cosmic joke that was beyond her yet she'd enjoy it nonetheless. She reached out for my hand.

Have you ever considered the phrase "out of one's mind"? As if someone who was confused, addled, or angry would no longer be using her mind. Was one in one's mind only when rational with full faculties? Well, Sumaiya was out of her mind for sure. It was more than encephalopathy; the pain medications had her higher than Mount Olympus. She stared at me with strangely inattentive eyes and began to speak, but I couldn't hear what she was saying. I stared back, noticing the slight oblique fold of her upper eyelids. Beautiful eyes. I figuratively slapped myself. I would be more attentive to her needs. I knelt toward her. She looked at me as though I were far off on a distant horizon. She blathered incomprehensively. I did hear her daughter's name, Asma, but couldn't trace it to anything rational. Before I could reply, she suddenly said, "We are not going back."

"No," I said softly. "No one is going back."

"Yes," she said and went quiet for a minute, looking at the heavenly ceiling of canvas. "You will take care of my girls. Asma, really. He will be fine with the younger girls, but she's willful. She will need guidance."

She closed her eyes and drifted off to sleep. She did not need me to agree or confirm.

I turned on the table lamp, which was a replica of the Eiffel Tower but looked more like a lonely oil derrick in the middle of a desert doily. What was that anomaly doing in the medical tent of a refugee camp?

How to Write to
a Young Girl

You were able to visit Asma and her family in Malmö, not me. You had a speaking engagement at the university there last summer, and you dropped by. I loved that she had to squeeze you into her busy schedule. Even though school was out, her off-season was filled with numerous activities, organized and not. She suggested that you take her and her scout troop out for ice cream — seventeen double-scoop cones!

I skype with her once a month, and she texts me regularly, but my guidance, if we could call it that, is primarily through letters. That's what she wanted.

"Send me a letter," she said. "Once a week. Not more than that because that would be too much. One letter that tells me what you did that week so I will know what to expect as a doctor."

Once a week, I write. I tell her what surgeries I did and how I performed them, what incisions where. I even go as far as telling her how many times I had performed the procedure and how comfortable I felt doing so. I tell her about my patients, both the easy and the difficult ones. I explain briefly each situation, how I talked to the family, what I said to the patient, what the nurses said. She is a dry sponge for medical information. She berated me in the beginning for writing to her as if she were a child, for explaining the diagnoses in simple terms. She did not appreciate that. I was to treat her like any physician. She wanted a full anamnesis. She could look up any of the difficult words. She was no dummy. She knew how to use Google, after all. I complied.

Her mother was right. Asma is willful. And I adore her.

Dream House Maintenance

Your father built the house of his dreams in his home village in the mountains of Lebanon, not far from the house he grew up in, the one his father had built. Before he broke ground, your father, though not very religious, did what every Druze man should when building or buying something new. He visited one of the Druze elders, a man in his late eighties who lived in a tiny village that was difficult to reach, hidden in a verdant valley encircled by high mountains. Your father asked the elder to bless his new home, which the man did by writing a little prayer on a piece of paper, which he folded and put in a small envelope that was essentially another folded piece of cardstock paper, a Lebanese origami. Your father placed that blessing, no bigger than a child's finger, between the first two stones laid down for the house. The house of dreams was finished in 1974.

And what a house it was. Overlooking the city of Beirut, it was sleek and modern, distinct and sui generis,

melding into the hills around it but unlike any other building in the area. In the middle of the house was the pièce de
résistance, a glassed-in room with an open-air top, in which
grew an old olive tree. But then your father covered the top
with chicken wire and began to fill that room with birds, all
kinds of birds. Canaries at first, for the song. Goldfinches
to sing back. Then local larks, finches, warblers, and bee-
eaters. When he included the first weavers, your father had
to fill the room with dried grass and dead plants so those
yellow things with feathers could build their intricate nests.
He brought in nightingales, but they didn't sing. From the
Netherlands, he purchased imported birds of paradise with
ridiculously long tails. The aviary became his passion.

Everybody loved it. Even you, cynical you. But were
you cynical then?

You have often written that 1974, when you were fourteen, a year before the civil war started in Lebanon, was
the single happiest year of your life. You found out that
you could pass for normal for short bursts of time, after
which you had a good hiding place: your bedroom with the
never-ending bookshelf in the new house. You would be
able to make it. Not a happy existence, but still—survival.
Existence, in and of itself, was an accomplishment. But
violence descended, only it wasn't directed at you person-
ally as you had expected. The Lebanese civil war erupted,
and you were bundled up and sent out of the country for
safekeeping, the young emigrant.

The house remained, though. Throughout the early
stages of the war, nothing touched it. Pressed and flattened
between the first two stones, that tiny paper prayer worked
its magic. Every time you visited during those first few years

of the war, and you did that quite a bit, you noticed that the house stood proud, not a scratch. Every house in the village had a pointillist array of bullet holes, but not your father's. A missile would fall in the orchard, a grenade would explode on the main road, but the birds in your father's house kept singing. A miracle if ever there was one. Christian militias, Druze or Muslim ones, they couldn't harm your father's house. The Syrian army, Palestinian fighters? The house existed beyond the ravenous cruelty of the war and its mundanity. Bullets, rocket-propelled grenades, missiles, they all bypassed it, swerved and detoured. The wonder lasted for seven glorious years. But then the Israelis invaded.

Would the Israelis understand paper prayers? Could the talisman protect against the evil eye of an invading army? Was Druze juju translatable into Hebrew?

A most definite yes, it seemed. Phylacteries were as common among Jews as they were among the Druze.

There were a couple of close calls. When the tanks arrived on the hill above your father's house, a general's megaphoned voice warned the village not to harbor any terrorists, the latter defined as anyone who was not welcoming the neighborly Israeli invasion with enough cheer. Fifteen thousand Lebanese were killed within the first two weeks of the Israeli invasion, which obviously meant they were all uncheerful terrorists. If the villagers did not want to be shocked and awed by having their homes bombed into oblivion, they should raise a white flag on the roof to indicate that there were no unfriendly terrorists in the house. Your mother stripped all the linens off the beds and hung the white sheets on the roof's laundry lines. She worried that would not be enough. For two days, while the tanks loomed above her home, your mother ran back and forth along the laundry lines, shaking the sheets to make sure they were seen from above. Possessed by Lyssa, the spirit of madness and frenzy, your mother set herself up between the folds of each sheet and swayed her arms back and forth, then moved to the next sheet and the next, for forty-eight hours in a row.

The prayer blessing worked on the Israelis, with a little help from your mother acting like a Halloween ghost on meth. Not a scrape, not a blemish on the house.

A week after your mother shook the sheets, a young Israeli soldier knocked on the large mahogany door. Your parents saw a shy, scrawny, mild-mannered boy. He looked fourteen at best, your mother told you, his glasses too big for his face. She wanted to drag him to your room, order him to get out of that idiotic uniform, grab a bath, pick something normal to wear from your closet, and then she would feed him. The soldier, speaking fluid Levantine Arabic, apologized profusely for disturbing them, so much so that your parents began to feel guilty for appearing intimidating to the poor boy. He had heard the birds, he told them, all the way down the street. He followed the sounds to the house, just as Melquíades, the gypsy in *One Hundred Years of Solitude*, found his way to Macondo by following the song of the birds. Beautiful singing — some trills the boy knew, but some he could not identify. He was going to study ornithology, you see. He was obsessed with birds, like his own father was. He hadn't been sure where the birdsong was coming from until that day, when he finally had a break. He was not supposed to wander on his own, he said, but the siren song called to him. He begged for permission to see the birds, if only for a moment. Of course your parents let him in. Your father may have despised the Israelis, but a young man who loved birds couldn't be a terrible person.

The young man was stunned when he saw the glassed-in room. Sunlight inside the house, the outdoors indoors, and birds, a profusion of birds. He had a look of such longing that your father forgave his trespasses, almost his country's as well, but not quite. The coffee came out, the entire hospitality accoutrements — almonds, candies, chocolate — even in the middle of a war, one must be prepared for guests. When your mother complimented the soldier on his Arabic, he explained that his mother was Druze and his father Jewish. He spoke Arabic with his mother's family and Hebrew with his father's. He had problems, he said, answering your mother's questions. He was Jewish, but not technically since his mother wasn't, and he wasn't Druze, because his father wasn't. He felt homeless, he said, which of course elicited hostly homilies from your parents: their home was his home; he would always be welcome, the usual stuff. He asked if he could visit again when the Israeli army withdrew. "On the way back" was how he phrased it. Surely, this invasion would not last long. Of course, your parents assured him, if they were still around, if he remembered, then his visit would be most welcome.

You didn't know whether he remembered, but luckily your family was no longer around.

The Israelis went insane, bombing Beirut incessantly. Even though the house wasn't in danger, your family decided to pack as much as they could and left for the safety of Damascus. Your parents left as soon as the Americans got involved.

The Israelis forced the Lebanese parliament to elect the head of the Phalange as president, and he was assassinated soon after. The Israeli army surrounded the Sabra and Shatila refugee camps, and the Phalangists massacred thousands of women and children as Ariel Sharon smoked his hookah and cheered from the sidelines. Oh, the hand-wringing at the UN.

Israel decided it would occupy only the south of Lebanon. The civil war flared up again. The American marines got involved in the war. Unfortunately for your family, Americans don't understand paper prayers. Druze juju would not translate to English. Blessings were not America's forte.

One morning, for reasons no one could fathom, the battleship *New Jersey*, cruising in the Mediterranean a tad off the Lebanese shore, fired its sixteen-inch shells into various villages in the mountains, killing who knows how many. One of those shells fell through the roof of your father's dream house, incinerating everything. The structure remained standing for the most part, roofless but standing. Nothing inside was unharmed. The birds—the birds were roasted alive.

After its murderous foray into Lebanese politics, the *New Jersey* was retired, the last of its kind. The shell that destroyed your home might have been the last sixteen-incher to be fired. Don't you feel special?

The Americans? A man drove a truck full of explosives into the US barracks just outside of Beirut, killing 241 young marines. Reagan withdrew all his forces, washing his hands of irrational Lebanon, calling the Lebanese terrorists, terrorists, terrorists that kill innocent peacekeepers. Why couldn't they fight fairly, like decent people, using battleships, fighter jets, shock and awe?

Your mother would phone you in your small apartment in San Francisco. Your father was devastated, she told you. He didn't know what to do anymore. The house was more than his pride and joy, she explained. The house was him, and he was the house. The battleship destroyed him. He had no idea who he was anymore. He tried to be stoic; he was a man's man after all. He'd tell her that they would build another house, maybe buy an apartment in Beirut or start anew and move to Paris. But she had caught him surreptitiously weeping on more than one occasion, whenever he thought no one was watching. She wished you were there to comfort him, but what could you do?

What could you do? You were in graduate school. You had to get another degree in order to become a productive member of an evil society. You gobbled up hamburgers and quenched your thirst with Coke. You dove into gay sex clubs every night. You were assimilating, for crying out loud. You did not wish to remain an outsider in your adopted country. How could you explain to your father that you were not coming back, that you were choosing to become a citizen of the country that destroyed his dream with a single sixteen-inch shell? Which side were you on?

You would try to become an American, become one with people who would rather see your family dead.

Either you are with us or you are with the terrorists.

Rapefugees Not Welcome

Late afternoon found the four of us back at the cookie dispensary in Moria watching another impromptu soccer game between pup tents, the brightness of the boys' smiles a contrast to the lacy gray air with its veiled light. The cookie shack overlooked the tier below, where the game was, which was one tier above another level of tents, which in turn was above the lowest rung, where the riot police still picnicked not too far from the public bathroom that they did not use.

Emma seemed more agitated than usual, as if she'd woken up from a fearful dream. Mazen and Rasheed watched the young men kick the ball around, the latter more wistfully.

"I can't help feeling that waiting here is a mistake," Emma said between sips of dark tea. The lipstick on the Styrofoam cup was a shade lighter than the same on her lips.

Mazen nodded his head a few times in agreement, his top-heavy hair wobbling like a silver crown. He kept track of the smorgasbord of peopled scenes around him, his eyes darting here and there with a modicum of discretion: the soccer boys, the pup-tent refugees, the young volunteers in neon, the riot police in brutal gear, the cookie pushers, and our conversation.

A moist, limp breeze wiped my face like a towelette. One of the players kicked the ball too hard and it soared. We all leaned right, following its flight, four heads nodding in unison as the ball bounced down the hill.

"I'm hearing rumblings," Emma said. "Unpleasant ones. Something happened on New Year's Eve in Cologne. There are no official reports yet, but the talk online is that refugees sexually assaulted dozens of women. It's not good."

For some reason, whether the changing light or my darkening mood, I couldn't take my eyes off the fetid pool next to the public bathroom, whose chocolate-colored surface seemed to be turning opalescent. A young girl poked at something in the pool with a stick, over and over.

"I've heard the same," Rasheed said. "And it might be more than dozens. Early rumors are that migrants harassed hundreds of women in the subways. It's being said that it was an organized attack."

"Organized how?" Mazen asked.

"Not sure," Rasheed said. "It seems that a few dark-skinned men, as they're calling them, attacked women during the New Year's celebration. They're saying over one thousand young men arrived at the revelries around Cologne Cathedral in large groups and began to attack German women."

"That doesn't seem right," Mazen said.

Torn pieces of Styrofoam, breadcrumbs, and small bones were scattered on the ground next to a boastful dandelion. No other greenery could survive, the earth scarred by cigarettes quickly extinguished.

"It doesn't matter whether it is or not," Emma said. "Even one incident is terrible, and not just for the victim. Some will use any crime by a migrant to try and close the borders. Everyone will be in an uproar. Nazis go insane if one migrant so much as looks at a German woman. Can you imagine what will happen when this thing becomes public, organized sexual assaults by groups of migrants? My lord."

"I don't see how migrants could organize," Mazen said.

"It doesn't matter whether they can or not," Emma said. "It's a catastrophe."

A hesitation in the free-for-all of a soccer game. A young man stood over the ball. No one attempted to tackle him. An instant. All the players glanced toward the incline behind the makeshift midget field before the game resumed. Two Greek policemen marched up the cement walkway. Unlike their friends below, they wore no helmets, carried no riot shields, no visible polycarbonates of any kind, but they did have their side guns and batons, as well as their bulletproof vests. They felt less threatening and probably felt less threatened. They walked slowly in sync.

"I love men in uniform," Rasheed said. "Sorry. Couldn't help myself."

Three volunteers, young men, followed the policemen up the hill. American sounding, they chatted loudly, like noisy sparrows trying to outshout each other, paying little heed to anything but each other and their cell phones. They sauntered with slow shuffling steps as if on a promenade in their own sacred garden of Hera. One of them looked up, noticed me watching, and smiled generously, as if I'd caught him in the midst of a ritual I couldn't possibly fathom.

"I'm leaving," Emma said. "Taking the night off. Make myself a hot bath and disappear in it."

New Year's Eve, Cologne

What happened that night in Cologne? The information was slow to emerge. We didn't hear much during the week we were on Lesbos. When the news finally erupted, it spooked me.

On New Year's Day, the police press release described the previous evening's events as peaceful. Not much out of the ordinary had happened, they said. The usual large crowds celebrated outside the historic cathedral and around the train station—revelry, merriment, alcohol, and fireworks. But what the police and the newspapers related later was an entirely different story. On New Year's Eve some fifteen hundred men, described by the authorities as having "a North African or Arabic" appearance, most of them sloshed drunk, descended upon the celebratory scene. At some point they broke into gangs and formed rings around young women, refusing to let them go. Some of the men groped victims while others stole handbags, wallets, and cell phones. The women screamed, fought back, tried to escape, but many found it almost impossible to free themselves. Witnesses described the atmosphere around the train station as aggressive, ominously violent, and intimidating. Fireworks were thrown into the crowds to increase the tension. Several women were raped.

Were these attacks organized beforehand? Who were these men? Why did it take so long for the reports to filter out?

Among the early arrests, thirty-one suspects were identified by name, including eighteen asylum seekers. The thirty-one were nine Algerians, eight Moroccans, four Syrians, five Iranians, two Germans, an Iraqi, a Serb, and an American. I tried to find the American's name or which city he was from but wasn't able to.

There was one report that was more heartening: a group of Syrian men surrounded an American woman, protected her from assailants by forming a ring around her, and then led her back to her friends.

Of course, in response to the assaults a large number of asylum seekers and darker-skinned refugees were attacked all over Europe. Xenophobia spiked. The repercussions of the Night of the Long Fingers, as it was called, were seen everywhere.

A monosynaptic response, the knee was hit in Cologne, and legs kicked out in Warsaw, in Budapest, in Paris, everywhere.

Antirefugee political parties grew in power.

Syrian refugees went into limbo.

The Cave of Shanidar

In spite of quite a bit of evidence to the contrary, I like to think of the world as kind, of humanity as decent if flawed, my misinterpretation of the just-world fallacy. I like to think that we humans try to do the right thing.

Between 1957 and 1961, at a burial site inside a cave called Shanidar in northern Iraq, archaeologists discovered the fossilized remains of eight adult and two infant Neanderthals, dating from around sixty-five thousand to thirty-five thousand years ago. Found with them were hundreds of stone tools, as well as bones of wild goats and tortoises. Nine of the ten remains were lost, along with fifteen thousand cultural artifacts, during that mess of shock and awe in 2003, when US forces invaded the country, destroyed the infrastructure, and chose to protect the oil ministry building but not the National Museum of Iraq.

The most famous of the ten Neanderthals was the one who was discovered first, called Shanidar 1 but known as

Nandy among his excavators. He was remarkably old for a Neanderthal, somewhere between forty and fifty, yet he displayed severe trauma-related deformities. He had a withered right arm, no hand or forearm, and a deformed right leg. He was also apparently deaf, as his ear canals were blocked by exostoses. His day-to-day life must have been excruciatingly painful, yet he was seemingly cared for by the community.

Among the numerous discoveries at the burial site were clumps of pollen representing a large variety of flowers, from grape hyacinth to yarrow. A debate still rages among archaeologists about whether these flowers were part of Neanderthal burial rites or were introduced to the site by jirds, a variety of rodent.

I prefer to think that my ancestors and yours would care for the weakest among them and then bury him with garlands of flowers. Go, dear one, we send you away with yellow cockspur and daisies, cornflowers and hyacinths.

Shanidar 3 does not have a nickname that I know of. He is in the United States at the Smithsonian National Museum of Natural History. An immigrant! He, too, was between forty and fifty years old and was found in the same grave as Nandy. He had a wound to the left ninth rib, a severe cut deep enough to have collapsed his lung. Shanidar 3 is the oldest known individual who was presumably murdered.

My ancestors and yours were also killers.

Malawi, Mon Amour

One of my favorite people in the world is a cousin of Francine's or, to be more precise, as precise as one can be within the limits of the English language, her first cousin once removed. Pete Jones had a generic name, a unique story, and a disarming smile. I'd known him for a long time, since he was in junior high. Francine was close to her cousin Esther, his mother. They grew up together. Pete was a bright, ambitious boy: in the top five percent of his class, quarterback on his high school team, dated a cheerleader, had all the accompanying perks accorded to special young men in the United States. More important to his family was that he aced his SATs and was accepted by many of the schools he applied to. He chose Northwestern because he was a Midwest boy, but he never attended. Changed his mind.

He shocked everybody by enlisting in the army.

His decision was surprising, although it shouldn't have been. He was quite articulate about why he wanted to join the army and fight. It was the summer of 2002, at the height of jingoism after the World Trade Center attack. He felt that the terrorists had hurt his country and he wanted his country to hurt them right back. Bush would soon declare his intention to bomb Iraq back to the Middle Ages, and our Pete felt that it was his personal mission to humiliate al Qaeda, the Taliban, Saddam, and all those people over there.

His mother vehemently disapproved of his decision. Esther and her son argued for weeks. Some of their yelling matches became legendary in their family. The phrase "What has Saddam ever done to you?" turned into a family catchall for situations that were completely crazy or nonsensical. Two Thanksgivings ago, Esther complained that her grandchildren were running around her dining table yelling: "What has Saddam ever done to you?"

Pete was shipped to Afghanistan not long after, then Iraq. He hardly spoke to his mother for three years. Their relationship remained strained until he returned home in 2006 broken and one leg short.

He told Francine that his youth was taken away from him in one ruthless swoop, in one cruel explosion. He was not yet twenty-two, on a desert road in Iraq with his troop. The vehicle had some malfunction. While they waited for it to be fixed, his superior denied him some minor request. Pete turned around, sulking and walking away, whining to himself, and kicked at a stone. He couldn't remember much else other than waking up in suffocating heat in a makeshift hospital bed in a bright room with high windows and without his right leg below the knee.

He returned home an amputee, downtrodden and inconsolable. He immured himself within high walls of despair.

His mother couldn't get through to him. He wouldn't speak to friends, wouldn't leave his room, which Esther had kept intact waiting for his return. The VA therapist was not able to help and neither was Francine. I remember walking into the house one day after his return and experiencing an immense weight as soon as I crossed the threshold. Pete's phantom leg would get cramps, which his brain thought of as real, and the house brimmed with a phantom gloom, which we all recognized as real.

Had he not sulked, had he listened to his mother, had he gone to Northwestern, had he anything, he would have remained a man. Without his leg, he said, he was half a one. He was no longer whole, no longer inviolate.

He was unable to talk to anyone, not his family, not his old high school friends. Everyone he knew seemed to be living in an insular world, desperately trying to stave off anything that would remind them of their own pain, and he felt he was nothing if not a reminder. He understood that his friends wanted to avoid him as much as he did them.

He decided that was no accident: losing his leg was what was meant to be. A teaching that he was not learning, a Buddhist karma or dharma or something. Not an accident, not random, not a desultory fluke. Fate could not be capricious. There must have been a point. He had done something wrong and had to pay for it with a miserable life. His great loss must have some significance.

As Francine says, "Insanity is the insistence on meaning."

She has a talent, though, my Francine. At his lowest, his weakest, when she was unable to break through to him and his mother was at her wit's end, Francine left him a book of poems by Frank Bidart, the first of which was about a man who had lost his arm. The poem began brilliantly with instructions on how to bandage your stump (firmly, firmly, in order for the stump to remain cone-shaped) and ended with a revelatory line about how blood, amputation, and rubble gave the city of Paris its grace. That, however, was not what Pete read in it.

In the poem, the narrator had an illumination: the solution to his pain was to forget he had ever had an arm. The lost arm had never existed. Pete had become obsessed with the image of who he was, a true man, of what was lost. Once upon a time he had two legs. There was a man called Pete who could walk without a hobble, who could run like an antelope, who could play the manly game of football. The memories crushed him, and he must therefore cut them off. He would start anew, seeking oblivion. Memoryless, he'd launch himself into a new world. And he did, or at least he tried.

Pete boarded a flight to Lilongwe, Malawi, with a small duffel bag and his prosthetic leg. Once again, during the next three years he would hardly speak to his mother, his friends, his family. He would try to reinvent himself as a packless wolf. He would later tell Francine that he couldn't be around his mother because she reminded him of who he was. He felt that the way she looked at him day to day was a further violation. The wolf limped across the Malawian countryside, stayed in the poorest villages, helped build houses and dig wells, taught children in various small schools. For a while, Pete found a home in that country.

It was during his African sojourn that he and I grew close. He needed medical advice, and he had less of an issue with me than with Francine since I wasn't his mother's cousin. I began to receive calls whenever one of the village children became ill. I helped however I could.

He lasted for three and a half years in Malawi. The country had settled his mind and his nerves, he told me. Yet the longer he stayed, the more he realized that something about what he was doing in Africa was dishonest. He couldn't put his finger on what it was at first. Yes, he was lonely, but that wasn't exactly the problem. He was not among his people. The chasm between African Americans and Africans was immense. As time passed, he began to realize that whenever he visited a new village, he would feel guilty. He began to understand that he was using the pain of others to alleviate his own. He couldn't keep going, he told me. As much as he was helping, he could no longer live with the fact that he was using the suffering of poor villagers to satisfy his sentimental needs. He needed them to suffer, he told me, in order to feel needed, in order to reinforce his privilege.

He couldn't go on pretending. After all, he said jokingly, he wasn't white.

One day while on his exercise walk, he heard the song from *Titanic* on his handheld transistor radio, and the damned thing wormed itself into his ear and made itself a home. He couldn't get rid of the voice of Céline Dion looping in his head. And when he returned to the village where he was staying, a number of the women were humming the song. He saw that as a sign. His heart most certainly could not go on and on. He returned home.

Happy ending: back home he began to work with an attorney on the South Side who specialized in tenant rights.

He was still there. Surprisingly, or maybe not, he fell in love with and married an Iraqi woman from Michigan. He worships his twin girls. And to this day, his mother is still trying to get him to go back to school.

He wanted to cut off his past, he once told me, so he could smother his dreams. His mass-produced dreams had all been designed for men with two legs. Whenever he looked in the mirror, though, there was only the inevitable image, the one leg. He thought he'd forgotten much while in Malawi, but it turned out he'd only put things aside. He'd locked his past in a kist that wasn't terribly secure. It worked temporarily, giving him time to settle his soul. After a while, he realized that without his past he couldn't be whole, yet he wasn't whole anyway. He could keep trying to forget or ignore his past, or he could reclaim who he was. Neither choice would make him whole; neither would make him true. No amount of optimism could return what he'd lost.

What to do? Go on, he said. Go on and on, as much as he loathed that stupid song. Go on and hope for bespoke dreams.

The Boy with the Midas Touch Touched Himself

"I can't believe it," Mazen said. The sun appeared from behind low clouds, casting a bit of pink, and suddenly his face was lit like a stage actor's, his hair given a sacred halo. "How could refugees organize? Many of these people have never owned a computer, but all of a sudden now they're supposed to be able to create sexual-assault Facebook groups. I can't see it."

"I can," Rasheed said.

"You can?" asked Mazen, more surprised than annoyed at being disagreed with.

"Of course," Rasheed said. "They're young men, after all."

"Come, come," Mazen said. "Not all young men are rapists. I most certainly wasn't. I know my son isn't."

"Your son is gay," I said.

"He's bi," Mazen said, flipping me the bird. "He went out with a girl once in high school, and he was a gentleman."

The sun seemed brighter all of a sudden, easing the bluish cold a bit. Half of my now-darker shadow lay on the ground, and the other half fell off the short cliff toward the soccer players.

"The reason not all young men are rapists is that we distract them," Rasheed said. "Sports, football." He nodded his head toward the soccer game below us. "Superhero movies, the internet, porn, and so much more. Unless we keep these boys entertained and preoccupied, they'll keep our world in turmoil for the next half century."

"That's an overgeneralization," Mazen said, "and completely unfair."

"Maybe," Rasheed said, "but look at them. Look."

For a minute or two, the three of us, sipping coffee out of paper cups, watched the delirious soccer game one tier below. Young men having fun, running, jumping, not caring that they had commandeered an area between pup tents where families lived, that all the other refugees had to walk around the claimed field. A prone old man marked one of the field's sidelines. He slept on his side, with a hand under his cheek, his lips parting and shutting every time the ball whizzed by.

"Look," Rasheed said, again nodding his head but this time to three young Syrian men on the cement walkway. They sauntered up the hill with shuffling steps, preening and swaggering, as if on a promenade on their properties. Another young man, with narrow eyes and a dark-green overcoat, an Achilles in training, leaned against a wall, seemed to be waiting for something. He sulked, looked like he disapproved of the three boys, of the soccer game, of the camp, of the whole wide world. He loathed the errors and blunders of creation. He, too, inspected his property, and found it wanting.

"We live in a world that promises these young men that they will rule it," Rasheed said. "What happens when they find out it's all a lie? If you're supposed to be the top dog, and suddenly you have to rely on others to throw you scraps?"

"No one promised me I could rule anything," Mazen said.

"That's because you're special, dear," I said.

"Many young men everywhere feel that the world owes them something," Rasheed said, "but in our lands it's double trouble with mothers' irrational adoration of their sons. These boys grew up believing they were meant for great things. Opportunities were supposed to rain upon them. Do you know what Iranian mothers call their baby boys? Doodool tala. *You're my doodool tala, aren't you? Come to mama, doodool tala.* We don't have an Arabic equivalent, though we really should. It means golden pee-pee. How can a young man not demand that the world kneel before his gold penis?"

All Hail the Mighty Harold

You were raised in the desert of Kuwait in the 1960s, a time when it was a desert in every sense of the word: sand, heat, and technology's greatest gift, air-conditioning. There was nothing to do. Your family and you were expats, strangers in a barren land.

You read.

You read everything in sight, anything within reach. You started out with comic books, of course. You began before you could put letters together to form words, let alone words to form sentences. Superman and Batman, Wonder Woman and the Justice League, Archie and Jughead, Asterix and Obelix, Casper and Richie Rich, Tintin, Little Lulu and Little Lotta, Lucky Luke and Baby Huey. You graduated to Enid Blyton books: The Famous Five and The Secret Seven series.

As a child you knew more about how to serve tea in the afternoon than how to converse with Kuwaiti kids.

A story: You were about seven. It was Thursday morning, the weekend for you, but your father had to work. You
were in the living room reading, maybe one of the Secret
Sevens. Your mother yelled your name from her bedroom.
She spoke loudly and slowly, in a tone she used whenever
she wanted to be exquisitely understood. "Call your father
right now. Tell him to bring a doctor right away. I'm fainting. It's an emergency." You did as instructed. On the phone
your nervous father asked how your mother was, and you
replied, "She's in her room, probably fainting." He arrived
not ten minutes later. He walked into the living room, found
you sitting in his chair reading. Incredulous, he asked you
where your mother was. You replied again that she was in
her room. You grew nervous. You were reading in your
father's chair since it had the best light. If he didn't return
to work, he'd reclaim it and you'd have to use another. Your
Egyptian neighbor, a doctor, rushed through the door. You
pointed to the bedroom. An hour later, your father came out
of the room and lectured you. You should have checked on
your mother. She had fainted, hitting her head on the vanity
as she fell. She woke up bleeding. That was when she called
to you. Then she fainted once again. Your mother had only
told you to call your father. You did that. She didn't say she
needed you. Your book did, so you'd returned to it.

As a child you knew more about how to fight injustice
than how to understand that your mother was in trouble.

But your mother understood, for she, too, was a reader.
She would read in one corner of the living room and you
in another, the two of you in your antipodal armchairs,
feet tucked under butts, books held up at eye level, lost in
another world, a world richer than Kuwait's oil-laden desert.

It wasn't long before you began to pick up her books. At the time she read mostly best sellers, the only books easily found in expat bookstores. Frederick Forsyth, John le Carré, James Michener, Jacqueline Susann, and . . . Harold Robbins.

You read them all, of course (*Sparkle, Neely, sparkle!*), and more, much more. The writer who captured your heart toward the end of your preteens was your dear Harold. It wasn't just the sex, although that certainly was a big part of it. You were twelve, after all. His was a much-maligned oeuvre, you once wrote, whose value to sexually deprived young boys was underappreciated. The sweeping emotional dramas, the grand betrayals, the triumph of good, and the delightful sentences (*She stroked his penis with two fingers*) were perfect reading when you were twelve.

A charming fact: Let any used Harold Robbins book fall open to the creased parts, and one would find all the dirty bits. This spine-drop technique worked anywhere in the world. You even tried it on a Robbins book in a house in Chengdu, China. Worked every time.

The book that snared you was *The Carpetbaggers*. You couldn't put it down. Summer in the mountains of Lebanon, you were twelve, cocooned on a couch, and your cousins — all girls, all older than you, all taller teenagers — insisted that you accompany them on a walk. Fresh air and all that. They dragged you out, chatting, giggling, strolling along the mountain road. You lagged behind a few steps until you were able to open your paperback. You read as you walked. A large truck was parked on the side of the road. Lost in the wholesale vengeful world of *The Carpetbaggers*, you walked right into that

truck and slammed your head against one of its brake lights.
Your cousins couldn't stop giggling for a week.

Fortunately, or unfortunately, infatuations fade, and
rather quickly. You had another cousin, three years older,
whom you'd desperately looked up to. You spoke to her
about your love.

"I must read that book of yours," she said, and she did.

You were disappointed but mostly astounded that she
wasn't crazy about it, not even a little.

"What about the story? What about the adventure?"
you asked.

"Such a story," she said gently, returning your dog-
eared copy, "I'd rather see in a movie. I like my books a bit
different."

It took some months, less than a year, for you to lose
your infatuation with Robbins and his cohort. In those days
you fell in and out of love with writers quicker than Byron
did, but that book, *The Carpetbaggers*, was a marker. After
it, you began to read books that were "a bit different." You
began to grow. You still read everything in sight for quite a
while, but Robbins began to sound childish to your adoles-
cent ears. The fact that you now considered the book puerile
was proof that you had finally become a man.

Your bookshelves smiled with new weights and colors.
Rejected though it might have felt, your faded lightweight
pocketbook still found a place between your new loves.

When the Lebanese civil war started in 1975, you were
fifteen. You were shipped to boarding school in England
and after that to the United States. Your family didn't leave
Lebanon. You returned regularly during those years, once

every six months or so. You slept in your room in your house in the mountains among your books.

In 1982, with the open involvement of the Israelis, and the Americans soon after, your parents knew that your house and your village were no longer safe. Your mother packed the valuables, the sentimental and the expensive, and shut the house down. She packed your record albums, hundreds of them, and your books.

She saved your books. On your shelves in San Francisco, you have a few hardcovers from those days: Iris Murdoch's *The Sea, the Sea* and *Henry and Cato*, John Fowles's *The Magus* and *Daniel Martin*, *The Complete Works of William Shakespeare*, and the book you treasured most, Naipaul's *A House for Mr. Biswas*. She didn't save any of the paperbacks, definitely not *The Carpetbaggers*.

After the American battleship *New Jersey* sent a sixteen-inch shell through the roof of your house, burning it in the process, your family didn't have the heart to inspect the house for four years. The fact that various armies and militias camped in it during that time had something to do with the lack of inspection. The Israelis, the Syrians, the Druze, Christian, and Muslim militias all were guests in your house.

In the summer of 1988, your father took you up to look at the remains of your home, what was once his pride and joy. He'd been to the house before that visit, but it was your first time since your family left four years earlier. He joked that it was in better shape than most of the Roman ruins in the country. Political and obscene graffiti covered the half-destroyed walls. There was no ceiling and surprisingly no floor: the parquet, the stone, the marble, all looted. Toilets, faucets, wiring, pipes, bathtubs, furniture, bookshelves, everything was gone. The house smelled of decay, cordite, and urine. Your room, which was once red, was now blood gray.

But in one of the corners of the room lay the old copy of *The Carpetbaggers*. It no longer had a cover, and some of the pages were missing, although you didn't check which ones. Ragged, it barely hung together. It was the only thing in the room that hadn't been stolen. You couldn't tell how many fighters had read it.

You didn't take it. You didn't even pick it up off the floor. You left it there. You might have thought it was too dirty or something. You never saw it again.

Years later, you would begin to write. You no longer had the unfettered time to read everything in sight. Your tastes narrowed. Your close friends considered you a literary snob.

You had a dinner party not too long ago. One of those dear friends arrived bearing a gift. He intended it as camp, to poke fun at you a bit. He wished to pinprick your pretensions. Not knowing anything about your history with the book, he'd found an early hardcover edition of *The Carpetbaggers* at a garage sale for one whole dollar, a used copy, clean and crisp. He bought it for you as a joke. He was stunned when you burst into tears upon receiving it. Your dinner guests were alarmed watching you weep with the book in your hands.

When you write in your study, the hardcover sits in one of your bookshelves. All you have to do is turn your eyes left of the computer screen, and you can see it, at home between Alain Robbe-Grillet and Marilynne Robinson.

Plan Your Honeymoon
on a Greek Island

We were supposed to go back to the hotel, shower and change, and then head out to the city center for dinner. Rasheed wanted to take Mazen and me to a café overlooking the water, a hole-in-the-wall with decent food. Mazen, however, sidetracked us. While waiting for Rasheed to finish with his group, Mazen walked around and chatted people up. I watched him approach a young couple who seemed to be, like him, promenading up and down the sloping road of Moria. They chatted, their voices turning livelier and livelier, as if they were old friends who had found each other after a long separation. The boy and girl were likely still teenagers, twenty at most, obviously in love, his hand not leaving hers. She was small and slight and talked with her head down, her sand-colored straight hair covering most of her face, like a poppy preparing to fold her petals as evening descended — nyctinasty in human form. They wore matching blue trench coats that somehow managed to look ill fitting on both.

Mazen called me over. I should meet the newlyweds. They'd gotten married less than four weeks earlier, he explained with no little excitement. This was their honeymoon. Instead of wedding gifts, the couple had asked all their relatives to chip in whatever they could and they'd use the cash to escape. They told the same stories of bombings, killings, and humiliations, of red tracers that would make the night blush, but their tales of woe sounded less horrifying since they seemed happy. They were together, they'd escaped, and they were safe for the time being. How could they not be joyful, they asked, even in the midst of sorrow. They seemed blissful, like two lucky teenagers who'd discovered sex for the first time, and that was probably because they were.

A honeymoon, Mazen said. This was their honeymoon. When he repeated himself like this, it usually meant that he wished to say something important, and I was missing what it was. This was no honeymoon, he said, not here. They were staying in the barracks with all the cots, all the other families.

"Oh, we're grateful for that," the boy said. He had brown eyes with green rings around irises that could not look away from his bride for more than two or three seconds, if that.

"These are the best beds we've slept on since we left home," the girl said. "When we traveled by bus, I'd wake up from a night of interrupted sleep with the worst neck pain. This isn't bad, and everyone in the barracks has been exceedingly kind."

"Who cares?" Mazen said. "You can't have a honey-moon with people sleeping in the same room with you. That's like going to a vegan restaurant when you're hungry. It won't do. We'll get you a hotel room."

The boy and girl were flabbergasted. No, as much as they appreciated the offer, as much as they would love to have a room all to themselves, they couldn't afford it, and they most certainly would not allow Mazen to pay for it, absolutely not. Back and forth the argument went, and it kept going for at least five minutes as each side pulled the fraying rope in their tug of war. No, he couldn't, shouldn't. Yes, he would, he must.

"We don't have to pay for a room," I finally interrupted, surprising myself. "We already have one. My brother will offer you his room for a couple of nights, and he'll sleep with me. That wouldn't cost anybody any extra money. It's the least we can do. Please honor us by accepting our hospitality."

I did not have to look at Mazen to know he was moved. I could feel him. I heard him gasp.

"Are you sure you'll be comfortable sharing a room?" the girl asked. "Would we not be imposing on you?"

"My sister and I shared a bed when we were children," Mazen said. "It's been about fifty years, but you don't forget how to share a bed with your sister. You never forget." He paused, but only briefly. A crease of a smile flickered across his face. "I know how to kick her when she snores."

Baptize Your Way to Better Hair Care Products

You met Farid and Maysa Chahar in 2014. A recently married couple, they were sharing a storefront with two other families in an abandoned mall not too far from Tripoli, north of Beirut. Maysa was four months pregnant with her first son. They explained during the interview that they needed to find different living arrangements. There was only one bathroom shared by five stores that had over fifteen families living in them. They had to resort to using a converted bedpan, which was not pleasant when there were two other families in the same room. You tried to help, but they were able to figure out better housing on their own. They found the priest.

This priest in the mountains of Lebanon decided that Jesus would have helped refugees. He took it upon himself to care for some of the Syrians overrunning his country. At first, he began to help his coreligionists. He allowed Catholic Syrian refugees into his church; he cajoled various households in the village to take in families, offered food to everyone. Just as important, if not more so, with the help of Western NGOs, he initiated a program that helped settle these Christian families in Europe and Australia. Why Australia? Lebanese had been immigrating to that island since the late 1880s, and it was said that over one million Australians had Lebanese ancestry. Also, in this case, the Australian government had refused to accept any Syrian refugees who were not Christian. The priest was more than willing to comply with a condition like that.

He was happy, doing his God's work. But why stop with Syrian Catholics and Maronites, he thought. Why not try his hand with some Sunnis, Shiites? No Druze, though, and definitely no Greek Orthodox or Syrian Orthodox for that matter. Melkites were all right, but no apostate Anglicans, no Protestants of any kind. And that was where the Chahars came in.

He asked a Lebanese family to take the young Muslim couple in. Farid was able to find the odd job here and there, but as he had explained to you, his family was going to be in trouble unless he found permanent work, which was difficult in Lebanon with so many other refugees. He would need to take his family abroad. He told you that the priest would help if they converted, that most countries in the West would move their application to the front of the line if they were Christian. Unlike Australia, most European countries were more discreet about their discrimination. Thankfully, his name wasn't Mohammad or Ali. The priest wanted them to make a decision sooner rather than later, before their child arrived. All they needed to do was to take a few catechism classes and be baptized in a bathtub of some kind. Not as easy as converting to Islam but not that much of a problem since they did have the time. Oh, and they had to give up on the religion of their fathers and mothers, the one that had provided them comfort for all those years. For a better future, for their child, they were willing, Farid said. May God forgive them their betrayal. They were dunked.

You saw them again not too long ago in Gothenburg, where they had settled. Maysa's son was now running around, and she was pregnant again, thirteen weeks. She enjoyed working part-time as a cook at a small café and day care center.

How was she adjusting, you asked. Quite well, it seemed. She and her husband had jobs they liked, they were learning Swedish, he had suddenly become quite fluent, whereas she still had a bit to go, and their son was their pride and joy. Was she having any kind of difficulty?

"My hair," she said, "my hair. I didn't have as much trouble as I thought I would when I removed the hijab, but no one told me how bad this cold weather is. Do you know what flyaway hair is? I certainly didn't. And that's different from the frizzy hair I get when it's cold and humid. Now I spend most of my time worrying about how my hair looks. Do you know how many different kinds of hair care products there are? I can't believe I'm spending money buying sprays and gels. We worried about our hair back in Syria, but this weather messes everything up. Don't tell anyone that I went to the local mosque for the first time this week."

What's Wrong
with Greek Spices?

We had to sneak the married couple into their room since
they had no papers. Mazen lied to them, telling them that
their meal in the hotel's restaurant was included in the room
rate. They should eat as much as they could. After he moved
his bags into my room, he had to rush to the restaurant and
prepay with his credit card. The cost of the room and meal
would end up around sixty euros per night, and I had to
figure out a way to pay him back. His finances were not
in great shape. My loans had been supporting him for the
last few years.

Rasheed drove us to the city center since he knew
where we were going for dinner. I sat in the back seat while
the boys in the front rekindled an argument that had been
burning for generations: which was the superior cuisine,
Lebanese or Palestinian? The "we make the better okra
stew" discussion lasted a whole ten minutes. The amusing aspect of such a discussion was that the difference

between the two cuisines was barely noticeable to any but the dedicated food connoisseurs. Back and forth they went discussing culinary likes and dislikes. Who had the better oranges? Obviously our knafeh was tastier. They disagreed on whether hummus was originally Lebanese or Palestinian, but any fool knew that it was not Israeli. That was ha-ha-ha laughable.

"The restaurant we're going to has the best Greek food on the island," Rasheed said. "I know that's not saying much, but we don't have many choices."

"Greek cuisine is an oxymoron," my brother said. "They ruin everything."

"True," Rasheed said. "Let's say that this restaurant is the least offensive."

"Why would you add béchamel to a moussaka? That doesn't make any sense."

"Exactly. It mutilates a perfectly good dish."

Now you know why the boys liked you so much so quickly. When we saw you at the restaurant, you may not have made much sense at first, but the one thing that had their hearts fluttering was this: when the food arrived, you said that Greek food felt to you as if an incompetent chef was given all the correct ingredients to make a fantastic Lebanese meal and proceeded to fuck it up by using the wrong mixtures. They found that delicious.

Caught at Last,
Caught at Last

You, pocket-size and folded, stowed yourself in the farthest corner of the restaurant surrounded by empty tables — away, away from everybody. The place faced the promenade and the sea, but your eyes would not abandon the tattered paperback in your hands, your head bent, your reading glasses almost falling off the flat tip of your nose. Hundreds of little Post-it notes bloomed from the book, from both sides of the pages. Your forearms pressed against the edge of the table. The paper napkins and faded silverware were still in the bread basket, no menu, no food yet. Mirrored walls encircled the restaurant's interior, which made everything feel cold and airy, too fluorescent bright. A chemical apricot scent enveloped us.

A waiter, wearing black shoes polished to a shine, pointed to a table, but I walked over to say hello to you. Mazen and Rasheed followed. The waiter stood like a panther about to pounce, with a pugnacious look on his face. He regarded me as if I had crossed the gods of Olympus. And your face lifted, a reticent expression. You looked up at us as though we were something far off on a distant horizon, something you couldn't discern. Our hovering at your table disturbed the light you read by. All I had to say was hello in our language, and like a good Lebanese boy, you jumped up to greet us respectfully, removing your reading glasses, your hand asking for a shake.

You were reading Hans Fallada's *Alone in Berlin* — a little portentous, don't you think? How many times had you read that one?

I announced myself — here I am — told you we'd met before, and you apologized for not remembering. I introduced Rasheed and my brother. There was a moment of awkward silence before you extended the requisite invitation to join you. You were stunned when I accepted, so shocked that Mazen nudged me with his elbow from one side and Rasheed from the other. I didn't care that your invitation was insincere. I wasn't going to let you get away from me, not again.

I have to tell you that you have the worst poker face, particularly when you're feeling vulnerable. The look you gave me when I thanked you and pulled out a chair was priceless. Your eyes were about to roll out of their sockets and tumble along your pronounced nasolabial folds.

We sat down. You and the boys a mite awkward, unsure what to say. Luckily it wasn't long before the waiter brought your order over, a feta dish heated in a clay skillet, swimming in herbs and olive oil. You had to share, of course. We waited for you to take the first taste and hand out judgment. It wasn't bad, you said. It was wrong. And then you proceeded to make the bad chef pronouncement, at which point the mood at the table shifted, everyone relaxed and agreed wholeheartedly. It wasn't terrible, Rasheed said, as he had a couple of bites out of the skillet. Why would you include oregano, Mazen said, as he sampled more of the dish. The ingredients were fresh, though, and you finished off everything. You wiped your lips with a piece of bread. We ordered another of the same dish.

You seemed to gain weight and confidence with each bite, asking Rasheed about his work in Jerusalem, about his volunteering in Lesbos. Mazen told self-deprecating jokes I'd heard a hundred times before about his ineptitude at selling stocks. At first, you skillfully evaded our questions about you. Mazen interrupted my third or fourth failed attempt to get you to talk about your work—he hadn't read you—by asking about your being on Lesbos. You couldn't stay away, you said. The images of the arriving boats seared themselves into your retinas and bored a hole in your heart. You told us that you'd worked on and off with Syrian refugees for years, all the interviews you'd done. There was an absurd number of refugees in Lebanon, you said, and more arriving every day, yet the country seemed to go on as if nothing was happening. Life in Beirut went on. You were not surprised, of course. You'd been through similar things before. During the civil war in Lebanon people trucked along. In San Francisco, the nicest and most compassionate humans were able to step over an unconscious homeless man if he blocked the sidewalk without even noticing what they were doing. You tried to find a way to write about refugees and break the wall between reader and subject. You said you wanted people not to dismiss the suffering, not to read about the loss and sorrow, feel bad for a minute or two, then go back to their glass of overly sweet chardonnay. But you failed, of course. And then the first crack in your veneer. You said, in a whisper, that the only wall you broke was yours. Your head bent forward again, shadowing your face and badly managed goatee, your chin coming to rest on the darker green collar of your sweater. A single long breath and you were back up again, alert eyes and a bittersweet smile.

Rasheed asked what you meant by having broken your wall.

"Nothing," you said. "I was overwhelmed a little, that's all. Don't mind me. Everything grew to be a bit much, and luckily I'm not exactly needed right now, what with the storms and weather. I will be fine. Everything will work out."

"Do you know what was too much for you?" Rasheed asked.

"Nothing really," you said. Your eyes darted from one of us to the next in an incompetent attempt to assuage our concerns. "It was the wrong time for me to come here. That's all, really."

"Where are you staying?" Rasheed said.

Your smile flickered for a moment like a lightbulb in a socket with loose wiring.

"I don't remember what it's called," you said. "It's about ten minutes south of here, a cozy hotel close to the sea."

"We're on an island," Rasheed said. "All hotels are close to the sea."

"You were staying in our hotel," I said. "I saw you leaving."

"I ran away," you said. "I had to find a hotel that was away from everything. But I'm doing better now. Okay, when I made my plans to come here, I thought I'd be able to help a little in this world that was falling apart. I never expected that I'd end up hiding in a hotel room. No, I didn't. But I'm okay now."

Later that evening, after our stint at the port, you'd correct your statement. Lesbos not only broke your wall, it broke you.

A Girl in Every Port,
but All the Boys in One

A couple of shifty seagulls eyed us as we left the restaurant. Rasheed suggested a postprandial walk to the Mytilene Port, something he did as often as he could trying to help the refugees who were waiting to board the last ferry to Athens, their next stop. You tried to get out of accompanying us, some excuse about bedtime and reading time, but I wouldn't let you, and this time Mazen and Rasheed joined in. My brother told you we weren't done with your company yet. You took another tack. You said you should return to your lonely hotel because there was a group of four Greek aunties who were playing cards in the restaurant, which also functioned as the lobby. They had arrived at around three in the afternoon and were still going strong by the time you left for the restaurant. You needed to go back to see if they were still there. It was an emergency, you joked.

When I was growing up in Beirut, my father's two younger sisters used to play cards with three friends four afternoons a week, Mondays, Tuesdays, Thursdays, and Fridays. They would begin exactly at four in my aunt's apartment one floor above ours, and the last hand was dealt at precisely eight in the evening. I mentioned that to you, and you said your father had a similar schedule, that he played with the same group of friends every weekday afternoon for over thirty-five years, and they stopped only when your father passed away.

"They could still be playing for all I know," you said. "They may have found a substitute for my father and kept going, you know, like replacing a battery."

"I miss that," I said, though I wasn't exactly sure what it was that I missed, what it was that I'd lost. "Are our aunts still playing?" I asked Mazen.

"Of course not," he said. "Auntie Ilham died eight years ago, and Auntie Laila moved in with her second son even though she no longer recognizes him."

The city of Mytilene was built some three thousand years ago, but the town center and marina had adjusted to serve the needs of the twenty-first-century tourist. As we walked from the marina to the port, there was a bigger variety of stores — more banks, grocery stores, well-lit cafés filled with evening locals, sprinkled with refugees. The two didn't look that different, but the state of their comfort and that of their clothing were clear indicators of who was who.

The port itself was busier than I thought it would be, and darker. There were no streetlamps or much lighting of any kind, leaving the air in blacks and blues scumbled over purples. A cold wind scalloped the water around the only docked ship, the giant ferry going to Athens. It could carry hundreds of people, but it looked like there were no passengers on board. Rasheed explained that the ticket to Athens cost eighty euros per person and that many refugees would have given their last penny to the Turkish mafia in control of the crossing between Izmir and Lesbos, thinking that they'd have finally arrived once they landed in what they thought was Europe. Most of the people waiting at the port did not have enough to cover a ferry ticket.

We walked through a sea of teenage boys that parted gently to let us through and coalesced again as we passed. I remembered that you were nervous around crowds, but you looked more astonished than frightened. Most of the boys were speaking Farsi. I assumed they were Iranian at first, but then I noted the epicanthal fold of their eyelids and realized they were Afghan, probably Hazara. We came upon a group of kids speaking Arabic, three girls and a boy, huddled close on a bench. They didn't seem concerned at all, chatting about nothing in particular. The eldest girl, perhaps no more than twelve, chestnut hair bursting from under a woolen cap, warily watched our approach. I said hello, introduced myself, asked where their parents were. The eldest said they were taking a walk and would be returning soon. I wondered what emergency would force the parents to leave their children in a strange place surrounded by a hundred teenage boys or, worse, whether these kids had been abandoned. But Mazen took over again. He talked to them, found out which Syrian village they were from, after which he joined them in chatting about nothing at all. I asked him in English, hoping the kids would not understand, whether we should be worried that their parents were not there. Once again that evening he regarded me as if I were speaking some language that no human had spoken before.

"This is my younger sister," he told the children. "I'm older by one year but wiser by more, many more. She moved to America a long time ago but forgot to take her brain with her. I kept it in a fine jar, which looked rare but was made in China. Every time we get together, I give her back her brain, but it takes a little while for her to adjust to it. Just as she gets back to normal, she returns to America and forgets her brain again."

The children snickered. One of the girls told Mazen that he was a big liar, like her dad. She accused him of adding salt and pepper to every word that left his mouth. Mazen denied the accusation with no little ardor, insisting that he was most honorable. Why, he had never lied in his life ever, not once. Everywhere he went he was called Mazen the Truthful. The girl, the cutest among them, asked me if I forgot my brain, to which I shook my head no.

"Of course she'd say that," Mazen said. "She forgets. Here, let me show you the jar I keep her brain in."

He patted his jacket, pretending to search for my lost brain. Where oh where had he put it? The girl stood up, laughing and pointing at him. "You can't find it because there is no brain!"

The parents finally appeared. As their daughter said, they had simply gone for a Proustian stroll before boarding the big boat. Mazen talked to them briefly before they were on their way to the ferry with their children, their belongings, and their tickets in hand.

"You've been away for too long," he told me.

"I was surprised that they would leave their children alone," I said. "After all they'd been through."

"Why is it that you live in such a safe place yet consider the world so dangerous?"

"I'm an American."

You stood with Rasheed quite a ways from us, surrounded by about twenty boys who looked like they were all talking to you at once. I wondered if you felt you were being crowded by the boys, but it didn't seem so. You didn't move away from them no matter how close they got. One boy kept pointing to your phone, but you didn't seem to understand what he was saying. By the time Mazen and I neared, Rasheed was asking the boy to slow down, for he was speaking much too fast. He didn't understand Farsi that well, Rasheed said. The boy grinned.

"He wants you to look at his music video on YouTube," Rasheed said. "He's a musician. No, he's a singer-songwriter, he says."

"On phone," the boy said in English. "On phone."

You had trouble tapping in the right web address, your fingers too old to be phone nimble. You gave the boy your phone. He held it in his small hands as if it were the queen's crown jewels. "Ooh," he said. "So nice phone." He proceeded to tap the screen maniacally, his thumbs a veritable blur, and voilà, a video began playing. The four of us were the guests of honor with front-row seating for the tiny screen, and the rest of the boys rough-and-tumbled their way to some angle of viewing behind us. Onscreen, the boy sang only slightly off-key, danced to a disco beat in front of a large mirror, delightfully cute in a coiffed do and besequined all over. The tune sounded hummable, but I couldn't understand a word, wasn't even sure what language the song was in, though the boys behind me were in awe. Chatter, chatter, a hand with pointing forefinger would appear over my shoulder, and another boy would begin to clap to the beat of the song.

"That's wonderful," you said, and the boy beamed in gratitude. Why was it that those boys thought you were someone of importance or someone who cared about who they were? Had Rasheed told them you were a writer? Because after the video ended, one at a time, they told Rasheed what they did or what they wanted to do, so that he would translate for you. This one was a carpenter, a mason, a cook, a shepherd who was willing to be retrained, sporting a worn jacket lined with lamb's wool, a couple of sizes too large. You took it all in, nodding your head, hearing them—you, the witness. This one was the youngest of twelve, all of his family still in Afghanistan; that one had a brother in Brussels, a cousin in Brazil, an uncle in Denmark. Your head bobbed up and down, your gaze focused on each speaking boy, your concentration that of a believer listening to his gods. This one's name was Najib, that one Mumtaz, and of course no less than five Mohammads. The teenagers were dynamic, so alive, as noisy as starlings chattering as they settled at sundown. Every single one of them told you he was eighteen. You kept asking, and they would say eighteen. Rasheed repeated the word so often that the boys no longer needed him to translate their age. I'm eighteen, I'm eighteen, they chirped. Not one of them looked older than fifteen, sixteen at most, with faces rarely, if ever, touched by razors.

"They don't have any money to buy a ferry ticket to Athens," Rasheed said. "They're completely out."

"But Athens isn't even their final destination," I said.

"They're stuck," he said. "There is a Swedish NGO run by an Iranian immigrant that comes here some nights with extra ferry tickets, but it doesn't look like they'll be around tonight."

I noticed you getting antsy again. You glanced left, then right, took in all the boys. You moved closer to Rasheed, whispered something in his ear. Rasheed smiled, repeating the word "certainly" a couple of times in Arabic. You two began to walk away. The boys didn't seem to mind, remaining in their own group, talking, arguing, gesturing wildly as if in a scene from an Italian movie, swimming in hormones, having what appeared to be a good time. I ran after you. Mazen ran after me.

"Where are you going?" I asked.

"To buy ferry tickets," you said.

"There are about a hundred boys out there," I said, trying to catch up. I, the voice of reason.

You stopped, your gaze not leaving your shoes. Rasheed threw a smile toward you, a life jacket, but you didn't notice. He lifted his arm to console you but didn't follow through with the motion, returning it to his side.

"I can't afford eight thousand euros," you said, paused for another moment, then started marching again into the dark night. "But I have a credit card."

I thought at first that you were going to buy one hundred tickets. You had me worried. You seemed determined. We followed in step, exited the port's gate, and crossed the street. The ticket office was around the corner, which I felt was a good thing: the boys who might be watching us wouldn't see where we were going.

The office, an old-fashioned travel agency, was over-bright and plastered with tacky tourist posters on all of its walls. Would a resident of a Greek island dream of a beach vacation somewhere else? You walked in first, held the door open for us, waited for Rasheed to lead the gaggle of us to the sole agent at a wide, bedraggled desk.

Rasheed, in English, said, "We'd like to buy ferry tickets to Athens."

The agent, a young man in his thirties, handsome and peppy, tuned himself to high sparkle. If he were in a United States high school, he would have been a cheerleader. "Would that be four?"

"No," you said, handing him your American credit card. "I want ten tickets."

The young man didn't blink. He produced a supply of tickets and counted out ten.

"What happens to them in Athens?" you asked Rasheed.

"I'm not exactly sure," he said. "They'll have to be processed again before moving on, if they're able to do so. This is one leg of a long journey."

"A drop in the bucket, I know," you said. "But I can help ten boys on this part of their passage."

Rasheed decided he could afford two more tickets. Mazen looked at me. Without speaking and letting either you or Rasheed know, he was asking if it was okay by me for him to contribute. He said he could afford two tickets as well.

"I'll buy ten as well," I said. "That'll make it an even two dozen."

The march back was less military, more hesitant. How would we distribute the tickets? We decided we'd let

Rasheed, the most experienced, deal with it. The starlings we'd left behind were still grouped together, the numbers remained at around twenty-five or a little more. Rasheed entered the circle, spoke his slow Farsi. The boys grew quiet but more excited, like stalking predators waiting to spring. Rasheed would hand out a ticket, and the boy who took it would leave the group, pick up his belongings, and rush toward the giant ferry, disappearing into the dark. One, two, until all twenty-four tickets were gone and only two boys remained standing before Rasheed, visibly the youngest by quite a bit. They hadn't been able to push through to the front. They looked about to break out in tears.

Rasheed held his hands out to show he had no tickets left. The words for "sorry" are similar in Arabic and Farsi, so we all understood him.

"No," I found myself saying, but apparently not as loudly as you did.

"Come with me," you told the boys in English, and they understood you. One picked up his tattered backpack, spoke rapidly to the other. His voice hadn't broken yet. They were thirteen at most. They stood before you, clutching their bags, smiling and waiting. And back to the ticket office we marched. I told you I could pay for one of the tickets, but you assured me you wanted to do it, as if it were some form of penance.

When you handed the boys their tickets outside the travel agency office, they hugged you, both at the same time. You looked perplexed, unsure how to hug them back. Then they turned to my brother and hugged him so fiercely he began to weep. I couldn't remember the last time I'd seen him cry. When it was my turn, they hesitated. Should they or shouldn't they? They looked ecstatic. I moved toward them with my arms out.

We watched them run across the street, heading back into the port. Beyond the gate stood at least a dozen boys looking at us, and behind them more and more boys, and more, ad infinitum.

Learn a Language,
Bed a Spy

Did you ever ask Rasheed how he came to speak Farsi? I knew he spoke Arabic, Hebrew, and English fluently. Of all the other languages he could have chosen to learn, why would he pick Farsi? That was a story in itself.

When he was much younger, he began an affair with an older married Jewish man. Even though they had to keep their relationship secret — they couldn't even be seen together — they lasted for more than five years, meeting in a friend's office three or four times a week. They kept telling themselves that it was just sex, and in a strange way it was. Rasheed told me that his lover had this fantasy of being ravished and sexually used by a dominant Arab, and Rasheed obliged. Rasheed had to curse and belittle his lover in Arabic while he was inside him, had to smack him figuratively and spank him literally. It was the best sex either one of them had had up to that point in their lives. They were able to sustain the erotic charge for about a year and a half, and just as the novelty of being sexually humiliated by an Arab began to lose its luster, the Israeli whimpered in Farsi during one of their sessions, a slipup, only one sentence. When they were done, Rasheed's lover would not elaborate other than saying that he was learning Farsi. He wouldn't say why. He didn't have to since this was a couple of years after the Iranian Revolution. To spice up their now-flagging sex life, Rasheed began to learn Farsi as well. Soon he was able to belittle his lover in broken Farsi; he moved from calling him sharmouta to calling him jendeh, much to his lover's delight.

For me, the best part of this story is trying to picture Rasheed as the butch one in any relationship.

I don't know if you heard this either, but Rasheed sent me an email recently telling me that there are many young Afghan boys in Athens working as prostitutes. Sex work is the only thing these boys can do to survive. For five euros, a European gets to fuck a young boy. Only five euros. I don't know how long this has been going on, but I do hope that the boys we sent forth to Athens are long gone by now.

A Toddler by Any Other Name Is Still a Toddler

Do you remember the photograph of the dead boy who washed up on a Turkish beach, the one that went viral and prompted international response, all the breast-beating and hair pulling around the world? Aylan Kurdi, remember? There were demonstrations in Germany, in Canada, in Cairo. People held signs mourning the losses of Aylan and humanity.

Rasheed saw the photo in the paper while having his morning coffee in Jerusalem, and by afternoon he had booked his first flight to Lesbos with three other nurses. He wasn't sure what moved him to take such a quick and decisive action. He thought it had to do with the fact that he had seen numerous photos of dead Palestinian children in Gaza or the West Bank but wasn't able to do much about those kids, never able to help.

In Gaza itself, an artist created a gigantic sand sculpture of the toddler on the beach. The sculptor left the natural color of sand for the three-year-old's skin tones, but used red sand for his T-shirt, blue for his shorts, orange for the soles of his shoes, and so on. Gazan children played all around it. There were reenactments of the death on shores in Rabat, Morocco, and the South of France, where dozens of people wearing the same color clothes as Aylan laid their bodies on the sand.

Emma, too, saw the picture that same morning as Rasheed. With tons of makeup and fitted sweaters, she boarded her first flight to Athens less than three weeks later.

A month ago, you told me that you tried to research the events of New Year's Eve 2016 in Cologne, the night that was used as an excuse to shut the doors to refugees worldwide. You sent out feelers through friends at Human Rights Watch and Amnesty International. And yet you couldn't figure out what exactly happened that night. Everyone had a different story; little was actually documented. You thought that was strange.

Well, here's something just as weird.

The boy's first name was not Aylan but rather Alan. It must have been misspelled early on, and no one corrected it until it was too late. His family name was Shenu, but once the family arrived in Turkey from Syria, they were called Kurdi because of their ethnic background.

Years later, it is the rare person who knows this.

Years later, there are still contradictory stories about what happened on that boat on the morning of September 2, 2015, before it flipped and the young Alan gained a *y* as his cuddly corpse floated to shore.

Do you know of the Turkish poet Cemal Süreya? The name Süreyya is spelled with a double *y*, but he lost one of them in a bet with another poet, or so the story goes and is still going. Cemal died sometime in the early nineties. Maybe his *y* remained behind for a while, waiting patiently for the right opportunity to come along, and suddenly, years later, a toddler's body appears on the Turkish shore, calling for it:

Here I am.

Another Kurd,
Another Drowning

His name was Baris Yagzi, all of twenty-two, drowned on April 23, 2017, off the coast of Turkey, when the refugee boat he had boarded sank in the Aegean, killing at least sixteen people, including children, and leaving only two survivors—a pregnant woman from the Congo and another from Cameroon. The usual story, the boat would have been barely safe had it carried only one-fourth the number of passengers. He was one of hundreds of thousands of refugees who sailed across those seas, one of thousands who died doing so.

He had dreamed of going to Brussels to study music, but his visa application was rejected. He grew desperate. He paid smugglers thousands of dollars for a seat on one of those boats. He was Turkish, not Syrian. The picture in the paper showed a boy of uncommon pulchritude, a young Apollo and his instrument, his head supported by the violin's chin rest, dark, brooding eyes looking at a point somewhere to the left of the camera, eyebrows of an ancient relief, a beauty mark on his left cheek, a perfect imperfection.

Baris washed up on the Turkish shore clutching his violin case, his fingers squeezing the life out of what gave him life. He would not let go even as he drowned. Within the case lay his instrument, that wooden vessel, and sheets of music of his own composition, now wet and unsalvageable.

You texted me a link to a newspaper article about Baris when it first appeared. You typed only one word: Arion.

In ancient time on our island, this Lesbos, Arion, he who would invent dithyramb and coin its name, came to be. The greatest musician of his time, the boy won a competition in Sicily. On his way back to Lesbos, carrying his lyre and prize money, the ship was waylaid by pirates who stripped him of his riches and offered him a choice in how he was to die: be stabbed and then buried properly once on land or be thrown into the sea and drown. What to choose, what to choose? Arion asked if he could sing a last song before dying, one that would help him decide. The boy raised his voice in praise of Apollo, the god of poetry and the greatest lyre player of all. The boy's song was so pure that dolphins floated on the water's surface to listen, and Apollo, he who had once skinned Marsyas alive, heard the boy.

When the pirates threw young Arion overboard, the dolphins carried him and his lyre to the safety of shore.

But not Baris.

Where have the dolphins gone?

Where the gods?

How to Live Forever, According to My Grandmother

I must not have snored. Unkicked and bruiseless, I woke up to the muffled sound of Mazen singing an old Fairuz song in the shower. His side of the bed looked hardly slept in, not unusual for him. When we were children, he barely moved once he shut his eyes, waking up full of cheer and energy each morning, his pajamas adding not a single crease during the night. It didn't seem that much had changed with him. I, on the other hand, had slept in a T-shirt and underwear for the first time in decades.

I got out of bed as soon as I heard the water turn off. I needed to use the bathroom.

"Out, out," I said, while banging on the door.

I had promised to meet Emma at the Kara Tepe medical tent that morning. We had to make sure Sumaiya was getting the care she needed and to prepare the family for what was to happen once she passed away.

As we parted to drive to our separate hotels the night before, I asked you to join us for lunch. You declined; our port adventure was enough for you. I insisted, and you attempted a couple of your numerous bad excuses. You couldn't, you could already feel the headache that would develop the next day, some funny excuses, all not believable. Then Mazen said that if you did not promise to come, he would handcuff himself to you. Rasheed insisted that you had no choice. I should tell you that they were both worried. After you drove off, Mazen said we shouldn't let you spend too much time on your own. He didn't think you were suicidal; no, he compared you to a grieving widower, and you know the Lebanese wouldn't allow a griever to be alone till enough healing time had passed. You had to join us.

Mazen came out of the bathroom with a towel wrapped around his privates and another around his head. He blocked my way in for a moment, looking a bit too pleased with himself.

"I remembered I have to show you something before we leave," he said as he strolled past me. He removed the bath towel around his head with a ta-da flourish, as if he had a white rabbit under it. "Well, make you listen to something. You'll love it." He would tell me only after I showered and dressed, since the surprise was supposed to knock my socks off.

He had me sit next to him when I was done, his laptop before us on the only table in the room, what passed for a desk and dinette in one.

"About seven years ago, I drove to our mother's village in Syria," he said, "which turned out to be great timing

because much of where I visited is gone now. I got to see
Aleppo before much of it was leveled. But the idea of the
trip was to visit our grandmother before she died and to see
where we came from. Our mother was driving me crazy
at the time, and I needed a break. I thought I would visit
the one woman who drove her crazy. Our mother loathed
hers, you know that. I was able to spend a day with our
grandmother, and it explained a lot. I could see from whom
our mother inherited her craziness. And, you know, you."

I punched his shoulder, not too hard but not soft either.

"She did remind me of you a little," he said, "except
that you're only half insane. I thought at first it was some
kind of dementia, but no, her crazy was her every day. She
loved to lecture and berate, roamed her old house at night
scolding mirrors for hours. I arrived, fresh ears, and she
began to give me advice. I had an idea. I asked if I could
record her because I needed to remember her guidance. Do
you want to hear your grandmother talk?"

As if I had a choice. He clicked the Play icon on his
computer, and this craggy, hoarse voice began to speak, an
old Syrian dialect, strong and clear, enunciating every word.

*You don't reach eighty years of age without being right, and
I'm ninety-nine,* our grandmother said from the laptop's
tiny speakers, from the beyond. *So I've been right for a long
time. Don't argue with me. I'm telling you this: each human, every
single one of us, is born with a predetermined number of heartbeats.
There is nothing anyone can do to change how many times your
heart will tick. God, in all his glory, has already assigned you
a specific number. You might die of old age or of being kicked in
the head by a donkey. Doesn't matter. Cancer, car accident? The
number of beats was already written on a piece of paper stored in*

God's lockbox. Each of us will find her own way to die when the beats have run out.

It is written. We grew up with this saying, that everything has already been written by God or Fate or what have you. Destiny was set, and one lived best by aligning oneself with what was written.

The secret is to make sure the heartbeats last for the longest possible time. If you ask me, exercise is the stupidest thing ever invented. Why would you want to waste heartbeats on purpose? All those runners, the swimmers, the football players, they will all die.

Her voice sounded pure, had the strength and fluidity of certainty. It would have been difficult to guess she was ninety-nine had she not stated it.

Any work that has to be done can and should be done slowly. Think tortoise. It lives to one hundred and fifty years because it is smarter than humans. Do your work deliberately and unhurriedly, whether it's around the house or to earn a living. Relax. Don't ever walk fast. Be methodical. Keep your heart rate slow.

And never get angry. It's not worth it. Even though I was married to the stupidest man in history, I never lost my temper. How stupid was my husband? Well, let me tell you. He was the only one who immigrated to Brazil, the land of untold riches, in order to make money, only to return two years later having lost everything.

I don't approve of movement in principle. It increases your heart rate. When I married, I moved into my husband's house and never left it. I didn't spend a single night in any bed but mine. I didn't travel. I stayed home when my husband sailed to Brazil. He was supposed to call for me when he settled in the New World, but he never did. He wouldn't have known how to settle without me. I'm not even sure he'd have known how to call. I told him that, but he didn't know how to listen. He had dreams, my poor, stupid husband, but they didn't last long, and he didn't either. I've been a widow for over fifty years. He was angry all the time, and he smoked a lot, which also increases your heart rate. He was handsome when he was young, so that helped.

Your mother wasn't smart either, but did I let her upset me? Of course not. And she was never satisfied. She wanted to see the world, to become someone of consequence. As if that was what's important. She wanted to travel.

Travel? No, of course I had no interest in travel. I visited the city only twice, both times with my husband, and let me tell you, I was not happy. Too many people, too many everything. It was not good for my heart rate.

No, I did not wander the world. I wandered sitting still.

It might have been a good thing she died before this last war began.

I told you I don't like movement. I was born for a sedentary life. I cooked, I cleaned the house, everything carefully. I worked my root garden. I loved my grandchildren. Most of all I loved my embroidery. I loved my needles and my threads more than I loved anyone.

If you ask anybody within twenty villages who has the best threads of all, they'll tell you it's me, even to this day. I could do all manner of embroidery, no one was better. My pieces were sought after. Lucky was the bride who received a wedding shawl from me.

In the early days, when I was newly married, I bought my threads from a peddler who arrived in the village on a mule-drawn carriage. He would save his threads for me. Silk threads of the brightest yellow from China for you, he would tell me. This blue is from Italy, this earth red from Morocco, only for you. Look, this green wool yarn came to me all the way from Germany, he would say. It matches your eyes. Come with me, he would say. Let me take you away. Ride with me, you can sleep where you will, walk out when you want, you can choose your bread, your dress, your company. He wanted me to fly with him, to taste a life beyond my life. He said his mule had seen more of the world than I had.

The peddler was stupider than my husband, who brought me back beautiful woolen threads from Brazil, bless his heart.

I did not need to go with him to see the world. I sat in my comfortable chair, the canvas on my lap, the needle leading a thread, each entry point a heartbeat. Delay and delay each cross-stitch, delay and delay each heartbeat, and suddenly I'm above yellow China. I soar over azure Italy. Is this Morocco's red I see before me?

No, I did not walk the world. I flew above it, and I soared.

Don't contradict me. I told you I'm always right. Don't argue with me. Of course I flew on my threads. Why would you believe that a woman could fly on a broom but not on threads, why?

I'm ninety-nine, and I can still thread a needle by candlelight.

Regain Your Virginity
with Moisturizers

Wind but no rain yet. Even without the rain, the inexorable sadness of the lands of the Mediterranean could not be ignored. The olive trees outside Kara Tepe stood sleeping, soughing instead of snoring, weary in the grayish cold. I parked the car, zipped up my jacket before exiting. Mazen, next to me, matched my movements, except that his eyes seemed to get stuck on a faint oily stain on the belly of his parka. As we entered the camp I told him no one would notice it. He informed me that wasn't the point. He knew, and since he did, the stain grew to the size of continental Europe. In his mind, of course, he added.

Refugees stood about the camp. We walked into a motionless and cold world, too quiet for that many people up and about, no one moving but Mazen and me. Two women chatted before one of the larger tents. There was no television, one was telling the other, both head scarfed and heavily layered. From the snippets of conversation we heard passing by, it seemed that the talked-to woman was a recent arrival. There was no privacy, the first woman said, no kitchen for cooking, nothing to pass the time, all the waiting with little to do. Not much to look at either, what was she supposed to do, admire sunsets or something? She prayed—that was how she entertained herself—talked to God, who didn't seem to be listening much these days and who never talked back, tongue-tied as usual.

The dirt beneath my feet seemed frozen, as if dreaming of snow. I shivered, trying to shake off the chill, trying to get rid of winter.

"I should still be in bed," Emma said, appearing next to us as if by a Swedish magic spell. "See all the things I do for you."

"As you mentioned for the hundredth time," I said.

"Well, it's freezing," she said. "My bed is comfortable and warm. I left a gorgeous young man in it. I left while he was still asleep. He'll wake up and wonder what happened to that stunning being he spent the night with."

"Didn't take you long," I said.

"George is quite different from Rodrigo, less talented but more charmingly innocent. He was a virgin until last night."

Mazen chuckled. "You deserve a medal," he said.

The whole family was attending Sumaiya, who looked wan, more noticeably jaundiced. A gray blanket covered her undulating chest, a limp oxygen tube tickled her nostrils. Sammy looked terrified, his wife imperturbed, her face slack. She fixed her sight on some point along the canvas's snow-white ceiling, oblivious to the ebb and flow of her daughters around her. Asma whispered into her mother's ear, giggling with an effort that would rip her apart if she kept it up. Another daughter ate the remains of Sumaiya's breakfast, which sat on the laminated fiberboard table. Both Sammy and Sumaiya smiled upon seeing us, his smile nervous, hers drugged beatific. She clutched a distended makeup bag of cloth covered in Palestinian embroideries.

I asked Sammy what happened to the imitation crocodile handbag. He explained that a number of the Syrian ladies in camp had heard that Sumaiya liked her makeup but hadn't brought any with her when she escaped. They gifted her some of what they had. It wasn't much, they told Sammy, but he had to accept the offering. The ladies were sure to be able to replenish their paltry losses with better products once they settled in Europe. Sumaiya had no makeup on her face.

I asked how she was doing. Sammy began to speak but stopped when his wife reached for my hand. She nodded happily. Well, she said. She was doing well. Emma was going through the patient report. I didn't need her to tell me that Sumaiya was not doing well at all.

"Are you in any pain?" I asked her.

"No," she said in a soft, almost ethereal voice. The scarf was the same one she'd worn the day before.

Mazen spoke up. "Come on, girls. Let's leave the doctor alone so she can treat your mother. Come on. We can go outside and play a game or, even better, look for a second breakfast." His eyes searched mine. Mine glanced quickly at Sammy, and my brother understood. "And you too, Sammy," he said. "Help me find some food and let the doctor work in peace."

Sumaiya's eyes were wide open, staring at me in wonder, then at Emma, who was checking her IV. I took off my jacket and hung it on the back of a chair. Sumaiya, still admiring Emma, tapped a finger on my hand.

"She looks like a houri," Sumaiya said. "I must be dying and going to heaven, because it's what I see. Don't tell the children."

I couldn't help but laugh. A virginal Emma was difficult for me to imagine. The real one wanted to know what Sumaiya said. I told her, having to explain the word "houri" and its origins. Her reaction surprised me. She almost teared up, her face flushed; even her hands, which reached out to Sumaiya's, seemed to have more color. She asked me to thank Sumaiya.

"Her skin is soft," Sumaiya said. "Like fresh milk. Not dry like mine, which is more like powdered milk."

Emma sat on the bed next to Sumaiya. She rummaged through her pockets, came up with a small bottle of blue plastic.

"Don't tell her it's my last one," Emma said. "I'm telling you because I want you to admit that I do all these things for you. I want a signed receipt from you saying: 'I don't know what I'd do without my best friend, Emma.'"

She undid the square knot of the scarf from around Sumaiya's neck and poured the moisturizer onto the palm of her hand. She applied it thoroughly to Sumaiya's face and neck, massaging the patient's skin with a delicate touch. The familiar scent of the cream must have soothed Emma, her face smoothing out before my eyes as if by osmosis. And Sumaiya—Sumaiya purred in pleasure, like a contented cat being visited by bliss. Emma's fingers repeated movements that had been memorized for years and years, middle and forefinger swipe above the brow, thumbs around the mouth folds, pinky under the eyes, up, down, side to side. When she was done, Emma held the bottle up for Sumaiya to see, unzipped the cloth makeup bag Sumaiya was clutching, and placed the moisturizer inside. While the bag was open, I noticed an unused box of Garnier Nutrisse hair dye before Emma zipped it back up.

Sumaiya turned, and in a voice that seemed quite sane, she said, "Kill me."

Give Me Autonomy
and Give Me Death

It had rained while we were cocooned inside the medical tent, as it should have. Every now and then, dolor could be contagious. Sumaiya had cried. I cried. We had every reason to, the sky and its attending clouds let loose for a while. Emma, Mazen, and I walked to my car. The world around us was glazed with a sheen of rainwater.

"You're not thinking of actually doing it?" Emma asked.

I couldn't wait to get to lunch. I was suddenly ravenous. I could eat a horse, a camel.

"Of course I am," I said. "She asked me. I must consider it. I'm surprised you think I shouldn't."

I shouldn't have told Emma, but I couldn't think of any believable lie when confronted. She'd been there, seen Sumaiya's reaction and mine. I'd promised Sumaiya that I wouldn't tell anybody, not her family, no one. I'd broken my promise already, with Emma, with Mazen, of course, and would do so once more with Francine when we talked.

"What do you mean?" she said. "I believe in the right to patient-driven euthanasia but only when the patient is capable of making the decision. Sumaiya isn't. She just isn't. She's not thinking straight. She probably has encephalopathy, and she's high on morphine to boot. I understand her wish, but she's not able to give consent in her current state. How can we be sure what her wishes are?"

Mazen's eyes lit up; his brow scrunched. I held my forefinger up to his face so he wouldn't interrupt.

"Stop it, Emma," I said. "Almost all euthanasia discussions are held when patients are high on pain medications. You know that. It's the nature of the beast. I'm the one who has to consent. She asked for my help, and heavens, she was more than clear about why she wanted it. She had thought it through."

"But—" Emma tried to say more, but I would have none of it. I held my forefinger up to her face as well.

A moment later, I was stomping more than walking on the muddy ground. I was moving and they were trying to catch up. My shoes squished with each step.

"She's not a child, Emma," I said. "She may not be educated, she may not have seen much of the world, but she was able to enunciate precisely what she wanted better than you or I would have."

"What did she say?" Mazen asked. "What did she say exactly?"

Again, I held my forefinger up, but this time only to indicate that I needed a minute. I didn't want to cry. When Sumaiya asked me, she began to weep, and I allowed myself to join her. Tears bathed my eyes. Her words hit me hard in the stomach, in the diaphragm. I could not stop myself from sobbing. I did not want a repeat. I needed to keep moving.

She'd said she wanted my help in ending her life. She was dying; it was a matter of time. She wanted to decide when that time was. Her family would move on only when she was gone, so it had to be done. She'd brought them all the way here. They now had to go on without her. She couldn't wait for death to arrive naturally. She'd had enough with the not knowing, enough with the waiting. Ever since the war in Syria started, she'd had no control over her life or that of her family. God, Fate, bombs, the government, Assad, the disease, Daesh, little boys with machine guns and a few hairs sprouting on their faces that she could have removed with a good scrubbing, everything and everyone had more control over what happened to her. She'd had it. Enough. She wanted autonomy.

"That sounds clear to me," Mazen said.

Emma took in a long breath, exhaled. "To me too," Emma said. "But please don't ask me to help you. I don't think I could deal with it. I believe in the right to end one's life, but I don't want to be the one who does it."

"I'll help," Mazen said.

"I'm grateful to both of you," I said. "If I decide to, I'm able do it on my own." I tried a joke to lift the mood. "That's why they pay me the big bucks." Neither of them found it funny.

Emma said she wouldn't join us for lunch. She'd try to convince George to get back into bed.

"You've made the decision, haven't you?" she said.

"I told Sumaiya I had to think about it," I said.

How to Live in Chaos, According to Your Aunt

The four of us were back at the Greek restaurant of the night before, still complaining about the food. Closer to the kitchen, we could watch the cook cutting carrots into coins and hear her humming a tune to herself. Rasheed made some joke about promising not to take you to the port after lunch. I was dragged into the conversation, couldn't stay within my tumbling thoughts of Sumaiya. When the grilled red mullet arrived, Mazen made a small plate of it with lemon and olive oil, adding a half clove of garlic and a pinch of salt. Fishing a small piece with a bit of bread, he brought it to your lips, and you nibbled meekly and gratefully from his proffered hand.

Mazen then asked the question that had been on my mind. "Do you know why you found this trip overwhelming since you've worked with refugees for so long? Is the suffering of the Syrians here more pronounced than for those you talked with before?"

No, not at all, you said, on the contrary. The refugees you met in Lebanon regaled you with much more horrifying tales, their destitution was much worse. In the haphazard camps of the mountains, the situation of the Syrians was more untenable. Interviewing the child beggars on the streets of Beirut left you horror-stricken. No, you weren't exactly sure why this trip broke you. Maybe when you returned to your psychiatrist's couch, you might be able to disentangle some of the threads of this noose. You had some ideas, but you weren't sure.

"When I talked to people in Lebanon," you said, "I was always the writer. I did the interviews officially. I would go around with a handler from UNHCR, and she would introduce me as a writer of some significance. There was a barricade between the person I was talking to and me. I could hear the stories, and no matter how sickening they were, I felt protected. I was able to listen dispassionately, impersonally. They were stories, after all, simply stories. I deal with stories all the time. I haven't been able to do that here. Metaphor seems useless now, storytelling impotent."

Rasheed suggested you work with his group, and he would introduce you as whatever made you comfortable, the writer, the king of Siam, Robert De Niro, anything.

You felt lost on the first day you landed, you said. You sat next to a Utahn on the small jet from Athens; the Rockies were in his clothes: the khakis, the plaid flannel shirt, the day-hiking boots. A garrulous Mormon who wouldn't take the hint of the open book on your lap. He had to tell you how much seeing the suffering on television had affected him, how horrible he felt, how he started having uncomfortable dreams about drowning, a sign from his God if there ever was one. His doctor upped his lorazepam dosage because Xanax was no longer as effective. He couldn't consume his food with the same relish he did before the refugee crisis. He had to do something to get his life back in balance.

Rasheed thought he recognized the Mormon. He'd met him briefly a couple of days earlier, good guy, a bit ignorant. Rasheed said he didn't care what brought him or selfie-girl or the college kids to the island; he could put them to work.

You had come from Beirut, you said, and the Mormon forced you to switch to American mode sooner than you'd expected. You hadn't realized that you were still that split — discrete entities not quite melted in the pot, Lebanese and American, still an immigrant after all these years — until you came across a large group of Middle Easterners while driving from the airport to Skala Sikamineas. They looked odd, a group of twenty-five or so, haphazardly spread out. You had to veer around those who sat on the bitumen. How could they not realize that they might be run over? You hadn't expected to encounter refugees so soon, little more than an hour after you landed, after you'd extracted yourself from Mormon clutches. You turned your car around, drove back to them, lowered your window, and asked if they needed help. Please, said a man in his forties in English as he approached your car. Police, he said. Where is police? Not Syrian, he was Iranian. You informed him that you spoke Arabic if anybody in his group did. He gestured to an older woman sitting on a garbage bag of belongings. She stood up and you were taken aback. Your aunt who had died some thirty years earlier walked toward you. Uncanny resemblance, the cut of the gray hair, the dress and its colors, the swing of the arms as she walked. You couldn't help but stutter your greeting. She explained that they needed to talk to the police; that was what they were told by the Turkish smugglers. They had expected someone to be there at the beach, but they might have landed on the wrong one. Where was the police?

You were a child once more, trying to explain to your aunt that you didn't know what to do. It wasn't your fault. You had been in Lesbos for no more than an hour. They should register at a police station, but you had no idea where one was. You got out of your car and told her you would look for one on your phone.

A boy of about thirteen with underwear-showing jeans and upright hair that accentuated long black eyelashes approached you. He, too, looked as if he were related to you. Before any exchange of greetings, he told you he understood that a Mercedes-Benz was the most expensive car in the world, but where he came from there were lots of old ones that worked as taxicabs. You told him it was similar in Beirut. You tried to make him feel at ease. Wasn't that sweet, you thought, a boy and his obsession with cars. He delicately unwrapped a piece of cloth he was holding, from which he removed a Mercedes hood ornament, one that had been rubbed assiduously until it had a sparkling sheen. He told you he was hoping to sell the ornaments to fund his schooling, but he wanted you to know that he did not steal them. He'd gone to a junkyard and paid the equivalent of five dollars for a dozen of them. The owner of the yard told him he'd be able to make a fortune on them once he crossed into Europe. Could you help him sell one, because he was starving and needed to buy food?

You didn't know what to do. Should you look up the nearest police station on your phone first or explain to the poor boy that he had been gypped, that the dozen ornaments wouldn't buy him a sandwich? That the boy trusted you by revealing his treasure squeezed your heart.

You didn't get the chance to do anything. Two young volunteers in a gray Jeep who happened to be driving by slowed down to demand in broken English that you get off the road. You realized that you were now standing next to the boy and your almost aunt in the middle of the road and had not thought of parking your car but had left it where you stopped, blocking traffic, you Lebanese you. You got back into the car to park it, and the volunteers took over. They called for a bus and organized the group into small family units to wait. By the time you rejoined them, one of the volunteers, his left arm browned from hanging out many a car window, wanted you to berate your aunt in her own language, wanted you to tell her in no uncertain terms that she should not allow herself or her children to wander onto the road, let alone settle on it. You were being hissed at, not spoken to. He wanted you to tell her that she would save a lot of time if she were better organized. She was no longer in chaos, he wanted you to explain.

You stood before your aunt and weren't able to say a word. You weren't a child who didn't know what to do. You were her age.

You looked rather pitiful telling the story. We could barely hear you. Your voice would have been audible enough, but you wouldn't look at us. You kept your head lowered, your neck bent at an awkward angle, like a bird preening its feathers. You appeared to be speaking to the improperly herbed cheese in the clay dish on the table in front of you.

You had trouble with the volunteers, you said, both the temporary and the NGOs. Not just those at the first meeting on the road, everybody. You loathed their selfies, their self-flattery, their patronizing righteousness, their callous self-regard, everything. And then you felt guilty for hating. You said you knew that in some way they were the best humanity had to offer. College kids were spending their holidays helping people instead of vacationing somewhere or, worse, interning for an evil corporation, but still, you resented much about them. You felt they had all the wrong reasons for coming to the island. They wanted to help in order to feel better about themselves, both the "Look at me, I'm the kind of person who helps refugees" kind of better and the "My life might suck, but yours sucks even more" kind.

You weren't any better, you said. You couldn't even do disaster tourism well. You came to a crisis area but ended up locking yourself in a hotel room, hiding from the people you had wanted to help.

You told us many things, but even though you would later try to convince me otherwise, you said nothing about panic attacks at that lunch. Do you think I would have let you off without getting you help or medicating you had I known at the time? No, telling us that you were overwhelmed and hid in your hotel room listening to opera was not the same thing as telling us you were having panic attacks. Paranoid fears, racing heart, fainting? Do you think I would have allowed you to drive had I known? By the time we met, you were doing better, but really, how stupid could you be?

Diomedes in the Congo

A year after your Lesbos trip, after multiple sessions sprawled on your analyst's couch, the picture of what happened to you would not become discernibly clearer. You were able to find more reasons as to why you were uncomfortable (you couldn't figure out which side of the divide you belonged on, your ambivalent feelings toward both volunteers and refugees), but those could not explain the abject terror that caused your withdrawal. What happened would remain a mystery.

You write your best work in mystery, however. You may not have understood much, but you ended up writing one of my favorite stories, "Diomedes in the Congo," the most self-eviscerating thing you'd penned. You transformed the onetime king of Argos and leader of the Greeks during the Trojan War into Diomedes, Dio for short, a Greek American mercenary fighting in the Congo. Pallas Athena still looked after him, though she no longer needed to make a stream of fire flare from his shield and helmet. His AK-47 could do that well enough. Similar to what occurred in the *Iliad*, the goddess offered her warrior special vision, allowing him to see the gods active in the war. He was able to see Dick Cheney fighting alongside mercenaries, Steve Jobs making sure his soldiers protected the copper mines with religious zeal, Muammar Gaddafi bringing the Pan-African troops into battle. Billy Graham and Ayatollah Khomeini danced a sensual milonga together, one slipping Bibles into pockets, the other Qur'ans. Your mercenary saw them all and could not bear it. Nothing was what it seemed. Humans were being directed by the whims of the gods. Poor Diomedes, had his vision been restricted to the gods of war and evil, he would not have been as traumatized. When he encountered the humanitarian relief efforts that accompany every war, he saw the activities of the gods of altruism, many of whom were known by one name. Some people were led to Africa by Bono, others by Oprah. Madonna exhorted the war baby adopters, onward Christian soldiers, and Demi's denizens tried to fight hunger.

Throughout the ages, humans have been warned against looking at the gods directly. None could look at the face of a god and remain sighted. Diomedes was blinded as soon as he saw the faces of the gods that directed his life, those to whom he had sold his soul.

In the *Iliad*, Athena warned her protégé to interfere with no god except Aphrodite, winner of Paris's apple. He should smite her if the opportunity arose, and arise it most certainly did when the king of Argos wounded Aphrodite. In your story, blind Diomedes mistook Angelina Jolie for Sally Struthers, his intended victim, and killed her. The murder of Angelina so horrified the people that they tore poor Diomedes to pieces.

How to Guide a Boy into Becoming a Man with Cognac

My insomnia courted cognac. I sipped Rémy Martin from the bathroom sink glass, which made my drinking at that hour seem wrong somehow, more illicit. My father used to say that cognac was the best remedy for insomnia, not that it would help you sleep, but rather it would make you enjoy being awake quite a bit more. I surprised myself still by how much I missed him. We were unable to understand each other, and he would not approve of the choices I made, but unlike my mother, he was a decent human being and would have wanted the best for me, whatever that meant.

I was eleven when my parents decided to have that horror of a talk with me. I sat on their bedroom taboret facing them on the edge of the bed, the vanity mirror at my back. They should have been able to see my front and back, to see me whole, to see my truth, so to speak. I was only able see their fronts, since as every religion tells us, demons have no back, only what they wish to present to us, false fear or beguiling dazzle. To this day, I can still picture the bedroom in my head as if I saw it yesterday, all cherry and blond pine, the vanity, the nightstands, the headboard. My mother's bed was always tightly made, of course. Nothing out of place, the room assaultingly neat and ordered. A flyswatter crucified on a small hook on the wall on her side of the bed, above a box of tissues and a stack of gossip magazines, both foreign and domestic, which I was not allowed to touch. There used to be an imaginary police cordon beginning at the bottom edge of the bed, beyond which we children were not allowed. The bottom of the bed was the limit. We couldn't go farther. What crimes were committed we couldn't investigate.

I sat on the taboret facing my mother and father. She, tight and mute, cleaved to his side, her face pinched. I must become a man, he said in a weighty tone. Did I want everyone to know what I was? Did I? I wanted to ask what I was, but I felt something shatter inside my head. I would spend my nights staring at an ocean of palpable darkness, wondering if anyone knew who I was, if anyone could see me.

My father, in a kind yet unequivocal tone, proceeded to trace the borders I was not to cross. In private, when I got older, I could do what I wanted, but discreetly, he said. In private, eat according to your taste, but in public, behave according to the public's. It was his fault, my father said. He wasn't spending enough time with me. I was learning the wrong lessons. Boys like me needed guidance to grow into men like him — guidance and direction and a clear map.

Until I matured and learned, I must watch my behavior and he would watch me.

Well, he didn't for long. In the blink of an eye — or after an eternity had passed — I grew older and found myself elsewhere, in a land where sunrises were more solid and people less so, a world made of paper and shadows, away from him, from her, from them, cast out of the Garden.

Yes, I was older now. I was doing what I wanted, which was to drink cognac at two in the morning. I had an inexplicable fondness for minibars and their mini bottles. I didn't dare turn my laptop on and disturb the darkness. Mazen treasured his sleep. I had to do everything quietly. I would have loved to go for a walk in the black of night, air out my musty anxieties, but I didn't think I could get dressed without waking my brother. I couldn't begrudge his making the offer to the newlyweds, but I did wish he were in his own room. My thoughts could spread out, loiter, and loll much more easily when I was alone.

"You can't sleep?" I heard him say in a sleepy voice.

"I am asleep," I said. "You're dreaming."

Once more, he laughed at an unfunny joke we'd had going for over fifty years. His laughter delighted me. Mine followed suit. Cackle, cackle. He was the wave and I its spray.

"Well, I'm up now," he said.

"Go back to sleep."

He was definitely awake now. I didn't know anyone who could leap from the innocence of sleep to wakefulness as quickly as he.

The window rattled softly, anticipating another storm. The fake creeping fig next to it quivered in its pot, plastic leaves rustling. I tried closing the window more firmly but was unable to make it budge.

"Have you decided when you're going to do it?" he asked.

"She decided," I said. "Tomorrow morning, or this morning."

I took another sip of cognac, which warmed me, releasing tension stuck in my neck muscles. A second sip melted the tangle of emotions caught in my throat, or in my heart.

"Do you have everything you need?" he said. "Do you have to get anything?"

"No, everything is already there."

"Really?"

"Yes," I said. "It's all about the heating pad."

I gulped down the last of my cognac, returned to the indentation on my side of the bed, and was out soon after. I slept like the dead.

How to Say Goodbye in Syrian

The sun was having trouble peeking from behind the clouds. It seemed weakened, as if the effort had exhausted it, a paltry circle up above. I was surprised and grateful to find Emma waiting for Mazen and me at the gate of the Kara Tepe camp. I'd assumed she would skip the procedure, showing up after to deal with the bureaucracy and burial arrangement as she'd promised. She looked glorious, more so than usual, beautifully applied makeup, a notable feature of which was blue pencil outlining the eye shadow. More dazzling than the sun that morning. She looked as if she had never been afflicted with original sin, citizen of her own garden, the Fall having nothing to do with her.

"I'm here if you need me," she said. "Never mind what I said yesterday. I can help."

I thanked her. She would be a great help. I assured her I had everything we needed and had confirmed the details the afternoon before with Sumaiya, who was going in and out of both consciousness and coherence at the time.

Kara Tepe was supposed to be a more humane refugee camp than Moria, but the main difference I could see was that the barbed wire above the Moria fences was concertina, whereas at Kara Tepe it was the more common three strands in a row. Someone had thrown a pair of baby shoes tied together with their laces onto one of the razor wires, the middle one. I couldn't remember whether that was a sign of a baby having been born or simply a good-luck charm. Mazen reminded me that when we were kids in Beirut, we used to see baby shoes tied to the back of taxis, so it was probably a ward against the evil eye. Below the shoes, laundry was clothespinned to the chain-link fence. So were plastic bags stuffed into plastic bags, forming clouds that looked ready to join their relatives up high. A gust of wind made the baby shoes swing like a pendulum. Or like a scythe.

A noisy group of preteen boys ran by, halting right before the fence, seven of them, all dressed in rags the color of ashes. A couple of them tried to engage a younger girl in conversation, but she wanted nothing to do with them. Among such a group, she looked regal, a child of Aphrodite herself. She moved away from the boys, the tops of her oversize rubber boots knocking against each other with a gentle slap. Within a few seconds, the boys began to collect stones and pebbles from the ground and launch them at the baby shoes. The noise level rose even though not a single projectile struck its target. The little girl, in her own world, on her own little island, examined the wet earth in front of her. She was covered in layer upon layer of clothes that once belonged to other children. Her face lit up, as if she'd had the greatest idea ever. Smiling, she sank her foot into the water-gorged clay, then pulled it back and gleefully admired her artwork. One rubber boot muddy, one not. A yellow plastic bag flew solo over the fence and landed at her feet. She lifted her muddy boot to stomp on it, but a gust winged the bag off before she got her chance.

I took out my smartphone to check the time, not yet nine. A drop of water landed on it, a rainstorm of one, and down the screen it streaked itself away. The air would soon feel fresher; less blight, but no smell of rain here, no petrichor, not in the camp.

In the medical tent, Sammy was the only one with his wife. He sat next to the bed, leaning in and holding her hand. He was whispering in her ear. I did not need to hear what he was saying to understand that it was endearments. As soon as Sumaiya saw us, she blurted, "I'm in pain and I'm cold." She said it loudly and hurriedly—in other words, as unnaturally as possible, which was not how I'd asked her to do it.

Sammy jumped up, brow furrowed, bushy eyebrows coming together as if commiserating. Did she need another blanket? Was the heating pad not enough? Should he fill the hot water bottle? I hadn't seen one of those in ages, since I left Lebanon all those years ago. Sammy explained that a few minutes after I left the afternoon before, Sumaiya asked for one. She felt that even though the heating pad might be better and more modern, it wasn't warming her up like a hot water bottle would. They couldn't find one anywhere in camp, so one of the young American volunteers had driven to a pharmacy in downtown Mytilene and bought one for her.

"Such a well-behaved boy," Sumaiya said weakly. She wasn't using the oxygen mask, relying on the nasal cannula. "Nice and kind." She looked better this morning, more vibrant, but her catlike eyes were butter yellow, the rings under them the color of a peach pit, and her skin was ashen, as if she had emerged from a vat of talcum powder. "He paid for the bottle himself and refused reimbursement."

"We tried to give him some money," Sammy said, "but he wouldn't have it, as if he were Syrian, one of us."

"He couldn't be one of us," Sumaiya said, "not with that pleated hair."

On the table next to Sumaiya's bed, someone had placed a small pot of African violets, a bundle of tiny yellow faces in purple bodies. Where had such living luxury come from?

I asked her where she was feeling pain, which was the signal for Mazen to suggest that Sammy and he step outside so I could examine Sumaiya in private. I asked them not to wander too far. As soon as they exited the tent, Sumaiya blurted out that she was ready. I asked if she was certain this was what she wanted. Emma whispered that we had to be sure.

"I want you to do it with the hot water bottle," Sumaiya said, "not the heating pad. That would work just as well, right?"

"Have you said goodbye to your daughters?" I asked.

She had, both yesterday and this morning. She did not wish them to see her corpse.

"Are you sure you don't want to tell Sammy? Don't you want to him to be here?"

He would feel too guilty. He'd worry about her not getting into Paradise for wishing to end her life. And she did not want him to witness her dying. She asked if everything was ready for her family to move on, all the documents signed, everything in order, her burial and funeral already set up. Did we have someone who could wash her corpse? I explained that if everything went according to plan, her family would be leaving the island tomorrow or the day after at the latest and would be in Malmö, Emma's hometown, within a week at most.

"Tell her to watch over them," Sumaiya said, reaching for Emma's hand. "Tell her to watch over my loved ones and I will watch over hers."

Emma broke down, began to bawl. I grew nervous that someone outside might hear her. She bent down and hugged Sumaiya, squeezing so fiercely that Sumaiya had to say, "Stop, I don't want to suffocate to death." It took me a second to catch the joke and laugh. I was grateful. I had been frightened of finding Sumaiya not quite lucid.

The sound of thunder and heavy rain grew louder. I hoped Sammy and Mazen had found shelter.

Emma clicked on the electric kettle to heat water. I took out four fentanyl patches, one hundred micrograms each, but peeled only three. That should be enough for respiratory suppression.

"This should ease your pain," I told her. "You will feel comfortable quickly. I'm going to put them on your back."

Would it be okay to place the patches on her front? She wanted to cuddle the hot water bottle and face upward, toward her God and His Heaven.

I pulled down the blankets. Emma and I lifted her shoulders to undo her gown. Her liver protruded from under her ribs and felt awfully firm. She looked pregnant. I placed the three patches along her abdomen and covered her with the gown. Emma handed her the old-fashioned rubber water bottle. Sumaiya clutched it to her above the fentanyl patches, smiling. Emma and I brought the blankets back up.

"You have nothing to worry about," I told Sumaiya. "Like I explained yesterday. It will feel a little like floating, like the lull of an easy tide of our Mediterranean. You'll feel less and less pain, and your breathing will slow. It's simple. I will be by your side the whole time."

I was about to sit down when I noticed panic visiting her eyes.

"What about Sammy?" she said. "I need him here. I can't leave without him here."

I asked Emma to find him, and as soon as he came back into the room, his wife chortled. She looked as if she wanted to say something, but ended up only grinning, as if she had seen an angel. Her whole body exhaled a sigh of relief. Sammy took the seat I thought I'd be using.

"Make sure the little one gets into her pajamas when you tell her to," Sumaiya told her husband.

The thunder stopped, the rain stopped.

I stepped back. Emma stood at the tent's entrance, a weeping sentinel. From seemingly out of nowhere, Mazen's fingers intertwined with mine. Together we watched Sammy recommence the whispering. With his forefinger, he tucked his wife's head scarf out of the way so his lips could have unobstructed access to her ear.

How to Say Goodnight
in Lebanese

Night was night on Lesbos; it erased all color. Away from the center of Mytilene, little was lit. Looking out the window, I saw nothing of the Mediterranean. I could imagine there was nothing there, a vast oblivion. The glass pane merely reflected the well-lit hotel room and me, the window turning into a mirror unmisted by what was behind it. The world outside was me — well, me and Mazen, since he walked out of the bathroom already in his pajamas.

"What are you looking at?" he said.

"Me."

"That requires serious contemplation." The window reflected us as a portrait, Lesbos Gothic, a brother and sister, he without the pitchfork. "Are you doing all right?" he asked.

"Yes, I'm okay," I said. "Nothing has changed since you asked five minutes ago."

He was worried because I'd told him that I hadn't done anything like this before, that I'd never helped a terminal patient end their life. I'd asked him if he thought that having experience would settle a physician's post-euthanasia turmoil, if there were any. I wasn't sure. Could it ever become habitual?

"Everything went exactly the way you said it would," Mazen said, his arm resting on my shoulder. "I have to say I'm impressed."

"It's what I do," I said. "I'm supposed to know how a body behaves."

"I'm supposed to know how the stock market behaves," he said, "but it never does what I ask it to. I can't believe people are more predictable than stocks."

"Bodies are," I said. "Not people."

I was doing all right. This was not post-euthanasia turmoil, maybe a bit of unrest. Sumaiya died peacefully, painlessly, and rather quickly, which was what she wanted. I wasn't sure I'd followed the oaths literally, wasn't sure I did or didn't do any harm, but I knew I'd followed them in spirit. Hippocrates shouldn't be able to berate me from his Greek grave.

"Let's go to bed," Mazen said. "It's been a long day."

"I shouldn't," I said. "I'd like to talk to my wife, the real one. Not you."

He wanted me to keep him company in bed until it was time to call Francine or he fell asleep. We would watch a movie on his tablet.

"Do you think the newlyweds are still enjoying their room?" I asked.

"Definitely, though not as much as we are."

I lay on my side facing the dark window, blanket all the way up to my neck. The pillow was too soft, and I had to use two of them. Mazen, playing big spoon, was behind me, his tablet before me. I had to hold it up. He put his head next to mine in order to see the small screen. I tumbled back into early childhood. My central nervous system released tiny, comforting angels coursing through the axon fibers of my being.

"This feels familiar," he said.

The euphoria did not last. Just as we did when we were children, we began to argue. Which movie were we going to watch? No shoot-em-up films for me, nothing that required thinking for him. I was too girly, he was too stupid. We didn't get to decide because Francine called. We answered on the tablet, and she got to see us in flagrante delicto.

On the screen, her face appeared, luminous and in full bloom. She had just woken up, five in the morning in Chicago, too early even for her. The halogen on her side of our bed was the only light in the room.

"That looks cozy," she said.

"I wish you were here," Mazen said. "A three-way cuddle is my ultimate fantasy."

"I couldn't sleep," she said. "I was worried."

"You didn't have to be," I said. "I'm doing okay."

"More than okay it seems," she said. "You look happy."

"I do? I'm not sure about that."

"You're glowing," Francine said.

"We were arguing about which movie to watch."

"Shut up and listen!" she said. "I haven't seen that look on your face in years. I can't remember the last time you were this happy, which makes me even happier. I miss you, and I miss that big lug on top of you. Come home."

The Plunge

Three months after Lesbos, you were with us in Chicago —
well, Evanston, to be precise. You had accepted a ten-week
teaching gig at Northwestern. You'd end up spending eight
of those ten weeks in our spare bedroom. You couldn't bear
the furnished apartment the university offered you, too generic, too beige, too dead. Not one shade of color that would
jeopardize neutral. You missed your cats, you said, so you
had to cuddle with ours. You missed your psychiatrist, so
you needed to lie on our couch, your head on Francine's
lap, complaining about everything and the cold weather.
The university recruiters tricked you, told you Chicago was
warmer in spring. What you didn't realize was that warmer
did not mean warm. There was always snow in April, just
a little less of it than in winter. Oh, the moaning. Oh, the
suffering. You were your usual bundle of triggers.

   You chucked the novel you were writing about Syrian
refugees and began one about what happened to you while

trying to help Syrian refugees, pages and pages that you
would scrunch and throw into the pit of despair. What
possessed you to try and write that? What did you think
you'd accomplish? Were you seeking some form of absolu-
tion, you fool, you? You went to Lesbos and turned into
a mess, or as today's youngsters like to say, you kirked
out. Did you believe that writing about the experience
would help you understand what happened? You still cling
to romantic notions about writing, that you'll be able to
figure things out, that you will understand life, as if life
is understandable, as if art is understandable. When has
writing explained anything to you? Writing does not force
coherence onto a discordant narrative. You knew that,
you told me that. But still, you thought this novel would
be magically imbued with your dreams of respite. Even
though none of the previous novels you wrote helped you
in any way, this one, you thought, would heal your pain.
Like a faithful analysand, you believed if you worked hard,
wrote long enough, you'd come across the clue that would
unravel the puzzle, the one key that would unlock your
mystery. Keys, if they even exist, darling, are not found
in literature.

    Why did you keep at it for so long? Did you believe
that if you wrote about Syrian refugees the world would
look at them differently? Did you hope that readers would
empathize? Inhabit a refugee's skin for a few hours? As
if that were some kind of panacea. You still hoped even
though it had never happened. At best, you would have
written a novel that was an emotional palliative for some
couple in suburbia. For a few moments they'd think how
terrible it was for these refugees. They'd get outraged on

social media for ten minutes. But then they'd pour another glass of chardonnay. Empathy is overrated.

You were grumbling about your novel. This wasn't working, that was the worst. Francine stroked your hair. I thought at first that she wasn't paying any attention since whining is your default state of being and she was reading a book, holding it in her other hand. In her usual quiet voice, she asked, "Have you considered writing about an American couple in suburbia to help the Syrian refugees? If you did a good job, Syrian refugees would be able to inhabit the skin of Americans, walk in their Cole Haans, empathize with their boredom and angst. I bet Asma would love a book like that."

You bolted upright, shocking all three of us. You tried to get her to repeat what she said, but she didn't.

You told me I should write my story. Maybe I could make sense of what was happening since you certainly couldn't. You were retiring. This writing thing was not for you. I should give it a go. You were not going to write another sentence, not one word. You hated writing more than anything. You could go back to working in a hardware store. Or you would write a novel about a Lebanese Frankenstein who creates a monster out of body parts belonging to victims of suicide bombings, a Shiite left arm, a Sunni right arm, maybe a Catholic brain, a Druze heart. Oh, you could do that one. It could work. Talk about internal struggle. Or you could write a novel about a second-generation Arab American whose Arabic isn't good but who is hired as an interpreter by the FBI regardless and proceeds to screw everything up royally. You could have fun with that one. A romp, yes, you could do something like that. You threw out one idea after another, each more outrageous, then discarded it. You would give up. Or you would write another novel. No, you could never write about Syrian refugees again. I should do it, you said. Maybe I could understand what happened, you said. I could unravel the mystery and find the key. Maybe I could come to terms with my past and heal my wounds. Ever delusional you.

I should write, you insisted.

I wasn't a writer, I said. I couldn't do it.

So, you plunged.

Acknowledgments

I am indebted to many who have helped with this book:

to the doctors who were kind enough to answer so many questions: Yana Najjar, Ethan Schram, Sophie Gadeon, Peter Pollack, and Fatima Karaki—

to Susan Stryker, who helped with all trans-related questions and quite a bit more—

to those who helped point and prod me in the right direction: Lina Sergie Attar, Lina Sinjab, Lina Sergie Atassi, Laure Chedrawi, Tony Chakar, Anissa Helou, Kim Ghattas, Zora O'Neill, Jeanne Carstensen, Marsha Williams, Brad Adams, Sarah Schulman, and Damian Ardestani/XOV—

to Alia Malek, Marwan Hisham, Molly Crabapple, and Rania Abouzeid for writing books that informed this one—

to those who read early drafts of the manuscript: Raja Haddad, Reese Kwon, Naheed Bashir, William Zimmerman, Oscar Villalon, and Pamela Wilson—

to Joy Johannessen, for her early editorial help—

to Elisabeth Schmitz, Deb Seager, John Mark Boling, and everybody at Grove—

to Duvall Osteen, Grace Dietshe, Maya Solovej, and everyone at Aragi—

to Nicole Aragi, of course—

and most of all, to all the Syrians who were generous enough to tell me their stories, who were kind enough to spend time, who always offered sweet tea.